AN EDUCATION IN THE
PRIVATE HOUSE

'Kate,' Mistress Judith said, 'tell Celia why you were punished this afternoon.'

Kate looked at her mistress with eyes wide with surprise, and then said, 'Oh. Yes, mistress.' She turned to me again. Her eyes were bright with incipient tears. 'I was a bad girl,' she whispered. 'I didn't lick fast enough, and I didn't play with my arsehole enough. So my mistress whipped my breasts until I started crying. After that I was a good girl and I licked my mistress again. I need to be whipped rather frequently, I'm afraid.'

AN EDUCATION IN THE PRIVATE HOUSE

Esme Ombreux

This book is a work of fiction.
In real life, make sure you practise safe sex.

First published in 2000 by
Nexus
Thames Wharf Studios
Rainville Road
London W6 9HA

www.nexus-books.co.uk

You can write to Esme at *esmeo@postmaster.co.uk*

Typeset by TW Typesetting, Plymouth, Devon

Printed and bound by
Cox & Wyman Ltd, Reading, Berks

ISBN 0 352 33525 4

Part One

YEARNING

The Private House
17 April
To Michael, the master of my heart
My darling, I know it's been too long since my last report. But if I'm not just a little bit naughty, how can I be sure that you'll punish me severely enough when I next come to see you?

Now – what have I been doing since I last wrote? I've been overseas again, setting up a branch in Italy. As always it's been a combination of frustration and fun. Acquiring suitably remote and spacious premises was the worst of it – the red tape is a nightmare. Of course, I made sure that my team had to seduce only the best-looking of the bureaucrats. I've settled for a modern villa, in the end, and I'm confident that we'll be allowed to make all the structural alterations: the mayor of the nearest town deals with the planning applications, and he just turns to jelly when I wear long black boots. His wife has discovered a charming devotion to little Valerie, too. They'll do anything for us.

Jem has insisted that the last portrait you did of me – the one where I'm tied to that vast dragon's head which is penetrating me with its tongue – should be hung in the entrance hall of the main House. Everyone says it's a masterpiece, and that I look beautiful, helpless and utterly depraved, but all the same it is very embarrassing. You can't miss seeing it when you come in through the main doors. People keep on asking me how long it took to paint, and how I was able to pose in such an uncomfortable position, and how you managed to capture the expression on my face. Of

2

course Jem and the others who know delight in making me tell the whole story. And so I keep on having to tell people: you constructed a wooden frame to represent the dragon's head; you tied me to it to show off my breasts and the stretching apart of my thighs; I didn't really notice how uncomfortable it was because you'd fixed a vibrator to the framework where the dragon's tongue would be; and after you'd taken enough photographs from which to paint my body you kept the vibrator switched on inside me all the time you were making sketches of my face. Can you imagine me, surrounded by a little group of visitors, like a guide in a museum, confessing that I came so many times I was sobbing, and that to achieve the expression of martyred ecstasy on my face you had Stephanie whipping my breasts as I came for the final time?

I've had to tell so many people about it, and every time I can't help blushing. And, of course, I get very damp and I wish that I could be with you. You beast. I'll bet you're getting hard just thinking about it.

Oh, Michael. I miss you so much. I'm touching myself as I'm writing this, of course. And I'm following your instructions precisely. I have understood exactly what you want me to do with the long, smooth stone you found on the beach and sent to me: I'm sitting on it, with the narrow end deep inside my arse. And with my left hand I'm pinching and squeezing my breasts. It's getting difficult to concentrate on writing, I can assure you. But I know I mustn't come until I've finished my report.

I'll try to get away one day next week. There won't be time for a sitting, but we can discuss some ideas for the next painting. And I hope you'll give me a very thorough spanking and come inside me. This stone is making me think that I'd prefer you to use my bottom, but it will of course be up to you. Perhaps the next picture should be something very simple: me with my bottom very red, and looking over my shoulder as I wait expectantly for – whatever you want to do next, more

3

smacks, coming into my vagina, or into my anus. Oh, Michael – I almost came then, just thinking about it. My breasts are getting very sore.

It's no good. I can't write any more. I've got to stop and finish myself off. I'm such a wicked girl. I'll see you soon. Please be very strict with me.

Always yours
Amanda

ONE

My involvement with Eloise and Anne began in May. It started with a letter, which had been addressed to me at the gallery where for a long time I had had an exhibition of some of my daubings.

The letter was forwarded to my flat by Tim, who owns the gallery. Tim claims that the only reason I have a permanent showing at his place is that I'm too lazy to remove my canvases, but I've a feeling my paintings lend the gallery a certain notoriety. Tim can never quite bring himself to ship the whole lot back to me, at any rate, and he's never once refused to pocket the commission on the rare occasion that he makes a sale.

My post consists mainly of circulars, bills, more bills, and final demands. Every now and then this gloomy cavalcade is enlivened by a cheque from Tim. More occasionally, on special, sacred days that make my spirits soar, I receive a report from Amanda. She had sent one such to me only a few weeks previously, and I knew that I could not expect another soon. Other handwritten letters are rare indeed, and I stared at the envelope for some time, savouring the unexpected flavour of the event and delaying the disappointment that I assumed would inevitably follow the tearing open of the seal.

The handwriting was round and regular, like a child's but very precise. The original postmark named a place I'd never heard of. The envelope was stiff and cream-coloured: it felt and smelt expensive. I opened it, and extracted a single sheet of cartridge paper. The letter, written in the same hand as the address on the envelope, went like this.

Emslove Cottage
5 May
Dear Michael

I apologise for troubling you. I have an intriguing problem with which I think you might be able to help me. But maybe I'm mistaken. I really don't know whether I should bother you at all. Perhaps, once I've written this letter, I won't have the courage to send it. Perhaps you're no longer associated with the gallery where we met, and this letter won't find you even if I do send it. And perhaps that would be for the best.

I'm sorry; I'm rambling. I should introduce myself. My name is Eloise Highfield. We met five years ago, when I came to view an exhibition which included some of your work. You came upon me rapt in contemplation of one of your pieces, and you asked me what I thought of it. I can't remember now what I replied – something silly, I expect – but we got into conversation. We met again, for dinner, but I'm afraid the fact that I live in the depths of the countryside seemed to make it impossible for us to remain in touch. I do hope you remember me. If you don't, then please ignore this letter. Don't read on – just throw this away.

I don't know quite how to proceed. It's the unusual subject matter of your paintings, you see. I find myself in a situation in which I simply don't have the expertise to make decisions. Your paintings lead me to think that perhaps you do have the relevant experience. The whole thing is made even more difficult and sensitive because the decisions I have to take concern a young woman: my pupil Anne, who is not yet eighteen years old.

I fear that writing to you about my problem is almost certainly inappropriate. However, if you receive this letter, and have read to the end, and if you don't regard it as an impertinent imposition, then please reply if only to acknowledge receipt.

Yours sincerely
Eloise Highfield.

I remembered her. I had been mooching around the exhibition, watching the visitors and trying to sort the potential buyers from the merely curious. As usual the former were so few as to be undetectable, and the latter were either tourists, who scurried away from the section devoted to my paintings as soon as they realised what they were looking at, or middle-aged men who had come to linger because they knew precisely what to expect.

And, I must admit, I like to hang around the gallery because it's an excellent place to meet potential models. Only a minority of the visitors are female; of these I find only a few who appeal to me; and of the few I admire even fewer are unaccompanied and linger alone to inspect my work. However, it's a safe bet that when a woman spends more than a few minutes staring at my canvases it's because she's at the very least intrigued by the subject matter. Under such circumstances there can be no better way of starting a conversation with a stranger than to introduce oneself as the artist.

I find attractive women irresistible, and as result I have fallen in love many times. I confess I am a serial romantic. Most of my recent lovers I have met on rainy afternoons in the gallery; many of them have returned to the walls of the gallery, fixed in oils or acrylics with the same care, affection and precision that I used to position and bind them in my studio – and in my bedroom.

I remembered that I hadn't been sure about Eloise Highfield. She was young – in her twenties, I guessed – and quite pretty, and she was clearly very taken with my work. For several minutes I had watched her staring at a large canvas on which I had depicted the slightly surreal scene of a woman, wearing only a feathered head-dress, a golden collar and golden ankle-chains, poised hesitantly in the open door of a suspended cage. I was pleased with the

7

tension I had captured in her limbs, and with the expression on her face as she looked over her shoulder into darkness.

It wasn't by any means the most erotic of the works on display, but it wasn't exactly tame, either. I find it almost impossible to paint women other than curvaceously, and the bird-woman's buttocks were prominent, well rounded, and quite clearly marked with the stripes of a whip. I had painted in the faint red lines as meticulously as I had earlier applied the lash to Clara, who had been my model for the work.

I had sauntered up to Eloise and had asked her opinion of the painting. Before she had had a chance to reply, I apologised for failing to introduce myself, and admitted that I was the artist. As usual I pretended to be timid. It seems to be expected of artists, and seems to be appealing. I have even been known to affect a slight stutter.

I have approached more than a dozen young women with this opening gambit, and each one has responded differently. I admit that I enjoy watching the expressions flit across a woman's face as she realises the implications of meeting the man who created the perverse image she has been admiring, and then as she decides how to react. I have seen several variations on the knowing smile; there have been one or two brazen grins. Stephanie, the most unashamed of all, had simply laughed, looked at the paintings, and said, 'If I go to bed with you, will you do those things to me?' I replied, 'Of course,' and ever since she has served me as occasional model, lover and studio assistant.

Most of my interviewees, however, have been more reticent. Many of them blush prettily; some simply stare at me with wide eyes, like schoolgirls caught in the act of buying cigarettes.

Eloise had seemed very timid. She blushed, certainly, but also turned her face away. She was at a loss for words, and in order not to frighten her off I steered the conversation rapidly away from the paintings and towards other subjects: the weather, the labyrinthine structure of the gallery, the city streets.

Gradually I had coaxed some information from her. She told me her name, and that she was a private tutor in a household in the country. She rarely came to the city. She would be here only a few days.

The day of our meeting had been in the late autumn, and although it had been warm in the gallery Eloise had been bundled up in a shapeless coat. She had kept her face cast down, and had glanced up at me only occasionally through large, round spectacles. I found I had no recollection of her hair. It had proved impossible, at that first meeting, to ascertain whether she had had any real interest in my paintings and whether her appearance was arresting enough to warrant pursuing her to pose for me.

I must have detected something in her, however, as I had asked to see her again. Over dinner the following evening she had proved scarcely less reticent, and she had stressed several times that she could not delay her return to her rural duties. I had taken her to the station, and as I said goodbye I mentally crossed her off my list of prospective models.

I had had no reason to expect to hear from her again.

I confess – to my shame – that I felt no thrill of excitement at the thought of meeting Eloise Highfield again. I can plead in extenuation only that I did not know then what I know now. And her letter was lacking in detail. All I had to go on then was my memory of a shy young woman, made mousier and duller by the dimness of my recollection, and the knowledge that she was five years older – and, I reasoned unreasonably, five years mousier and duller – than she had been when I had met her.

No, I fear that it was the mention of almost-eighteen-year-old Anne that kindled my interest. Eloise's difficult decision involved a younger woman and, it seemed, the kinds of sexual practices that I depict in my work. It was an irresistible combination. My curiosity was thoroughly aroused (as, no doubt, Eloise had intended), and after only a day I dashed off a reply to Eloise's letter.

I assured her that I remembered our two meetings and, with pardonable exaggeration, that I had always hoped we would meet again. I gave her some sketchy information

9

about my latest projects, and I hinted that my interest in the more unusual aspects of sexuality remained undiminished. I didn't mention that since I had last seen her I had encountered, and learnt much from, a world-wide organisation dedicated to the enjoyment of sexual submission*; the Private House does not like to be advertised to the uninitiated, and in any case I felt it would be undiplomatic to mention Amanda, my heart's eternal desire and my favourite inspiration. It is ironic that had I written merely the two words 'Private House' I could have saved myself the effort of composing the rest of the letter.

A few days later I received Eloise's second missive. This one was longer and full of details.

Emslove Cottage
8 May
Dear Michael
Thank you so much for replying. I'm glad to hear all your news, and that you are managing to make a living from your artistry. I confess that in normal circumstances I wouldn't importune someone I know as little as I know you – particularly a self-confessed sexual adventurer who specialises in suggestive paintings. But the circumstances are not normal: I've recently made discoveries that have turned my world upside down. I'm afraid you'll think my life has been very dull. Certainly I have no experiences that can provide the guidance I need now.

I'll start from the beginning and try to tell the whole story in an orderly fashion.

Twelve years ago I left college and applied for, and won, the post of private tutor to Anne, who was then six years old. I went to live with the family in their delightful cottage in the country. It was a small household, consisting only of Anne, her mother Celia, myself, and a succession of village girls who filled the post of live-in maid. The gardener lived out.

*As described in *Amanda in the Private House*.

Celia had borne Anne quite late in her life, and was almost twice my age. She was vivacious, elegant and witty, and was still very attractive. She ruled the household firmly, managing every detail from the kitchen expenditure to the planting of the spring bulbs. She was clearly wealthy: Anne had everything she wished for, and Celia was given to bursts of outrageous generosity to me and the other staff. As my salary was also more than reasonable, and the cottage was idyllic, and Anne was sweet-natured and intelligent, I had no thought of ever leaving.

While Celia and I were never close, I found her always entertaining. And I became very fond of Anne. It was a strange, cloistered, marooned existence, but I couldn't help enjoying it. My memories of those first few years consist of endless summer days: teaching arithmetic to Anne in the little schoolroom nestling right under the overhanging thatch; sitting in the garden with Celia, sipping long, cold drinks as we watched Anne watering her little flower bed and, it seemed, almost growing before our eyes.

Dark clouds came soon enough. Celia fell ill; recovered; fell ill again, and was diagnosed with a serious complaint. She refused to be treated: she would have had to abandon the cottage; Anne would have had to be sent away to school. It was never stated, but Celia and I both knew that by insisting on remaining at home, with only nursing care, Celia was relinquishing any hope of long life.

Her condition deteriorated, gradually and with periods of remission. She became frail, and walked with a stick; then had to resort to travelling by wheel-chair; and finally she was confined to bed. She remained clear-headed and strong-willed, and she continued to direct the household. Nurses were employed to care for her; accountants and lawyers were summoned to deal with the tidying of her affairs. I continued to be Anne's tutor, and with Celia's encouragement took on something of the role of mother or elder sister.

11

Celia died still possessed of a brittle beauty. Anne and I wept and grieved, but Celia's matter-of-fact attitude to her own impending death had prepared us well to bear the loss. Life in the cottage resumed its routines and was, it must be admitted, rather more carefree now that the shadow of death had swooped at last, had taken its prey, and had gone.

In her will Celia had bequeathed the cottage to her daughter; other assets were to pass to Anne on her twentieth birthday. I found myself the beneficiary of a substantial sum – on condition that I act as trustee of Anne's cottage, and that I remain there as Anne's tutor and guardian. Celia's will was that Anne should continue to be taught at home until she was eighteen. On her eighteenth birthday Anne's guardian was to unlock the chest at the foot of Celia's bed, in which Celia had deposited her instructions for Anne's further education.

After Celia's death Anne and I became very close: she was – and still is – a lively, precocious girl. She excelled in her studies, and I was pleasantly surprised to find that my role of tutor transformed easily into that of friend, or perhaps older sister. Mindful of Celia's wishes, and following my own predilections, I maintained the seclusion of our little domain. When Anne needed new clothes, for instance, I resisted her urgings that we should visit the shops in the nearest town, and instead ordered from catalogues; I did my best, I admit, to keep her in ignorance of modern society. However, I hadn't the heart to prevent her from walking with me into the village or reading my daily newspaper. I thought it cruel to forbid her all social intercourse.

I don't know whether I would have done better to keep her always in the cottage and its garden. As she grew older she began to fret at the isolation I imposed on her. Last year, when she was seventeen, she sat her examinations; in the summer we learnt that she had passed all of them, and at a sufficiently high level to be able to take her pick of colleges. Both she and I were overjoyed: I had known that she was accomplished, but

I had expected that she would have to take at least some of her subjects again this year. Our pleasure soon soured: Celia had been adamant that Anne should stay at the cottage until after her eighteenth birthday, but Anne could see no reason to delay her departure into the world. She wanted, quite naturally, to mix with people of her own age; she wanted to visit faraway places; she wanted to press on with her education.

The past few months have been difficult. I have coaxed and cajoled Anne into staying with me, but only by dint of stretching to breaking point my friendship with her. I have begged her not to leave me alone; I have reminded her of her duty to abide by her mother's dying wishes; I have tempted her with a one-year curriculum of exciting new academic work; I have permitted her to go alone into the nearby villages; and, in the end, I have resorted to pointing out that I control the household purse-strings. I think – I hope – that she and I are still friends. But I am painfully aware that the restrictions of our life together are chafing her.

Anne and I had both assumed that when she reached the age of eighteen, and Celia's final instructions were revealed at last, the result would be the dissolution of the cottage household. Anne would go to college; I would, perhaps, be allowed to stay on as caretaker while Anne was away – although the prospect of remaining there, with only my memories of Celia and Anne to keep me company, had little appeal. Anne's birthday is now less than a week away. As the day has approached she has become more and more excited and impatient; I confess I have felt only a growing dread.

A few days ago I could stand the suspense no longer. I convinced myself that it was reasonable that I should know, in advance of announcing the news to Anne on her birthday, the contents of Celia's letter.

Late at night, when I was sure Anne was asleep, I crept into Celia's room – almost untouched since her death – and, with my heart thumping, I unlocked the chest at the foot of the bed. By candlelight I saw the letter, lying on a stack of notebooks and albums. I opened the envelope, read its contents and sat on the floor, motionless with shock, until a drop of wax fell on to my hand and caused me to start. I tried to gather my thoughts. I glanced into the notebooks and albums, but the words and illustrations depicted scenes that my mind refused to comprehend. I was reminded of your paintings – and of nothing else I have ever seen or read.

I have enclosed Celia's letter herewith. You will, I'm sure, understand at once why I am at my wits' end. Not once, throughout Anne's childhood, have I chastised her – not physically. I simply don't know how to proceed. I don't know whether I should. I am distracted, and Anne has noticed. I'm sure she suspects that I have discovered something of Celia's wishes for her continuing education; I cannot imagine how she would react if she knew what I have learnt – how she will react, when I tell her, as I must, on her birthday. Will she be revolted? Angry? Fearful? I am at a loss to know how to deal with this problem.

In the few days since I unlocked Celia's chest I have dipped into the notebooks and albums. They purport to be a record, in words and pictures, of Celia's life when she was a young woman. I know that I have led a sheltered life, but I cannot believe that any normal person could fail to be shocked and amazed at her shameless autobiography. It had never occurred to me that any woman could willingly submit to a life of such depravity; that the life was that of Celia, my employer, my friend, my patient, seems still beyond belief. I can't make up my mind whether the account she has given is literal truth or sheer, perverse fantasy, or a mixture of both. You, I suppose, must have some knowledge of such things. Your paintings are more than merely erotic: they hint at the same unusual tastes as are wantonly celebrated in Celia's journals. And I must confess – although I know I shouldn't – that there is something perversely thrilling about reading Celia's accounts.

I hope that, when you have read Celia's letter, you will at least be able to offer some advice as to how I should proceed with Anne. Furthermore, however, I hope I can persuade you to come down to the cottage in time for Anne's birthday. I would be eternally grateful. I would feel much more confident when I broke the news to Anne. You could look through Celia's notes and scrapbooks – I suspect that you might find inspiration for a hundred works of art. And the countryside is very bucolic at this time of year.

I look forward – with some trepidation – to your reply. Please hurry: Anne's birthday is only a few days away.

With hope

Eloise.

With Eloise's letter was a second, shorter note: the letter that Eloise had found in her deceased employer's chest.

To Anne's guardian; not to be read or acted upon until the day of Anne's eighteenth birthday.

Eloise, I hope that you are still teaching Anne and that this letter is being read by you. If so, I am confident that you will do your best to perform my wishes; if not, I can only ask that whoever is now responsible for Anne's upbringing will do as her dead mother asks.

The journals that I wrote when a young woman, and which you will find stored with this letter, will reveal the life I used to lead. I expect you to be shocked, but please do not condemn: I lived life to the full, I enjoyed every moment of my subjection, and I regret not a single thing I did.

I knew, from a very early age, that I had interests that were a little different from those of my playmates. And if I have any regret at all, it is simply that once I was grown up I found no one with whom to pursue those interests until I had reached the age of twenty-six.

I have no idea whether Anne has inherited my particular appetites. I have done my best to bring her up in ignorance of my life before she was born, and without any influences on her budding womanhood.

However, I am determined that she should be given the opportunity to discover her own tastes and, if it proves that she shares mine, then I would like her to benefit, as early as possible, from the kind of education that I received only in my late twenties.

Therefore I propose that you undertake the following programme. On her eighteenth birthday, be generous with presents. Give her expensive gifts that symbolise her step from girl to woman: stockings, silk lingerie, perfume, expensive cosmetics, fashionably tailored dresses. Her own vehicle, perhaps. A set of keys for the cottage. Pamper her with the expressions of feminine adulthood.

Dress her in her new finery. And then tell her that now she is grown up, she is old enough to display her sexuality and to be chastised physically when necessary. You may show her this letter so that she knows that these are her mother's wishes.

Talk to her about masturbation. Get her undressed, and tell her to demonstrate to you how she plays with herself. If she needs instruction, instruct her. Before she has an orgasm, take her over your lap and give her a spanking. I suggest eighteen smacks. Let her continue masturbating until she comes.

Follow this routine at least once a day. The weather will be mild at this time of year, and therefore it should be easy to persuade her to remain generally unclothed in the cottage and out in the garden. If she seems reluctant, use the pretext of wishing to see her in her new, feminine, expensive, grown-up underwear. Comment frequently on the attractiveness of her breasts and her bottom. Remind her from time to time that if she wishes to masturbate she must do so only in your presence, and that you will spank her before she is permitted to reach a climax.

It will very soon become clear whether or not Anne has the potential to enjoy the regime. In fact, knowing my daughter as I do, I'm sure she'll refuse to co-operate even once if she finds the idea distasteful.

However, if you find that she takes some pleasure in the routine, or in some part of it – the exhibitionism or the punishments, in particular – then I would like her to receive a course of education at the Private House. This is the establishment at which I was trained, and I have no doubt that it is still thriving.

I am confident that Anne will have done well in her examinations and is now qualified to proceed to college in the autumn. Therefore I suggest that if Anne proves to be suited to the Private House she should be sent there during the summer. A couple of months should be sufficient to introduce her to a range of techniques and sensations, and to equip her for a lifetime of self-discovery.

Please follow my suggestions, however strange they might seem. I am no longer with you and Anne, and this piece of paper is all that remains to persuade you to grant my last wishes.

I send my love to you both and, whatever the outcome of the experiment I have proposed in this letter, I wish you both a life full of pleasure, excitement and contentment. I had such a life, and therefore don't waste a second more than you feel absolutely necessary in mourning for me.

Celia.

I could hardly believe my eyes. I stared at the two documents in my hands: Eloise's round, perfectly formed letters; Celia's more angular, italic script. I re-read both letters.

It was perfectly clear. Anne, brought up to be innocent of the world, would reach the age of eighteen in just a few days. On her birthday Eloise would follow Celia's instructions – from beyond the grave – and would give Anne her first spanking and then watch her make herself come. And Eloise wanted me to help. She wanted me to be present when Anne received her birthday surprises.

Most astonishing of all, Celia wished her daughter to be educated at the Private House. The House is a secretive institution of which only one in every ten thousand people could be expected to know, but I had the best of reasons to know of it: Amanda had been trained there, had discovered there the pleasures of submission, and now served the Mistress of the Private House as a senior negotiator in the House's international dealings. It was a remarkable coincidence.

Suddenly it all seemed too tempting to be true. Was I was the victim of an elaborate hoax?

My hesitation lasted no longer than the time it took for the idea to cross my mind. I've never been particularly worried about making an idiot of myself, and I long ago discarded any pretensions to respectability. I had nothing to lose.

I scribbled a note to Eloise. I would be pleased to offer my assistance, I told her. I would take the train tomorrow.

I left a note propped on my easel for Stephanie. While I was away she would water the plants, feed the cat, and no doubt turn my studio into the stage set for at least one extravaganza of debauchery.

I decided not to contact Amanda until I had had the opportunity to assess Anne. I packed a few summer clothes into a canvas grip.

There was nothing to do until it was time to leave for the station. I slept restlessly: I could barely recall Eloise, and had no idea of Anne's temperament or appearance, so that the fantastical excesses of my imaginings veered from the impossibly delightful to the ludicrously disappointing.

Would I have slept more soundly if I'd known just how intimately my life was about to become entwined with Eloise and Anne? I wouldn't have slept at all. I'd have been on the train already. Or I would have run on bare feet, under the stars, all the way to Emslove Cottage.

TWO

From the diary of Anne Bright
10 May

I let Josh touch my breasts! And it felt all tingly, like electricity. And we kissed, too, with lips *and* tongues.

Thank heaven for this diary. I think I'd go mad if I had to keep everything bottled up. And there are things that I can't possibly tell Eloise. I'm very fond of Eloise, really I am, but she doesn't realise that I'm grown up now. She still treats me like a child.

No, that's not fair. I know she's only doing what Mummy told her. And she treats me like an adult in most things. I think she's glad to have another grown-up person to talk to. I suppose it must get on her nerves, too, living in this isolated place. We're a bit like spinster sisters, Eloise and me, ever since Mummy died.

She's been acting a bit strangely these last few days. It must be something to do with my birthday. It must be. She thinks I've forgotten, but I remember her letting slip years ago that Mummy had left a special message about me that no one could see until I reached the age of eighteen. I bet she's read it. It's infuriating to have to wait until tomorrow.

And she received a letter this morning, too. She said it was just a bill, but I'm sure it was something more important. She's planning something, I'm sure of it. And I think it's all got something to do with me.

I suppose I'll have to try to be patient. It's only until tomorrow.

Now: I must write down what I did with Josh, before I forget how wonderful it felt.

I told Eloise that I was going to walk into the village to see if my Spanish and Philosophy textbooks had arrived yet at the post office. In fact I had arranged to meet Josh under the big oak in what he calls the Far Meadow (but which looks indistinguishable from any other field to me).

Lots of the young men who work on the farms have tried to talk me into going out with them, but most of them don't interest me. Their language is very crude: 'Show us your tits, love' and 'Nice arse!' – that's about all they can think of to say. Actually, I rather like it when they say those things – which I suspect is very naughty of me. But they don't have anything else to say.

Josh doesn't say much at all, at least when he's with his friends. He's tall and strong, and the others seem to respect him. He's the one I've always had my eye on, but as he didn't seem interested in me I decided that I could do without him. That's why I let Tom Hinch and then Rob Jerrold kiss me. But it was Josh I wanted.

And today I met him. Under the big oak. I was so nervous as I walked along the footpath. For Eloise's benefit I'd gone out wearing sensible trousers and a jacket, but as soon as I was out of sight of the cottage I took them both off and carried them in my bag. Now I was dressed to impress Josh, in my favourite sunbathing shorts (the ones I've spent hours shortening so that I can get a tan right up my hips and right up to my bum). On top I had on only the little pink T-shirt that Eloise thinks I regard as some sort of vest or undergarment, but which is really quite respectable to be seen in (well, almost).

As I climbed over the stile I could see a figure – white shirt, dark trousers – standing under the oak. Walking across the field, with the grass stems tickling my legs, I could feel Josh's eyes on me. I felt hot, and I don't think it was just because the weather was warm. It was a relief to step into the shade of the oak tree. Slightly out of breath, and I'll bet I was red-faced, too, I stopped in front of Josh.

He was still staring. His gaze travelled slowly up my legs, stopped at my shorts, continued up to my T-shirt, stopped again, and finally he looked at my face. He was grinning, and looking generally casual and gorgeous. I was blushing like mad, but I smiled back at him.

'Hello,' I said.

'Hello, beautiful,' he replied.

After that we were both a bit stuck for words. I put my bag down against the trunk of the tree. I confess that I turned my back on Josh and bent down low from the waist – entirely unnecessarily – so that he could see just how short my shorts were. And that I couldn't possibly be wearing any knickers under them. I straightened and faced him. We smiled at each other for a while.

At last he took a step towards me. 'Come here,' he said, 'and give me a kiss.' He held out his hand.

I reached out to touch his fingers, and I think I probably said something very daft like, 'Oh, all right, then,' which I suppose doesn't really count as putting up much in the way of resistance. But then, I didn't want to resist. I wanted to feel his hands all over my body.

I didn't have to wait. Josh is quite a rough kisser, I think (from my horribly limited experience). Enthusiasm, but not much finesse. His mouth tasted minty, though, which was perfectly pleasant, and I didn't mind what he was doing with his tongue because I was busy enjoying what he was doing with his hands.

It was as if the surface of my body was much more sensitive than usual. Everywhere his hands went I felt all shivery – a bit like being tickled, but without the attendant hysteria. In fact it made me feel kind of dreamy. And that was just when he was running his hands along my arms!

He seemed reluctant to touch my breasts. Perhaps he thought I'd scream, or slap him, or tell Eloise and get him into trouble. (Oh. I've just had a thought. I wonder if those are the things I'm supposed to do when

21

someone touches my breasts? That's the trouble with being brought up in the back of beyond – one simply doesn't know how to behave correctly.)

Anyway, his hot, strong fingers were stroking my skin and pressing into me all over the place: my shoulders, my arms, my sides, my tummy, and all the while we were kissing breathlessly. But my breasts were beginning to feel ignored, and I so wanted him to touch them.

So I just pulled my face away from his, grabbed his wrists, and moved one of his hands on to each breast. He looked quite shocked, but he recovered quickly and started to move the palms of his hands in little circles against my nipples, which were very firm indeed by now.

I lost track of things after that. As I've confided in these pages many times, I like to stroke my breasts and play with my nipples. It always makes me feel sort of warm and melting inside. But this was a million times better. I pressed myself against Josh – I wanted to feel him against every part of my body – and lost myself in kissing him as hard as he was kissing me. His hands went everywhere – grasping a breast, tickling a nipple, pressing into my back, stroking my bottom – but I wasn't aware of the specifics. It was the whole experience, and it was wonderful.

At some point I said something like, 'Stop a moment, and I'll take off my T-shirt.' Josh agreed, of course, and started tugging the hem upwards, but then he suddenly stopped.

'We can't do this here,' he said. 'Anyone might walk along the footpath and find us.'

At the time I thought he was being chivalrous, and I was touched. On reflection I suppose he might have been equally concerned about his own reputation and safety: I've heard that he has a girlfriend from Nether Lawrop, and she's said to have several older brothers who are very protective of her.

'We need somewhere more private,' he said, and he placed his hand on the waistband of my shorts and slid it down until his fingers were curled into the gap between the tops of my thighs. Yes, he was touching my sex place. My vulva, as it's called in my books on human physiology. He squeezed, and I couldn't help making a ridiculous squealing noise. It was like an electric shock going up through the middle of my body, except that makes it sound nasty and it wasn't nasty at all.

'Come up to the cottage,' I said. My voice was shaking. 'There's an old, locked-up outhouse at the back. I've found a way in on the north wall. It isn't visible from the cottage. Can you meet me there at about five o'clock? And can you do that again, with your fingers?'

'I'll be there, beautiful,' he said, and nudged his fingertips further in, as far as the material of my shorts would allow. I almost swooned.

Oh – I'd better stop writing now. I can hear Eloise opening the front door. Perhaps we've a visitor. Will I let Josh undress me later, in the old shed? Hang on, diary, for the next instalment!

Eloise had warned me that the cottage was isolated, but nonetheless I made the mistake of walking from the railway station. It was a balmy Spring day – sunny, and warm for the time of year – but after tramping for an hour and a half along overgrown footpaths, into countryside with fewer and fewer signs of human habitation, I began to tire of the rustic scenery. And my overnight bag was definitely growing heavier.

At last I came upon a wider track, which I followed as it wound between hedges bright green with new leaves, over the brow of a hill.

A gentle valley lay before me. A stream ran between irregularly shaped meadows, which sloped up to the surrounding woodland. There was only one dwelling in sight: facing south, its back to the ragged woods, sat a long, white-plastered cottage with two substantial wings. The thatched roof was so thick and overhanging that it appeared in places almost to touch the ground; diamond-leaded windows peeked from beneath thatched gables. The chimney stacks were tall and convoluted. Around the cottage were terraces and outhouses, and then lawns, and then flower beds, and then orchards, and then paddocks, so that it was impossible to discern the boundary between the grounds of the cottage and the surrounding countryside.

It wasn't difficult to see why Eloise had stayed here for so many years. I'm as cynical as the next struggling artist, and I have a particular aversion to chocolate-box images of the countryside. But it was impossible not to be charmed by the serene prettiness of the valley and the cottage.

Apart from the expected sounds of the country – birdsong, the rustle of leaves, the lowing of distant cattle – the valley was slumbering in a silence which persisted as I descended through meadows, between neat borders crowded with old-fashioned flowers and across a lawn that had recently been mown in precise stripes. It was hard to believe that the cottage was inhabited.

I knew, though, that this had been the chosen retreat of Anne's mother, Celia, whom it appeared had led a life of such debauchery that Eloise could not bring herself to describe any of it. And that the same cottage was now home to Eloise, who seemed to be more excited than appalled by her discovery of Celia's secret past, and to Anne, who would be eighteen on the morrow and therefore was about to be introduced to the pleasures of erotic punishment.

The juxtaposition between the serenity of the cottage and the potential depravity of its inhabitants served to add to my anticipation. As I walked up to the rose-framed front door I was aware that I was already half erect. I prepared a smile of beguiling frankness.

Eloise opened the door. We said 'hello' simultaneously, and she invited me inside, and we exchanged views about the clemency of the weather and the charm of the cottage.

Each of us was also taking the opportunity to take a good look at the other.

Eloise seemed to have aged hardly at all in the years since I had last seen her. I had to remind myself that she was now in her early thirties. Her big blue eyes had the brightness of youth, and the fine lines at their corners were hardly noticeable. Her straight, dark hair, cut in a bob, was lustrous and had no streaks of grey. My memory of her was unclear, but I had the impression that she was slimmer now than she had been. In fact, I realised as I let my gaze drift casually from her face to her body, she was decidedly slender: she was wearing a cotton dress whose tight belt revealed the narrow circumference of her waist and which showed off the elegance of her tanned arms and legs.

I confess that I was pleasantly surprised. I had expected the years of rustication to have dimmed her charms. Instead, the continuing semi-hardness of my member provided incontrovertible proof of Eloise's desirability.

'Enough of this chatting about the wonderful views,' I exclaimed. There was no need now to remain merely polite: I set out immediately to seduce and enthral. 'You look wonderful, Eloise. I'd say you'd grown younger if I didn't know it was impossible. You may consider me half in love with you already. And what about me?' I opened my arms in an expansive gesture. 'Have I changed?'

She giggled, which made her wide mouth look very attractive. 'Oh, gosh,' she said. 'I can hardly remember. I think perhaps you're even more rumpled.'

I affected despondency. 'Hair, clothes, or general demeanour?' I asked.

'Everything,' she said, still giggling. 'But don't worry, rumpled suits you. It's a very huggable sort of look.'

'Ah,' I said, and held out my hand.

Eloise had lowered her head, and was looking at me from behind a curtain of her dark hair. She was smiling. There was a long moment of silence, and then she extended her hand to mine. Our fingertips touched, we looked into each other's eyes, and our hands clasped together.

We moved closer, and stood there, in the hall, gazing at each other's face while a grandfather clock loudly ticked off the seconds.

'I'm glad you're not disappointed with me,' Eloise whispered.

25

'The thought never occurred to me,' I protested in what I think was a convincingly hurt tone. 'Would you like to show me round the cottage? This hall feels rather exposed, and I'd like to kiss you and play with your nipples.'

She moved closer to me, so that her breasts brushed my shirt. 'Later,' she said. 'We can go to my suite and I'll show you the notebooks that Celia left. But now you must be thirsty after your long walk. I suggest we have a cup of tea, and you can meet Anne. I think you'll be pleased with her, too.'

Twenty minutes later Eloise and I were taking tea in an oak-panelled parlour, with the French windows open to the courtyard beyond. We were waiting for Anne. Several minutes had passed since Eloise had called to her up the stairs, and Eloise seemed embarrassed that her protegée had still not appeared.

'She stays in her room more and more,' Eloise said. 'I suppose I thought that being brought up in the country and educated at home might result in her going straight from childhood to adulthood, without the awkward stages in between. But instead I think the awkward stages have just been delayed.'

I was about to murmur something reassuring when I heard footsteps on the stairs. Eloise looked up, into the corridor behind me. The expression on her face began as tense anticipation, which she transformed into a smile as Anne approached. Then, as I heard Anne enter the room through the door behind my chair, Eloise's smile froze and her eyes widened in alarm.

'Anne,' Eloise said in a stage whisper, 'go and get dressed properly. I told you we have a visitor.'

Anne's voice had the clear vowels of the well educated and the exaggerated, flouncing sing-song of the teenager. 'I haven't got any decent things to wear. Anyway, it's warm today. Who's the visitor?'

Eloise stood up. I followed her example, and turned to face Anne.

'Anne, this is Michael. He's an old acquaintance of mine. An artist. Michael, this is Anne.'

I held out my hand, almost in jest. One doesn't expect teenagers to be polite. However, I was in for a surprise. Anne took my hand and shook it firmly.

'Good afternoon,' she said. 'It's a pleasure to meet you. You've chosen a lovely day to visit us. I hope you like our little retreat. Eloise and I just love the place.'

She was tall, slim, blonde, and quite spectacularly pretty. Her blue eyes were darker than Eloise's, almost grey, and when she smiled her eyelids crinkled and her eyes seemed to sparkle. Her teeth were as brilliantly white as the sunlit walls of the cottage; one of the canines was slightly crooked, and although the flaw was barely discernible it seemed to emphasise the near-perfection of her mouth, and gave her smile an endearing little kink. Her lips were pink and moist, and filled me with a desire to bruise them with kisses.

'Enchanting,' I said. 'I didn't expect to find myself surrounded by such beauty. It's just a pity I don't specialise in landscapes,' I added, as I suddenly realised that my effusive comments could be misconstrued.

Anne's height – she was almost as tall as me, even though her feet were strapped into flat-soled sandals – was due to the length of her legs. And her long, shapely legs were entirely visible, as she was wearing only a pair of very brief shorts and a T-shirt that seemed to be a couple of sizes too small.

I decided it was pointless to pretend that I wasn't staring at her body. She didn't seem to mind the attention.

She was tanned, fit and lithe. Her skin glowed with youth and health. She would have looked like an athlete or gymnast had it not been for the generous size of her breasts, which were straining against the thin cotton of her T-shirt.

'I hope Michael is going to stay the night,' Eloise said, 'so you'll probably meet him again at dinner. But do wear something appropriate, dear.'

Anne tossed her head, causing her cascade of golden hair to fly from one shoulder to the other. 'All right, I suppose,' she said. 'But I haven't got any proper clothes, like I said.'

She turned and marched away, no doubt towards her bedroom. I watched her hips swing. I watched her oval buttocks, barely contained within the shorts, moving up and down as she walked. I reminded myself that on the following day she was to receive her first spanking.

I turned, to find Eloise watching me. Her bright blue eyes were wide and questioning.

'I can safely say,' I enunciated carefully, 'that even if I were obliged to leave here immediately, I could not in all honesty claim that this has been a wasted journey. Not one, but two delightful and beautiful creatures, immured in the depths of the countryside. I will certainly accept your invitation to stay.'

'I'm very pleased,' Eloise said. I noticed that her hand strayed to her left breast. 'I hope you can help me with advice about dealing with Anne. I really think you should read some of Celia's notes. I haven't read them myself in any detail. I wanted to wait until you were here. But I have extracted a section which seems to explain how she became involved with Anne's father. Would you read it?'

'Of course,' I said. 'Lead me to it. As long as I can steal a kiss on the way. By the way,' I added, as though I didn't realise that the information would almost oblige Eloise to let me assist her with Anne's birthday punishment, 'that establishment you mentioned in your letter. The Private House. I should have told you earlier, but I know the place. Been there, in fact. Know some of the people. I'll tell you all about it.'

From the notebooks of Celia Bright
I had a feeling that today was to be special. I have become accustomed to being summoned to D's house – a message delivered with a rose to my desk at work, a letter waiting for me inside the front door in the morning – but today D sent me a key to his house, with instructions that I was to let myself in. And he usually lets me know what he wants me to wear: a particular dress, or a specific set of underclothes, or no underwear at all, or perhaps just a general preference for a skirt

28

that can be unbuttoned down the back, or a soft blouse with short sleeves. Today his note states merely that I am to undress completely and wait for him in the study.

When I arrived at his house it was in darkness. When I put the key in the lock of the front door I found that my hand was shaking. Standing in the centre of the hall I listened to the silence. I was alone in the house. Normally the door would be opened by Thomas or Ruth. Both of them know why I come to D's house: indeed, both have at different times helped me to undress, and have held me down while D touches me or chastises me. It's not that D keeps no secrets from his domestic staff; it's simply that he has discovered that I become easily aroused by the embarrassment of being observed while D uses me for his pleasure. When they take my coat, or lead me into the drawing room, or bring me a drink, their faces remain impassive, their voices deferential. At such times it is almost impossible to believe that Thomas once held my arms behind my back and held a pad in my mouth to stifle my cries while D slapped my breasts, or that Ruth, with her hands around my ankles, has held my legs aloft so that D could play with my sex and my anus.

But today the house was empty. I wondered whether to light the rooms as I passed through them, but decided against it. I lit just one lamp in the study, to augment the glow from the fire in the fireplace. When he arrived D would be able to see my naked body highlighted by the subtle combination of dim lights. I undressed, and folded my clothes in a pile on a corner of the desk. I wondered whether to leave on my stockings and shoes: like most men D likes stockings and high-heeled shoes, and I knew that he would appreciate my legs in dark grey gossamer, with black lace edging, and red stilettos. However, he had specified that I was to be naked, and with some reluctance I removed everything from my body – even my wrist-watch and my necklace.

This, too, felt very strange. It occurred to me that never before had I been completely naked when with D.

I had always in the past retained something: stockings, shoes, jewellery, or at the very least the ropes with which he sometimes tied my wrists. To have nothing on at all made me feel ridiculously vulnerable – which was, I am sure, D's purpose. I guessed, too, that I would be made to wait for him, so that my feelings of foreboding would have time to breed and colonise in my imagination. What was he going to with me tonight?

The scent of my perfume – one of several that D had given to me – seemed overpowering. I touched myself between my legs. I proved what I already knew: I was wet there, wet with anticipation and longing.

I picked up my handbag and checked my make-up. I added another layer to the dark red gloss on my lips. I was wearing rich colours at my lips and lids, and dark mascara on my lashes. The style would have looked absurd in the daytime, as my complexion is pale, but it seemed appropriately Gothic for an evening in D's house.

I browsed along the shelves of books. There was no point in trying to read anything other than erotica: I thought it unlikely that I would be able to concentrate on anything else, and in any case I wanted to remain aroused for D. I found a slim novel that described the misadventures of a well-bred young lady who had the misfortune to be captured by a gang of barbarian bandits. I opened it at the first page, and started to read. I wandered to the fireplace, and stood before it with my legs apart, enjoying the heat on my bottom and thighs. The sensation reminded me continually of the fiercer heat I expected to feel when D came home.

I had read half of the novel, and had reached the point where the young lady, in order to avoid further punishments, had tearfully agreed to beg for the honour of taking into her mouth the bandit leader's prodigious member. My left hand had strayed between my thighs, as I was confident that the bandits would be unable to resist the tempting target of the lady's bare bottom as their leader instructed her in the art of fellatio – and I have a fantasy, as yet unrealised, of being spanked while licking D's penis. I heard the front door open, and then close.

My heart seemed to rise into my throat. D had arrived home. I wanted him so much that I was trembling. I fumbled the book into its place on the shelves, and knelt in front of D's armchair. I moved my knees apart, placed my hands together behind my back, and bowed my head. I had loosened my hair, so that it now fell from my shoulders and obscured my face.

I heard D's footsteps as he moved about the house. He went up the stairs; he came down again. Doors opened and closed. He was in no hurry to find me; he was making me wait. I felt the warmth of the fire on my face and my breasts, and another warmth, sending out tendrils of flame as it grew and slid downwards inside me towards the opening, moistening lips of my sex.

The door of the study opened, and the glowing logs flared. I could feel his eyes on me. I stayed still, letting him enjoy the sight of my body. At last I moved, lifting my shoulders to ease the strain of remaining for so long in one position. 'Hello,' I said, and pulled my hair back. I turned my face to look at him.

As always, my breath caught in my throat. I have known D for six months, and yet I am still never prepared for the thrill of seeing him. He was standing in the doorway, filling it; his presence dominated the room. He has to make no effort to have this effect on me. Today, when he found me in his study and I turned to see him, he was leaning casually against the door frame; his hands were in his pockets; he was smiling. He had changed into soft cotton clothes: dark trousers and a white shirt, open at the neck, sleeves rolled up.

He strolled into the room and sat in his armchair. I looked over my shoulder at him, but he seemed happy for me to stay where I was. He leant forward and ran his hand through my hair.

'Celia, you are an angel. Although I may have mentioned that before, I suppose. You're looking exquisite tonight. You seem to become ever more desirable. I don't know what I've done to deserve you. Come and sit with me.'

I scrambled to my feet and on to his lap. I love sitting with D in his armchair: he holds me in his strong arms, and I feel the warmth and hardness of his body. He seems like a giant, and I'm like an infant.

We kissed for a long time, like teenagers who have just fallen in love. Then, with my head resting on his shoulder and my lips grazing his neck, we chatted about the things we'd done since we last met. I had made a presentation to important clients; he had had a difficult board meeting. I told him about the play I saw last night. (Was it only last night? It seems like a lifetime.) We began to discuss whether to go to the opera at the weekend.

His left arm was warm and strong about my shoulders; the fingers of his right hand stroked my thighs, and occasionally brushed the tips of my breasts. I began to find it very difficult to concentrate on our conversation.

Some evenings we would stay wrapped around each other in the chair for hours. Sometimes, at last, D would hold my hands behind my back, part my legs and caress my wetness until I came, crying out softly and wordlessly against his chest. Sometimes he would ask me to undo his trousers and stroke his hot, hard, velvet cock; when he came I would catch his semen in my cupped hands, from where he would feed some of it to my lips with his fingertips.

Today, though, I felt unsettled. I couldn't help wondering what he had planned for me. I knew what would calm me.

'I know it's early,' I whispered, 'but would you spank me, please?'

D laughed. 'I intend to punish you later,' he said, 'if you'll let me.'

Even these words were troubling. D knew that he didn't need to ask me. 'That's all right,' I replied. 'It's just that I'd like a spanking now. Please.'

He held my face in his hands and stared at me, as if trying to find in my eyes the answer to an unvoiced question. He kissed my lips with exquisite tenderness. 'You know that I am yours,' he said. 'I'll do whatever you wish. Besides,' he added, with a grin, 'there's almost nothing that gives me more pleasure than smacking your bottom. Stand up.'

I stood before him. I put my hands behind my back, and shuffled my feet apart. I blushed, as I always do, as his steady gaze inspected my body. He gestured for me to turn round. I stood with my back to him. I could almost feel his eyes caressing my bottom as I bent forward.

'On my lap,' he said at last, and as usual at the last moment I succumbed to a strange reluctance – similar, perhaps, to the stage fright that afflicts actors – at the thought of placing myself in such an undignified position. So I went to the side of the chair, took a deep breath, and lowered myself slowly across the nearer arm, and down on to D's thighs, until my breastbone was resting on my folded arms on the other arm of the chair.

All doubt and anxiety sped away. I wriggled my stomach contentedly against D's thighs. His hand rested lightly on the small of my back. I felt safe.

He stroked my back and my buttocks for a while, making me wait for the first smack. He told me, in a low, loving voice, that he was going to spank my bottom until it was bright red. He touched the skin where he intended his smacks to land. I began to squirm with anticipation.

Then, as usual, I felt the gentle pressure of his hand between my thighs. This was the signal for me to move my legs apart. I sometimes think this is the best part of a spanking: the inexorable wave of shame that engulfs me when I realise that I am going to have to part my legs, and display not merely the most intimate parts of my body, but also the fact that I am so aroused that my juices have leaked from my vagina and have soaked the

33

whole area. At this moment D usually touches my labia, or runs a finger down the widening space between my buttocks: just a fleeting touch, but enough to remind me what he can see. If Thomas or Ruth is present the disgrace is almost too much to bear, particularly because I become even more excited. D likes to point out that he can see my cunt opening (he uses the vilest language when the servants are watching me), and my juice trickling out. If he touches me while he's talking I have to bite my lip to stop myself coming.

Today he amused himself by tugging at my outer labia, and smoothing my wetness into the fine blonde hairs there. The sensations were so wonderful that I found myself uttering little moans. I tried to clear my head; the spanking would begin at any moment, and I wanted to concentrate on enjoying the first smacks.

The first few smacks of a spanking are both the best and the worst. They hurt – they sting – and however much you try to prepare yourself you're never ready for that first slap of his hard hand on your soft buttock. But there's also a sense of release, of letting go. Sometimes I can't help crying out when the first smack lands, and the first few times D spanked me he stopped at once in order to ask whether I was all right. But it's a cry of relief, a cry of abandon. The punishment has started, and nothing else matters.

Soon, as you get into the rhythm of being spanked, the smacks stop hurting – or at least they merely add to a general stinging heat that spreads all over your bottom, and pushes in pulses, in time with the smacks, deep into your body.

Today D spanked me slowly. He likes to watch my buttocks move, being compressed by his hand and then springing back, with a fresh red imprint, to quivering, rounded readiness for the next smack. He sensed that I needed reassurance, perhaps, and he made sure that he interrupted his leisurely smacking at frequent intervals to touch my sex or my anus, and to tell me how adorable I am. If one of the servants had been present he would have commented on the evidence of my arousal, and the firmness of my buttocks, and how much I liked to feel his finger testing the resistance of my tiny hole. Just the thought of it made me tremble with an incipient orgasm.

D's usual practice is to increase the speed and severity of his smacks at the end of a spanking. At the same time he pushes his left hand between my hips and his thighs so that he can press against the top of my sex, near the tip of my clitoris. I am invariably so aroused that I come quickly – and, to my shame, very loudly.

Today, however, he didn't finish the spanking properly. He just rested his hand with finality on my bottom, and stroked me, and told me that both buttocks were the colour of pink rose petals.

I moaned in frustration, and pushed my bottom up against his hand.

He laughed. 'That's all for now,' he said. 'More later, if things go according to plan. Now turn over and let me kiss you.'

My bottom was warm and tingling. I wanted him very much. As I sat curled in his lap, kissing his face, my hand went to the hard shaft cocooned in the soft cotton of his trousers. 'I want to take you inside me,' I pleaded with him. 'Please let me have it. I'm so ready for you.'

I wanted him to acquiesce: to let me release his manhood and kneel astride him so that I could sink on to it and feel it pushing deeper and deeper inside me. I expected him to resist: to laugh, and pull my hand away, and tell me to wait. But he did neither: instead a worried frown crossed his brow, and he looked searchingly into my eyes once again.

'Celia, my love,' he said. 'Do you always enjoy the things I do to you? And the things I make you do?'

I was perplexed. How could he doubt it? 'Of course,' I replied. 'Everything.' I was so worried I was close to tears. 'I love you,' I said. 'I love everything about you. Everything you do.'

His eyes appeared to be watering too. He was determined to catechise me. 'I know you will do anything I ask,' he said, 'but can you assure me that you always enjoy obeying my instructions? Does it always please you to obey me?'

These were very specific questions, and very precisely phrased, but I didn't at that time understand their significance. I stroked D's face and told him that nothing gave me more pleasure than doing as he told me – except kissing him, and holding him, and hearing his voice, and feeling his hands on my body.

This answer didn't entirely satisfy him, and he spent some moments deep in thought before shrugging, and giving me a rueful smile. 'Well, that will have to do,' he said. 'I'll just have to see how things fall out. Come along, my love: stand up, and lead the way upstairs. You know how I like to watch your bottom moving as you're climbing the stairs.'

'Where are we going?' I asked, looking over my shoulder as we ascended. I took slow steps, swinging my hips from side to side, inviting D to touch my reddened buttocks.

'To the bathroom!' was the surprising answer, but I had no time to wonder about our unusual destination because D leapt up two steps, swept me off my feet, and carried me at a run up the remainder of the stairs and into the main bathroom.

He deposited me on the seat of the lavatory, and stepped back to watch me. I didn't know what to do. I looked up at him.

'Well, go on,' he said. 'You know you want to.'

He expected me to pee. And he clearly intended to stay in the room. I felt my face turning as warm and pink as my bottom. I don't know why I felt so embarrassed. We had been lovers for several months, and had become accustomed to seeing each other naked. There had been times when one of us would wander into the bathroom to find the other peeing. We thought nothing of it. But this was different. D was watching me. He expected me to perform for him.

I opened my mouth to protest, but remembered that only a minute previously I had vowed that I enjoyed following his instructions. And it was true that it was now several hours since I had last visited the lavatory. I should have been ready to empty my bladder again.

But I couldn't go. The more I concentrated on trying to relieve the pressure, the more aware I became of D, sitting casually on the side of the bath with a grin on his face and his eyes fixed unrelentingly on my crotch. My face was blazing with embarrassment.

'It's all right,' he said. 'No hurry. I'll just wait until you're ready.'

I swore at him. He laughed.

At last a few drops squeezed from my clenched urethra; then a trickle; then a stream. I turned my face to the wall.

'Keep your legs apart,' D said. 'I want to see clearly. And don't turn away – look towards me.'

His words made me shudder, and I realised that as soon as I had started to pee I had become suddenly aroused. If he were to merely touch me there, just above the source of the stream, I would come. I moved my knees further apart, and looked at him. He was still smiling, but only because that is his natural expression. He was gazing at me with what I can only describe as awe. I imagined myself seeing through his eyes, and pictured this: Celia, naked, caught in the most intimate of moments, red-faced and almost weeping with humiliation, holding her legs apart to show off the fountain of sparkling liquid, aware of being watched, aware of the shameful, unstopp-able splashing of the little waterfall. I felt ashamed and ridiculous, but I knew that in D's eyes I was beautiful.

His eyes remained on me as I dabbed at myself with a tissue. Then in two strides he was in front of me. He pulled me to my feet and into his arms. He kissed me.

'I suppose this is some kind of cleansing ritual,' he said. 'It seems appropriate, anyway, in the light of what's going to happen. Now go and sit on the bidet. Facing the taps.'

He watched as I played a jet of warm water on to my vulva. The sensations made me catch my breath.

yourself,' he said. 'Turn off the water for a
.. Take the soap. Rub the soap against yourself.'
  pressed the slippery bar into my sex his hand
    ed slowly through my hair, continued down my
  ine, and brushed my outthrust buttocks in circles that
crept closer and closer to the sensitive, wide-open
furrow. I was so close to coming that I had to stop,
frequently and suddenly, and grip the rim of the bowl
to suppress the shivers of ecstasy.

'Take your time,' he told me. 'I don't want you to
come, but you must be thoroughly clean. Put the soap
down and rinse yourself now.'

The warm, pulsing water was as seductive as the firm,
lubricious soap. When D's fingers joined mine to ensure
that the water rinsed every fold of my vulva I felt my
imprisoned climax surging to escape, and only a sharp
word from D contained it. I took several deep breaths,
and managed to calm the shuddering of my body.

I begged D to take me, there and then in the
bathroom. I was almost mad with desire. I tried to grab
the front of his trousers: I think I intended to pull his
cock into my mouth. But he was implacable: I was to
remain on the bidet, but I was to turn round so that I
could wash my arsehole. He insisted that I try to push
the bar of soap into my little hole, even though it was
obvious that the bar was too big. Then he made me use
my fingers instead, inserting one and then two soapy
digits. In the short time I have known him D has
ensured that I have come to appreciate the erotic
sensations that can be generated by stimulation of the
anus. He squatted in front of me and watched my face
as my fingers slid in and out of my arsehole.

'Good girl,' he said. 'You see? You enjoy washing
yourself, don't you? Now rinse off the soap. See if you
can direct the water right up your arse, sweetheart.'

I don't know how I restrained my orgasm as water
squirted into my anus and trickled down my perineum
to join the water dripping from my vulva. And with D
watching me so intently, so adoringly.

'Now dry yourself,' he said. 'Then come to the bedroom.'

I was suddenly alone in the bathroom. I selected a towel from the heated rail and began to dab it between my legs. I went slowly. I needed some time to recover my equilibrium, and in any case I was so aroused that if I had rubbed myself carelessly I would have come. I applied a little talcum powder, and brushed out my hair. Eventually I felt ready to look at myself in the mirror.

I was surprised to see so little external evidence of my inner turmoil. My face was still blushing pink, my eyes were very bright, and my nipples were erect. But it was impossible to tell that I had just performed for an audience (admittedly of only one, but he was very appreciative) the most intimate toilet acts, and that I had found the experience not only utterly degrading but also almost uncontrollably exciting. I turned, and looked over my shoulder: my bottom's pink bloom was fading. I hoped D was going to punish me again.

I can't decide whether I prefer to come with D inside me, or when he's spanking me. Once, he let me kneel astride him while he lay on his back on the bed; when I'd taken all of him inside me, I leant forward to kiss him. I hadn't realised that his hands could reach my bottom, which must have felt very open, and temptingly rounded, as I was bent forward. Anyway, the point is that he was able to spank me (and play with my arsehole) while I rode up and down on his erection. We came together, rather more quickly than either of us expected. So that probably wasn't quite as good as some of the other times, when I've been able to concentrate on D's hand slapping against my bottom, or his penis filling me – but it would be wonderful to try it again.

And I still had no idea what D had planned for this evening. It seems odd, now, that I couldn't work it out. I put my hand between my legs to check that I had dried myself thoroughly. My bottom was dry; so were my pubic hair and the lips of my sex. My fingers paused in their explorations; with my desire still crouching captive

39

within me, and my mind full of memories of D's face, and his hands touching me and spanking me, I knew that I would be wet inside.

My fingers teased apart my outer labia, and immediately met hot moistness. I pushed a little further in: the inner lips were ready to open, and offered no resistance. The mouth of my vagina was sopping wet. Even though I had just washed and dried myself, it would be impossible to conceal from D the true state of my mind. I didn't care. I didn't mind him knowing that the mere sound of his voice is enough to set off the tingling warmth inside me.

I smiled at my reflection, and set off to find D in the bedroom.

He had removed his clothes, and was now wearing only a long, silk dressing gown. He looked immaculate and elegant, standing in the pool of light from the bedside lamp, reading through a document on the table.

He must have heard me enter the room, but he didn't turn immediately.

'You still look ravishing,' he said, with pretend sadness, once he had looked at me steadily for a few moments. 'Kneel at the end of bed, would you? Facing the window.'

I did so. He walked round the bed, looking at me from every angle, and then he carried a chair to where I was kneeling and positioned it a little way in front of me and slightly to one side. He sat down, and was close enough to stroke my face, my hair and my breasts.

'Celia, my love,' he said. 'I have something to ask you. I've been putting it off for some time, but I can't postpone it for ever. Do you mind if I talk very seriously for a few minutes?' His fingers combed through my hair.

I don't know why, but my first thought was that he was going to ask me to marry him. And I didn't know how I would react. It might seem strange, but I've never imagined myself being married. I've never sought a husband, because I've always been searching, consciously or otherwise, for someone like D. And I never really believed that men like D existed, until I met him.

His hand moved from my hair to my breasts. His fingers stroked down lightly to one nipple and then the other. I felt my areolas crinkling. He cupped my left breast, and squeezed it. His thumb pressed against the rubbery hardness of the nipple. I caught my breath as I felt my labia parting.

I have very sensitive breasts. Sometimes D can make me come just by caressing and pinching them. I knew that if I let myself think of nothing but the vibrant sensations running between my nipples and my sex I would soon start to climb towards an orgasm.

The black silk of D's robe was tented by his erect manhood. I wanted to reach out and touch it; I wanted to bring it to my lips.

But I had to consider whether I wanted to be D's wife. I wanted nothing but to be his lover. I have my own house; I have a career. On the other hand, I can deny D nothing. What was I to do? How would I answer his proposal of marriage?

'I know we haven't known each other very long,' D was saying. 'But it's obvious we're entirely compatible. You enjoy the games we play as much as I do, I'm sure of that. I think it's time to ask you to take a step forward. But it's a big step. I hope you're ready. And once I've asked you, things will never be the same again. If you turn me down, we may have to part. So I hope you understand my trepidation. I don't want to lose you.' He was silent for a moment. His finger and thumb closed on my nipple and held it firmly. 'Look at me,' he said.

I looked up at his face. His eyes were wide with hope and anxiety.

'Celia, my love,' he said. 'I want you to agree to be my slave.'

I had been so certain that he would propose marriage that it took a few moments for me to comprehend his words. I must have looked bewildered.

'I don't mean a domestic slave,' he said with a sudden smile. 'I wouldn't have you dusting my house. Or rowing in my galley, if I had one. I mean I want you as my slave lover.'

'Yes,' I said. It seemed unnecessary to consider the question for even a second. 'Of course. I am already your slave.'

He briefly pinched the nipple he was holding, and I gasped.

'No, you're not,' he told me. 'Not yet. As my slave you will be subject to me in all things. You will have to consider the consequences very carefully. Above all, you must realise that your agreement is irrevocable. Your enslavement to me is and will remain entirely your decision. If, after some time as my slave, you decide that you want your freedom then I will not deny your request. But we won't be able to return to being lovers, as we are now. It would be the end for us.'

At first I couldn't understand why this would be so, but as I thought about it I realised that D was correct. Once he had become accustomed to owning me, and I had become accustomed to being owned, it would be impossible to have any other kind of relationship.

'I've drawn up a document,' he said, 'which I think covers everything that I will require of you. But let me tell you some of the most important things you need to consider.'

I had no doubts. I wanted to be D's slave. In my mind I was still going over the ramifications of his proposal, but my body had no reservations: D would use me for his pleasure, he would bind me and whip me, he would make me do disgraceful, disgusting things, and I could feel my body's response to the prospect – it was seeping wetly from my sex.

'As my slave,' D told me, 'you will not be entitled to expect pleasure of your own. I may choose to let you enjoy the things we do together; from time to time it will no doubt amuse me to let you reach a climax. However, your purpose will be to provide pleasure for me.

'You will be punished regularly, and more severely than you are used to. I may indulge you from time to time by giving you a spanking, but you must expect to be whipped frequently. And you must submit willingly – indeed enthusiastically – to any punishment I choose to inflict. You should be aware that I will do my best to ensure that your body at all times bears the marks of at least one punishment. In addition to these regular whippings, I may punish you for disobedience, for any failure on your part to please me, and for the entertainment of myself or others. Do you understand?'

I was surprised at how readily I was prepared to accept this fate. I couldn't remove from my mind the image of D, standing over me with a whip in his hand, striking my body so hard that the marks would remain visible until our next meeting. I so badly wanted those marks. I would be so proud of them. They would remind me constantly that I was his.

'I understand,' I said. My voice was trembling. 'And if you carry on talking about whipping me, I'll probably come here and now.'

'Try to control yourself a little longer, Celia,' he said with a smile. 'There are a few other things you need to know. First of all, when it comes to marking you, I will probably want to have you pierced – at least your nipples, and perhaps your labia. I might choose to have you tattooed. As your body will belong to me, you will have no part in such decisions.

'Your sole purpose will be to give me pleasure, and as symbol and reminder of that fact I will use your mouth and your anus when I wish to come inside you. I won't use your vagina for my sexual pleasure – although I may punish you by hurting it, and it will probably entertain me to have objects inserted into it, and perhaps to let others fuck you there. You are already used to taking me in your mouth. You will quickly become accustomed to taking me in your anus. Knowing you, I'm sure you'll soon get to like being buggered. In the time we've been together we have often had sex so that we both reach a climax at the same time. If you become my slave this will cease to be a frequent occurrence. When I fuck you

43

your only concern will be to ensure that I reach the best possible climax.

'And as for your orgasms: once you're my slave you will come only when I give my express permission. You will not touch yourself, other than to dress or wash, unless I am present and have given you instructions. When I allow you to masturbate until you reach a climax it will usually be because I want to watch you or to show you off to others. Occasionally I will use my fingers, or an implement, to bring you to a climax: I anticipate that I'll do so either while you're being punished, or perhaps in public places, to demonstrate your servitude.

'I will require you to maintain your house and your job. Your apparent independence will contrast with the reality of your slavery, and your submission to me will seem that much more piquant for both of us. However, I will take control of your wardrobe, and I'll instruct you to dispense with all items of clothing of which I don't approve. As my slave you will not purchase any clothes without my permission. Unless I instruct you to the contrary you will not wear knickers or trousers at any time, whether I am present or not.'

He stopped talking, and let me absorb the implications of everything he'd said. It all sounded entirely reasonable to me. I would be whipped: good. I would devote myself to D's pleasure: even better. I would be marked as his property, and would be under his jurisdiction even when at my home and in my office: nothing could make me happier (in fact I can already see that the problem will be curtailing my smugness). And I would be permitted to have orgasms! It was everything I've fantasised about.

I looked up at his face. 'I'm entirely willing to be your slave,' I told him. 'I belong to you.'

He sat back in his chair and exhaled a sigh of relief. His face couldn't disguise the glee that he was feeling, but he remained in control of his voice.

'Thank you, Celia,' he said. He stood up, and went to the table beside the bed. He collected the paper he had been reading and set it on the floor in front of me. He moved away, and returned with a coiled whip which he placed on the floor next to the paper. It was short, with a thick handle and a broad tail. It was made of black leather. It gleamed and looked sinister, like a sleeping snake.

'This is the document I mentioned,' he said. 'Please read it, and think carefully about your decision. I'll return in fifteen minutes. If you are still of the same mind – if you are sure you want to be my slave – then you must not speak to me unless and until I speak to you, and you must remember to address me as master. I'll then have you position yourself on the bed with your bottom raised. I'll whip you hard. You will thank me, and use your mouth to make me ready to penetrate you. Then I'll introduce you to the discomfort of being buggered. After that I imagine I'll be hungry, so we'll go out to eat. You'll wear a black choker when we're out together, until your collar has been made.'

He left the room. I didn't glance at the paper: I had already made my decision. I spent fifteen minutes staring at the whip, trying to imagine the sound it would make as D brought it down on my bottom, and how much more painful it would feel than D's hand spanking me. I yearned to put my hand between my thighs as I entertained these imaginings, but that was now forbidden to me. The prohibition served only to increase my longing.

I heard the sound of the door opening. D entered the room. I lowered my head.

It is three hours since I wrote the above account. I am back in my own house now, and have just finished sorting my underwear. I will keep two pairs of knickers, both made of lace, if D allows it. The rest will have to go. I will be always knickerless from now on! I feel delirious with happiness. I love him. I'm his slave. He is my master. I feel contented, and utterly secure. I will sleep soundly tonight (but on my front!). Tomorrow I'll go out into the world with such pride, such confidence. I am invincible, because I am his and he is mine.

I can't stop looking in the mirror to see the stripes on my bottom. I hope they're still there in the morning. I managed not to cry out while D was whipping me, but although he used plenty of lubrication I couldn't help yelling when he went into my anus. It was so painful. D told me to shut up and keep still, for which I'm grateful. It helped me to endure the pain and to concentrate on letting him enjoy me, which after all is the whole point of being his slave. And I'm rather ashamed to say that after he'd been pushing into me steadily for a few minutes, I began to experience a whole new and wonderful series of sensations. The burning stripes on my bottom, and the heat deep within my sex, and the stretched, full feeling in my arsehole all seemed to combine and expand, and I found myself pushing my bottom back to meet his thrusts. I wanted him to fill me. I almost came when he did.

D must have been satisfied with me, as he let me have an orgasm after I'd helped him take a shower. We had both dressed to go out for dinner – I was without underwear, of course, and had a choker of black velvet around my neck. He sat back in his armchair in the study, and had me kneel in front of him with my skirt pulled up to my waist. He told me to put two fingers up my arse, to remind me that I had been buggered (as if I needed reminding), and then he told me to use my other hand to play with myself until I came.

I love calling him 'master'. I said the word under my breath, over and over, as my fingers took me over the edge of my orgasm.

[Marginal note]
D has told me to collate and maintain a record of my enslavement: a more complete account than I keep in my diary. The pages above are from my diary and were written on the day that I became his slave – a decision which I still have no hesitation in declaring was the best

I ever made. I will place these pages at the front of this notebook, which I'll fill with words and pictures about my years of submission. I suspect there will be several notebooks, in fact. I wonder who'll ever read this?

From the diary of Anne Bright
10 May (continued)
Well, I've been sent to my room – in the middle of dinner – so I might as well finish writing this. Honestly, Eloise treats me like a child. I think she hasn't realised that I'm grown up now. I certainly was not showing off in front of Michael (well, only a bit, anyway) and I was being no ruder to Eloise than I usually am. It's just not fair.

Michael's rather nice, I think. He jokes and laughs a lot. He's actually rather attractive, considering that he's even older than Eloise. I think she's jealous because he and I get on so well together.

I wonder whether he's really a proper, serious artist. He seems a bit too flippant. But then he has got lovely hands, with long, slender fingers. And he looks sort of scruffy. So maybe he is.

Of course, maybe I like him just because he's a man. I've met so few.

And I wonder what he and Eloise are up to. And what it's got to do with me. Eloise measured me this afternoon. And not just to see how tall I am, like she used to when I was little. She measured everything: neck to waist, around my waist, waist to ankle, around my ribs, around my bust (she became very embarrassed when she did that one). It was just as well I was wearing only my shorts and a T-shirt, after all. Which I told her, of course.

I suppose it means she's going to buy me clothes for my birthday. That's all very well, but I'm old enough to choose my own clothes now. I suppose I'll have to try to look all grateful and delighted when I open the packages tomorrow. I just hope she has the sense to get me some modern things.

47

Anyway, I was able to get away in time to meet Josh as arranged. Now, I've written previously about my exploration of the old outhouse. It's been locked up for as long as I can remember, and I've wanted to take a look inside ever since Eloise told me – years and years ago – that I must never go in there. The more I think about it, the more I'm sure that the stuff in the outhouse must have belonged to Mummy, although she never mentioned it when she was alive, and I don't remember her ever going there. It's as if the adults have pretended all through my life that the outhouse doesn't exist.

Well, I found a way in, about three months ago (see diary for 16 March!), but it was a bit too cold to stay there and explore. It's difficult to get in without being seen, so I've only been back once (see 19 April). And it's full of weird things.

It's just the most exciting place. It's not just because it's out of bounds, although that certainly makes it thrilling. (Maybe I am a naughty girl, as Eloise avers. I seem to get a thrill from doing things I shouldn't. But then, I don't know any non-naughty girls to compare myself with.)

No, the things in the outhouse are strange and wonderful. I've peeked under the dust covers, and there are big pieces of furniture that look at first sight just like ordinary chairs and beds and so on, but then when you look closely you realise that they've got extra bits, and bits missing, and straps and handles and so on. There's a big, black leather chair that looks like it comes from a dentist's. And a flat thing that's a cross between an ordinary bed and something out of a dungeon. In fact, because it's so dark in there, it makes me think I'm in a dungeon – and that's particularly exciting because, as I've confided in these pages many times, one of my favourite things to daydream about when I'm lying in bed is being captured by a gang of (handsome, naturally) ruffians and held prisoner in a dungeon. They chain me to the wall and threaten to torture me unless I tell them the information they want – and I refuse, obviously. I've usually got my hand on my breasts by this time, because it feels so exciting, or tucked between my legs. That's where the daydream ends, because I don't really want to be tortured. Well, not horribly, anyway.

Hanging on the walls of the outhouse there are things that make me wonder whether it used to be a stable. There are loops of leather, which might be reins, and other bits of leather held together with metal links, which look like complicated harnesses. And there are whips and riding crops, so I suppose the building must have been a stable. There's a small two-wheeled carriage under one of the dust sheets. No evidence of any stalls for horses, though. And I can't imagine what the lengths of chain would have been used for.

Oh. I've just had a very odd notion. It's almost too wicked to write down. But I will, because this is my private diary. What if the outhouse really is a dungeon? If you were lying on that odd bed, for instance, with your arms and legs tied up, you'd be at the mercy of anyone who wanted to use a whip, or one of those long, whippy sticks I found in the corner. It's just too exciting! They could tie you up in any position they wanted to. Oh goodness. I want to go to bed straight away and start my dungeon daydream.

And maybe that's why Josh –

But I'm getting ahead of myself. Josh was waiting for me, as we had planned, and after a bit of kissing I said we had to get out of sight. I showed him the loose boards I'd found, and I led the way into the outhouse. It was a bit of a struggle for Josh, as he's not as slim as me, but the prospect of taking off my clothes and a helping hand from me were enough to pull him through.

It's been sunny all day today, so we weren't prepared for the gloom. We held on to each other, breathing deeply, as our eyes adjusted. As we were touching anyway, it seemed natural to let Josh kiss me again, and soon his hands were stroking the front of my T-shirt and I was beginning to feel those lovely tingly, sticky, sinking feelings, all over my breasts and deep inside me.

Then, suddenly, he stopped. 'Bloody hell,' he said. 'What are those?'

He was staring at the implements arranged in rows on the walls.

'Whips and things,' I said. 'This used to be a stable.'

He looked at me as though as I was mad, or stupid. (And I think I realise why, now. But I've never been in a real stable, have I? How am I supposed to know what's obviously to do with horses and what obviously isn't? I know about things such as Pure Mathematics and the Metaphysical Poets. Josh is the country boy.)

With wide eyes he crept about, lifting the corners of dust sheets and whispering obscene exclamations at what he found under them.

He came back to where I was standing. 'This is a very weird place,' he said. I suppose I should have noticed the wary tone of his voice, but I was very excited and I wanted him to touch my breasts again.

'I know,' I said. 'Isn't it thrilling? I love it here. It's my favourite place.'

That was enough for Josh. I expect he already had reservations about seducing the poor little rich girl from the isolated cottage, and my enthusiasm for the dark secrets of the outhouse confirmed his worst fears. He pretended that he could hear someone approaching, and he almost ran to where the loose boards were letting in slivers of light. Within seconds he was gone.

I was not in a very good mood when I returned to the cottage. I went for a long walk in the paddocks, and returned late for dinner. Under the circumstances I think it's entirely understandable that I was 'grumpy and uncommunicative' during the first course. What does Eloise know about my life, anyway?

So it's my birthday tomorrow, and I might finally be given some idea of what's going to become of me. I'm getting to the point where I don't care, as long as I can go a long way from here. And as long as I can meet some people. Including some men.

That's everything for today. I'll take my clothes off before I write the very last bit.

That's better. I can hear Eloise and Michael talking downstairs. They don't know I'm sitting on my bed without a stitch on. They don't know that I'm touching my nipples. It feels so nice. Now: shall I start my dungeon daydream, or shall I read my favourite anatomy book? Anatomy first, I think. I'll prop the mirror on the pillows so that I can compare the picture in the book with the reflection. It's difficult to get the mirror at the right angle, and the book next to it, and me in front of the mirror with my legs wide apart, but it's worth it. I'm learning all the proper names: labia (outer and inner), vagina, anus, urethra, clitoris. The words themselves are exciting, but I like to touch each part in turn, and watch my fingers in the mirror; that's more than just exciting! After a while I use my other hand to stroke my breasts. Doing that at the same time as I'm touching the area near my clitoris is sometimes so exciting that it's almost painful. An anatomy lesson never fails to get me in the mood for a dungeon daydream.

I'm sure that these are the bits of my body that are to do with sex. They're the bits the boys all want to get their hands on. I can't believe that it's a coincidence that the only textbooks that fail to arrive here are the ones that have sections on human reproduction. It's the one subject that I can't seem to find a way to study. It's as if Eloise is deliberately keeping me in ignorance. And that's not fair, either.

THREE

On the morning of Anne's birthday I rose late. I'm not used to any other routine, and the dawn chorus of rural birdsong had no more effect in waking me than the vehicles rumbling past my apartment in the city.

I found Eloise in the kitchen, to which I had been drawn by the smell of coffee. She was standing in sunlight at the window, looking out into the garden. She had her back to me, and was dressed in only a voile slip which the rays of light rendered almost transparent. She hadn't heard me approach, and so I stood in the doorway and admired her admiring the view.

She was standing on her left leg; her right was bent at the knee, and only the toes of her right foot were touching the floor. As a result her hips were tilted very prettily, showing off the slim curves of her waist. Her head was cocked to one side, and the short curtain of her bobbed dark hair just touched her shoulder. She was a picture of slender elegance, and only a soft pencil and a sketch pad would have improved my enjoyment of the moment. My eyes kept returning to the soft cushions of her buttocks, their oval perfection draped in flimsy material that served only to accentuate their curves.

'Is there enough coffee in that pot for me?' I said.

She started, and turned. She was holding a mug in both hands. Her eyes were wide and her lips were parted. She could have been the model for a painting with a classical theme: a shy nymph surprised by a satyr at a sacred grove.

I would have had to lose the coffee mug, of course, but otherwise she was perfect. The voile slip could easily be transformed into a wisp of diaphanous robe.

'Yes, there's plenty,' she said. Her cheeks reddened. 'I'm not dressed. I must get something on.'

She took a few steps towards the doorway, and then realised that I had no intention of moving from it.

'Actually,' I said, trying hard to keep my voice level and reassuring, 'I think you look perfect just as you are. So don't bother to dress on my account.'

Her blush deepened, and her eyes pleaded with me. I held my ground.

'What about that coffee?' I said. 'I'm a desperate man. I'm not civilised until I've had my first dose of caffeine.'

She smiled at last, and lowered her arms. I didn't attempt to disguise the fact that I was looking at her breasts. The nipples were dark shadows beneath the voile, and jiggled enticingly as she moved. She turned slowly, conscious of my gaze, and placed her mug on the table. Succumbing to the pleasure of being watched, she stole glances at me as she stretched to take a cup from the top shelf of the dresser. She poured coffee into it and brought it to me.

'Thank you,' I said. 'That's wonderful.' I'm sure she understood that I meant her as well as the coffee.

'Michael,' she said, 'you know those pages from Celia's journal that I gave you yesterday afternoon? I read them last night.'

The coffee was black, its bitterness offset by a chocolatey thickness. Eloise's blue eyes were bright with excitement.

'Strong stuff,' I said. That covered both the coffee and the story of Celia's submission. 'What did you make of it?'

Eloise hardly needed to answer. Her eager eyes, her quivering lower lip and the stiffness of her nipples told me everything.

'Well, I've never read anything like it before,' she said. 'Do you think she was writing a story? I mean, it couldn't possibly be a factual account, could it? People don't really do things like that, do they?'

Looking at her over the rim of the cup, I reached out to touch her hair. She didn't move away, so I let my hand caress her cheek and descend on to her shoulder.

'Things like what?' I whispered, and pulled her gently towards me.

She was close enough to kiss. She smelt of rose-scented soap. Her voice was low but steady and businesslike. 'Today, if I am to abide by Celia's wishes, I shall have to make Anne masturbate in front of me, and I shall have to spank her. I don't have the first idea how to go about it.' When she looked up at me her face expressed no confusion, however: just pleading desire.

I knew precisely what to do. My cup was now empty, and I offered it to her. Instinctively she reached for it, and I opened my hand before hers was in a position to receive it. The cup slipped through her fingers and fell between us to the tiled floor. It broke with a crash that made her gasp.

'Clumsy girl,' I said. My gaze didn't waver from her eyes. 'You've broken the cup. That was very naughty.'

Eloise knew exactly what was going to happen next. 'No one will hear,' she said softly. 'I've told the gardener and the maid to take the day off, and Anne's gone out for a walk.'

I pulled her into my arms. We exchanged coffee-tasting kisses. Her breasts were warm against my chest, the nipples as hard as pebbles. I ran a hand down her back and caressed her buttocks: the delicate material of her slip slid deliciously over the swelling flesh.

'Are you ready?' I said.

She nodded. She was blushing again, and kept her head lowered.

'I'll give you eighteen smacks,' I said. 'That seems to be the appropriate number.'

She buried her face in my neck. 'Do you want me to – I mean, before I spank Anne I'm supposed to – you know.'

I waited, stroking her bottom and her hair.

'Do want me to watch me playing with myself?' she blurted at last.

'Not now,' I replied. 'Perhaps later. Aren't you already excited? Tell me.'

She looked up at me. 'I think I'm very wet down there,' she said. 'Do you mind?'

'On the contrary,' I said. I kissed her again, while my hand cupped her right buttock and my fingers pressed into the hollow where she admitted to being wet. She moaned softly into my mouth.

I kept my hand on her bottom as I led her to the kitchen table, which was a wide slab of old oak on sturdy legs.

My cock was uncomfortably hard inside my trousers. I wanted to be as undressed as Eloise was; I wanted to see her with her torso pressed against the table's top, her legs stretched wide apart, her arse open and projecting; I wanted to flog her buttocks and her vulva and then plunge my cock into her wet heat.

However, I knew I had to progress slowly. So I continued to hold her reassuringly and I guided her limbs gently as I said, 'Stand a little way from the table. Now lean forward and rest your elbows on it. That's right. And now dip your back, so that your bottom is presented prettily.' I kept my hand in the small of her back until it was arched downwards to my satisfaction.

Her head was bowed, and her dark fringe of hair was touching her forearms. 'I feel ridiculous,' she said in small voice.

I stood beside her, on her left. I placed my left hand on her back, and with my right I started once again to caress her buttocks through the flimsy material. 'You've been a naughty girl,' I said. 'Being made to feel embarrassed is part of the punishment. You want to be punished, don't you?'

Her reply was almost inaudible. 'Yes.'

I gave her bottom the lightest of slaps.

'Say please,' I said.

Her voice was a little stronger. 'Yes, please.'

I slapped her again, a little harder. 'And call me sir.'

'Yes, please, sir. I want to be punished.'

As I pulled up the skirt of her slip she gave a muffled cry of protest, but didn't move. I gathered the material in my left hand at the small of her back.

Her buttocks were flawless ovals, separated by a deep, dark cleft. I began to caress them with my hand.

'What a pretty bottom,' I commented. 'It's pale and cool now, but in a few moments it will be pink and warm.' The regular movements of my hand and the sound of my voice seemed to relax Eloise. When I was sure that she was comfortable and still I lifted my right hand from her bottom, very slightly increased the pressure of my left hand on her back, and then swung my right hand down with moderate force.

My palm landed with a loud slap on her right buttock. Eloise made no sound or movement. I smacked her in the same way on the left buttock, and then continued with six more, during which Eloise slowly lowered her head on to her forearms.

Her arse now had a blush of colour, and I stopped smacking her to stroke it for a few moments.

'Ten more to come,' I said. 'Move your legs apart.'

I wanted to see how readily she would obey instructions, and whether she would object to exhibiting her private parts.

She didn't hesitate, but moved her bare feet across the tiles so that her inner thighs and her vulva were displayed to me. Without being asked she kept her knees slightly bent and her feet on tiptoe, which had the effect of pushing her bottom out further.

My right hand drifted lower. She made a muted sound as it travelled down between her buttocks, but she kept still. My fingers then discovered why she was submitting so readily to the punishment and to my instructions: she was so aroused, so ready for sex, that her inner labia were wide open and leaking a trickle of lubricating fluid. Her profuse pubic hair was sopping wet, and the insides of her thighs were slick.

I curled my hand under her sex and pressed with my fingers at the top of her split flesh. She gasped and shuddered, and I could tell that only a little more massaging of that area would be sufficient to induce a climax.

I withdrew my hand, and she moaned. 'Very, very naughty girl,' I said. 'I can see that the final ten smacks are going to have to be very hard.'

Eloise murmured her agreement, and I resumed her spanking.

In truth the ten were not much harder than the eight, but by the final few smacks she was uttering a quiet 'Ah!' when each one landed, and what with the impetus of my palm and the wiggling of her hips her buttocks were dancing quite delightfully by the time I finished.

'Don't move!' I told her, and my right hand returned to her bottom to caress the heated ovals. I released the material of her slip from my left hand, which I slid under her stomach and into the gap between her thighs. As my fingertips began to tease the supremely sensitive fold of skin above her clitoris, I interrogated her.

'Did you enjoy your spanking, Eloise?'

She was, I'm sure, in the midst of a whirlwind of sensations from her stinging bottom, the soothing touch of my right hand, and the fires of pleasure being stoked by my left. She managed to mutter, 'Yes.'

'Then what do you say?' I insisted, removing my fingers from her swelling bud in order to allow her to concentrate.

She moaned again, with frustrated desire. 'Thank you,' she gasped.

My right hand administered a resounding slap, and she yelped.

'Thank you for spanking me, sir,' she said.

'That's better,' I told her. 'Now, would you like me to play with you until you come?'

She lifted her head and looked up at me through the curtain of her hair. 'Yes, please, sir,' she said, and smiled.

'Very well,' I said. 'In that case I'll place my thumb here, right on your arsehole. Can you feel that? Does it feel nice when I press in, like that?'

Her head had sunk back on to her arms. I could feel her pushing her bottom back to meet the pressure of my hand. She murmured an answer, with which I decided for the moment to be satisfied. There would, I began to see, be

57

plenty of time in which to teach her the correct procedures for submission.

'And then my fingers,' I went on, 'can touch you here, at the source of your wetness. Perhaps this finger can slip inside? And then another?'

Her vagina was tropical in its heat and humidity. My fingers slid into her without the slightest resistance – in fact her entrance seemed almost to suck them in. My erection twitched, and I again considered whether it wouldn't be more pleasurable to take her there and then, so that we could ride together into a joint and complementary ecstasy. But this was supposed to be for her benefit, and I contented myself with enjoying her little cries of pleasure as I moved my fingers inside her.

'And finally,' I said, leaning forward to place a kiss at the base of her spine, now cool and damp with her perspiration, 'I'll tickle you here. And then rub, very gently. And then tickle again. And then tug at these wet hairs. And then rub again.'

I didn't need to touch the tip of her clitoris. My fingertips danced around it, and after only a few seconds Eloise's breath started to catch in her throat and her vagina began spasmodically to grip my fingers.

Watching a woman having an orgasm is, I find, an unfailing delight. Whether she comes when I am inside her, or while I am smacking her, or as a result of the movements of my fingers or of her own, I feel almost as though I am sharing in the pleasure. I feel a sense of power, too, I must admit: a woman's orgasm is overwhelming, all-encompassing, and I feel pleasure and pride in creating sensations that reach the extreme of experience. In the end I'd have to say that I would rather submit a lover to a climax than to come myself: male orgasms are thin, brief, occasional things, genital spasms, mere spurtings of release, whereas women come with their whole bodies, and in their minds, and sometimes over and over again.

And women look and sound so beautiful when they're coming. Eloise's ragged gasps grew in volume and frequency; her body trembled. I was merciless, and continued to brush my fingers around her clitoris even as her gasps turned into loud cries. I pressed my thumb against her anus, and thrust my fingers into her vagina as deeply as I could. Her limbs shook and her body jerked. After what seemed like several minutes, her legs gave way and she collapsed on to the table.

Immediately I put my hands under her torso and pulled her upright. I clasped her to me, she rested her head against my chest, and I tucked strands of her hair behind her ears. Her eyes and lips were half open; her cheeks were flushed. She looked quite simply good enough to eat, and I kissed her face hungrily.

For a moment her eyes widened, and she looked up at me. 'Oh,' she said, and smiled. Her eyes closed.

I extended my arm under her legs and lifted her off the ground. She seemed to weigh almost nothing as I carried her from the kitchen to the morning room, and subsided on to a sofa with her on my lap.

We spent some time kissing lazily. I was very conscious of the pressure of her warm bottom against my stiff cock, and it seemed that she also had detected the unyielding hardness.

'What about you?' she said, wriggling a little. Now it was my turn to gasp. 'I've come – to put it mildly. It doesn't seem fair.'

I shrugged. 'Would you like to touch my penis?'

She nodded. Her cheeks were reddening again.

Through the thin material of her shift I toyed with one of her nipples, held it between my finger and thumb, and then squeezed until she gave a little cry of pain. 'Ask properly, then, and I might let you.'

She twisted on my lap and pressed her breasts against my chest. 'Please, sir,' she whispered, 'may I touch your penis?'

'Of course you may,' I said.

She moved her bottom so that she was sitting on my knees; now she could reach to undo my trousers. I could feel her fingers trembling as she unbuckled my belt. The tip of her tongue appeared from between her lips as she

59

concentrated on her task. Every now and then her gaze darted from my lap to look questioningly at my face, as if she needed assurance that she was performing correctly. It occurred to me that it could have been a long time – many years, perhaps – since she had last had a man's cock in her hands. So despite the increasing urgency of my desire, inflamed by the movements of her fingers as she undid the buttons of my trousers, I smiled and murmured words of encouragement. I told her that she looked astonishingly pretty, which was no exaggeration. I brushed my fingers against the front of her slip and watched her breasts jiggle.

Her finger closed around the stiff shaft of my penis. 'Gently,' I said, touching her nipples with the delicacy I hoped she would employ when touching me.

My erection was standing between us now. Freed from the constraint of my clothing it felt cooler; the danger of imminent release had passed. 'Hold it just below the glans,' I told Eloise. 'And a little less tightly. That's right. Now slide your fingers upwards, so that you pull the loose skin just over the rim of the glans. That's it, not too far. Little movements. Now pull back again, to just the below the rim. Ow! Not as far as that. Just a little way. Now do it again: gentle, little movements, just above and below the flanged head of my penis. That's perfect. It's very sensitive there – almost as sensitive as your clitoris. See how big and hard you're making me?'

Her bright blue eyes were as wide as saucers as she stroked me. 'It's so big,' she breathed, 'and so hard. But warm and soft to touch. If I carry on, will you come?'

'You'd have to do it faster,' I said, 'but don't. I'm rather enjoying the sensation of slow stroking. Now bring your lips closer so I can kiss you.'

We remained like that for some time, with our faces pressed together, her hands moving in my lap, and my fingers caressing the voile slip against the tips of her breasts. My excitement was intense, and the pressure was building to a point where I was becoming desperate for release, but I was determined to enjoy Eloise for as long as possible before I came. Images of things that I would like to do with her flashed into my mind.

When our mouths separated to take breaths I idly murmured, 'I'd like to smack your breasts.'

'All right,' she said. 'But –'

Suddenly I feared that I had taken a step too far. She had only just had her first spanking. Perhaps that was as far as she wanted to go.

'What is it?' I asked.

She looked into my eyes. 'I want to do something for you,' she said. 'It's only fair.'

'What do you have in mind?'

'Well,' she said with a shy smile, 'when Celia became a slave she was made to please her master with her mouth.'

My cock twitched involuntarily in Eloise's hand, and her smile widened. She knew that I would not be able to resist the proposal.

However, it was important to preserve the authority of my role. I did my best to look unimpressed. 'You can ask, I suppose. Get off my lap, take off that slip, and kneel in front of me.'

Eloise scrambled to obey. Naked, she knelt before the sofa where I reclined with my legs widely parted and my penis rising like a pole from my trousers.

'Please, sir,' she said, 'may I have your penis in my mouth?'

I leant forward. 'Yes, I think I'll allow that. You can kiss and lick my cock to start with, and then when I'm ready I'll put it inside your mouth and fuck you until I come. Don't swallow until I give you permission.'

She stared up at me for a moment. She seemed shocked at the coarseness of my words. I merely grinned at her until she lowered her head and inclined her body forwards.

I felt the moist warmth of her lips encircle the head of my penis. Her tongue touched the opening of my urethra. Then she pulled away.

'I haven't done this for a very long time,' she said. 'Not since I was a student.'

I reached out to stroke her hair. She looked adorable, gazing up at me with her open mouth almost touching the bulb of my penis. 'You'll remember what to do. Just keep your teeth out of the way.'

She kissed and licked the glans for a few minutes before looking up again.

'You taste wonderful,' she said. She bent forward, and then stopped. 'What if Anne comes back?'

'It would be very embarrassing if she found you in this position,' I told her. 'You'd better hurry up and make me come quickly.'

I lay back on the sofa as Eloise applied herself once more to the task of licking me. She had an agile tongue, and my last coherent thought was that she must have been a practised – and no doubt popular – fellatrix in her student days.

She licked in circles around the head of my penis: once clockwise, and then once anticlockwise, in the cool air outside her mouth, and then she pulled the glans into her mouth, held it between her lips, and in the warm wetness repeated the double licking. Then outside her mouth again; then inside. Again and again, with increasing speed.

I was unable to stop myself thrusting my hips up to meet her lips, and soon I knew that I would not long be able to resist the pressure that was building in my loins. I leant forward and placed my left hand on her head to keep her still; with my right hand I guided my shaft into her mouth, and began to pump it. With her lips stretched round my hard cylinder of flesh, and her mouth full of my oscillating glans, Eloise was no longer able to lick me, but she pushed upwards with her tongue in a rhythm that matched my increasingly rapid thrusts.

I felt the hot seed rising from my balls; I saw Eloise's breasts trembling each time I thrust into her mouth; I remembered the pinkening of her pale buttocks under the slaps of my palm.

I imagine I exclaimed some sort of hoarse cry just as I felt the semen rush through my member. It jetted into Eloise's mouth, once, twice, three times, and then again and again with decreasing force.

I wanted nothing more than to throw myself back into the depths of the sofa and close my eyes. But I have been playing games of domination and submission for many years, and I know that my role carried with it certain responsibilities. So I controlled my breathing, remained sitting upright, and kept my hand on Eloise's head.

'Don't move,' I gasped, and kept her waiting until I was completely in control of myself.

My penis was still firm. I pulled it slowly from between her lips. 'Very good,' I said. 'I'll let you do that again one day soon.'

She looked up at me with a pleading look. Her lips were pursed and her cheeks were distended. Her mouth was still full of my semen. She had remembered my instruction.

I stroked her face, and then cupped my hand in front of her. 'Let some come into my hand,' I said.

She pouted, and a dribble of creamy fluid slid down her chin and into my palm. Her cheeks were aflame: she must have found this procedure as degrading as I found it aesthetically pleasing. She looked beautiful: her face was red, her eyes were bright and wide, her lips and chin were slick with semen. I felt a twinge of ache in my penis as it began to harden again.

I used my fingers to anoint her face with my come: I applied it to her eyelids, her jawline, her upper lip, her throat. I told her how appealing she looked. And at last I said, 'All right. You can swallow now.'

With a sob she gulped back the mouthful of viscous fluid. She gagged, coughed, and swallowed again. She licked her lips. She wouldn't look up at me, and I wondered whether she was about to start crying.

I put my hand under her chin and lifted her face. 'Was that good?' I said. 'Do you like the taste of me?'

She nodded, blinking back tears. Perhaps she had thought that, having used her for my pleasure, and in a particularly humiliating way, I would no longer have any interest in her. I had to convince her that nothing could have been further from the truth.

'Well, then,' I chided her, 'what must you say?'

'Thank you, sir,' she whispered.

'For?'

'Thank you, sir, for using my mouth,' she said, more confidently.

'Eloise, you are truly wonderful.' I bent to kiss her forehead. 'Come and sit with me. Let me hold you.'

We huddled together on the sofa. I felt drained – quite literally – but content. And excited, too, although I had hardly the energy to express it, because Eloise was pretty and very desirable, and was mine to play with. And I was sure that she was as happy as I.

We kissed and caressed each other, and together fell into a doze – from which we awoke with a start.

'Was that the door?' Eloise whispered. 'Is it Anne?'

I held her in my arms and we listened to the silence extend for several minutes. Simultaneously we breathed out sighs of relief.

'I must get dressed.' Eloise kissed me and jumped from my lap. 'Come with me. We have to talk.'

Eloise's bottom was no longer pink, but the two perfect ovals still mesmerised me as I followed them upstairs. I watched sorrowfully as in her bedroom she concealed her body under a cotton dress.

'Well,' she said, combing her hair, 'now I know how to smack Anne's bottom. And her behaviour last night gives me the pretext to do it. But I still don't see how I'm going to persuade her to masturbate for me. And I'm supposed to do that first, before the spanking.'

'Presents first of all,' I reminded her. 'Given the amount you've spent on her, and the quality of the merchandise, she ought to be suitably grateful and agreeable to almost anything. Then again, she is a teenager.'

'And the other thing,' Eloise said, coming to sit beside me on her bed, 'is the question of whether you should be present throughout this strange ritual. Anne doesn't know you; on the other hand, she obviously likes showing off to you. She'll probably feel even more inhibited with you present; on the other hand, I'd feel much more confident if you were there. I don't know what to do.'

'I think I should be there when you give her the presents,' I said – I'd already considered the matter and had decided on the best course of action – 'and then we'll see whether Anne objects to me staying while she tries on the clothes. If she's prepared to let me watch her modelling her new, grown-up lingerie then I think we can assume she's happy to let me watch whatever happens next. And,' I added, 'I've been thinking about the masturbation issue, too. The question is: does she masturbate already? Has she already worked out how to do it, when she's alone in her room, or in the bath?'

For a moment Eloise looked like the prim tutor she was accustomed to being. 'I haven't the first idea,' she said. 'How could I possibly know?'

I smiled. 'The bedtime reading is usually a give-away. While she's still out, I suggest we take a quick peek at whatever books she has secreted under her bed.'

'I don't know.' Eloise looked anxious and slightly angry. 'It's an invasion of her privacy. After all, she's an adult now. How would you like to have people poking around your bedroom?'

'They'd get a shock if they weren't broad-minded,' I said. 'But seriously, this isn't about us gratifying our prurient curiosity about a teenage girl's sexuality. It's a matter of doing everything we can to abide by her mother's last wishes. Anne is about to face a test. If she performs well she will be given the opportunity to be trained at the Private House. That's a privilege, and we have to do our best to help her succeed.'

Eloise giggled, put her arms around me, and placed a hand on the front of my trousers. 'Oh, I see. Well, since you put it that way, I can only agree with your suggestion. Shall we go and satisfy our prurient curiosity?'

From the diary of Anne Bright
11 May. My birthday! Hurrah (I think).
Oh my goodness what a morning. So much has happened that I don't know where to begin.
Begin at the beginning, Anne. That's always the best. So: what did I do first? It already seems a long time ago. I think – I'm not sure – but I think my whole life is changing today. Which I suppose is what happens when you become an adult. But not quite this suddenly. And the afternoon is still to come.

Keep calm. Concentrate on this morning. It was another sunny day. I went out for a walk.

I wasn't feeling sunny. There were no presents waiting for me when I woke up. Eloise was moping about the house in her negligée, and had nothing for me but a 'Happy Birthday'. She said I had to wait until later. I'm so fed up with waiting. So I was rather brusque with her, and went straight out.

I suppose I intended to stay out all day, so that Eloise would have to wait for me for a change. But there was no one I knew to talk to in the village. I saw Tom Hinch and a couple of his friends on the other side of the green; usually they'd come over and try to chat to me, but today they just stared. I wonder if Josh has been spreading stories about me already.

I took the long way home, through the woods, but there's a limit to how long one can extend a purposeless stroll through the countryside. And I couldn't help wondering about my presents, and about the instructions Mummy left about my education.

So it was still morning when I returned to the cottage. I wanted to go to my room without Eloise knowing I was there, but as I was going up the stairs she called out, 'Anne! Come down to the drawing room when you're ready. We've got lots of surprises for you.'

'We.' So Michael was still there. That cheered me up a little. In my room I brushed out my hair and changed my clothes – although, of course, as it turned out I needn't have bothered.

I found Eloise and Michael sitting together in the drawing room. I think it occurred to me at the time that they were looking very pleased with themselves, and that I would do my best to attract Michael's attention by flirting with him. Once again, a rather futile resolution considering what happened!

And all my attention was immediately taken up with the mountain of parcels piled on the floor. I hadn't expected so many presents. I was speechless.

'Come in, Anne,' Eloise said. 'As you can see, there are lots of packages for you to open. As I think you've realised, there are things we will have to discuss now that you've reached the age of eighteen, but I'm sure you'd like to open your presents first.'

'So start unwrapping,' Michael added. I got the impression that he had helped Eloise in selecting the gifts. I suppose I might have felt resentful at his intrusion, but I was so excited that it didn't occur to me.

I started to tear the wrapping paper from the boxes, bags and parcels.

I've made a separate list of all the presents. They're all wonderful. And everything is so grown-up. There are no children's things at all: not a single cuddly toy, no casual clothes in indeterminate sizes 'to grow into', no plastic jewellery. Everything is real, and obviously expensive.

At first I was most pleased with the luggage: a complete matching set of suitcases and soft cases and make-up cases and even hat boxes. And a big leather briefcase. I loved it all, because it was so significant: it meant I would be travelling, and I so wanted to get away.

But then I looked again at the jewellery: earrings and necklaces and rings and pendants, all in white gold and utterly sophisticated.

And the cosmetics! Oils, creams, powders, colours, perfumes – all from one of the most expensive ranges. I confess I reached the point where I was squealing with delight each time I opened another of the little, gold-embossed scarlet boxes. I wanted to try them all immediately. I would be able to make myself look just like a fashion model.

Every now and then I remembered to look up from my hoard of booty, and I would find Michael and Eloise looking indulgent and excited. They seemed to be as delighted as I was. Several times I jumped up to hug Eloise. I seem to remember saying, 'Thank you, thank you, everything's marvellous,' over and over again.

'It was your mother's idea,' Eloise said at one point, 'and Michael helped me to choose most of the presents.'

That gave me an excuse to hug Michael, too, which made my head swim for a moment. The boys from the village are all very well, but Michael – well, he's a real man.

'You're an adult now,' he told me. His hands felt big and strong around my waist. 'You're a woman, not a girl. You should try on the clothes we've found for you.'

And so I started rummaging in the tissue-paper-packed boxes, and as soon as I had pulled out a dress I stripped down to my knickers.

I don't really know why I was so shameless. It's not as if I make a habit of letting people see me undressed. I started locking the bathroom door when I was twelve, and no one – not even Eloise – had seen me wearing just my knickers from then until today.

I was just so excited, and so wanted to show off my new clothes. And I must admit that I was enjoying the effect I was having on Michael: he was now looking at me a lot more than he was looking at Eloise. And it's partly Eloise's fault: she didn't stop me. With each item of clothing I discarded I expected to hear her asking me what I thought I was doing, and telling me to remain respectably dressed. But she didn't say a thing. She just smiled.

So anyway, there I was in just my knickers, surrounded by presents, and suddenly very aware that my breasts were naked. I pulled on the dress I'd selected, and to cover my embarrassment I turned away from Eloise and Michael, to find myself looking at my reflection in the big mirror over the fireplace.

I could hardly believe it was me. The dress was quite simple: it was made of dark blue crêpe, and had a halter top and an ankle-length skirt. It fitted me perfectly, and I could feel the silk clinging everywhere to my body – except on my back, because when I turned and looked over my shoulder I discovered that the dress was entirely backless. Even without make-up, without shoes, and with my hair loose, I looked as though I'd walked off a catwalk. My waist looked tiny, my legs looked long, and my tits looked huge.

I mean, Eloise has always told me that I'm pretty, and the boys I've met seem to think so too. And I've seen pictures of models and actresses, and I'm sure that I'm not deluding myself in thinking that I'm as tall and slim and blonde and busty as the best of them. But in that dress I looked special. Grown-up. Stunning. Not a pretty girl any more. A desirable woman.

I stole a glance at Michael. My face went bright red, because he was staring at me with a look that I can best describe as that of a hungry wolf presented with a lamb. And although I looked away, I wasn't quick enough to avoid catching his gaze. His eyes looked straight into mine, and I had to hold on to the mantelpiece for a moment as the most indescribable sensations sort of shivered down through my insides.

I tried on all the clothes. There were more dresses, and some separates, and shoes with high heels. Everything could have been made for me: the fit was perfect. The skirts were cut to show off my legs; the cashmere sweater tickled my breasts.

I identified the sensations I was feeling: they were very similar to those I can induce when I daydream in bed, particularly when I touch my breasts and between my legs.

I was feeling so excited and dreamy (both at the same time – it was woozily wonderful) that when I'd tried on all the dresses and blouses and shoes and skirts and scarves, I didn't think twice about starting to try on the tiny, lacy underthings.

That was when Eloise stepped in.

'Anne, darling,' she said, 'that's enough trying on of new clothes, don't you think? Take all your presents up to your room now.'

It was exactly the tone of voice she uses when she's treating me like a particularly dim-witted infant. It was clear that as far as she was concerned I was still 'little

Anne'. I was so angry and deflated that I burst into tears, which did precisely nothing for my self-esteem or for my credentials as an adult.

I shouted quite a lot. I hate you, it's not fair, all I want is to get away from this bloody awful place – that sort of thing. I find the odd swear word gives Eloise a real shock. Then I came upstairs and locked myself in my room.

And here I am writing it all up, only minutes after the events. It was a bit stupid of me to get so angry. The presents are all fantastic.

I can hear Eloise and Michael walking up and down the stairs. And whispering to each other. They don't sound very upset – in fact I'm sure Eloise is giggling. That's how much notice they take of my anger and distress!

They've gone now. I've just unlocked the door. All the parcels are in a big heap on the landing. I'll try to carry them in without making a noise.

Well, I wasn't entirely silent, but Eloise and Michael didn't try to interfere. I could hear them talking downstairs.

I've got all my presents with me in my room. They're still all wonderful. I've also retrieved from the landing a big sandwich – cheese, tomato, pickle – which Eloise must have left for me, and a note which says:

Dear Anne
You're being a silly girl. Here's something for your lunch. When you have calmed down, and when we're ready, we'll call you to the study. We have to have a talk with you about your behaviour, your responsibilities as an adult, and your future. Dress smartly: this is an important day.
With love
Eloise.

Well, I don't know what to make of that. When I've calmed down, indeed. I'm always calm, except when Eloise exasperates me. How dare they just summon me to appear in the study!

But I'll have to go, I suppose, when they call me. I'm still desperate to learn about going away to college. Mummy must have left some very specific instructions. I do so want to get away from here. I want to be free.

I was sitting once again on the sofa in the morning room, and Eloise was once again sitting in my lap. Anne's room was at the other end of the cottage, and we considered it unlikely that she could overhear us.

'Do you think it's time to call her?' Eloise said.

I kissed her ear and squeezed the breast I held cupped in my hand. 'Let her wait a little longer,' I said. 'If she's sullen we've got yet more of a pretext for punishing her.'

'The way she's been behaving lately,' Eloise said, 'we don't need any more pretext. She really does deserve a spanking.' She wriggled her buttocks on my thighs and kissed my mouth. 'I just hope you don't find her bottom more appealing than mine.'

I said I thought it unlikely, although in fact I had every expectation that Anne's rear would prove at least as spankable as her tutor's. 'You think it will be all right for me to be present, then?' I added.

'She saw you watching her while she was trying on her new things,' Eloise said. 'And so did I, by the way. She may refuse to let me punish her, but I get the impression that she'll take any opportunity to get undressed in your presence.'

'I hope so,' I said. I undid the top three buttons of Eloise's dress so that I could more easily caress her breasts. 'Now then,' I went on, 'we mustn't allow our concern for Anne to divert our attention entirely from our own amusement. Are you getting excited about the forthcoming interview with Anne?'

'I'm not sure that excited is quite the right word,' she said.

'Oh, I think you should be excited.' I ran my hand up her calf, over her knee, and on to the inside of her thigh. 'Shall we see whether you're getting excited already?'

'Oh,' she whispered, as she realised where my hand was going. She nestled her head on my chest and began to kiss the front of my shirt.

71

My fingers reached her knickers. I ran my knuckles back and forth along the taut cotton between her thighs, at first as lightly as a breeze then, suddenly, pushing hard against her vulva, and then once again very gently. She made little noises in her throat which I felt as vibrations against my ribs.

I pulled aside the material and pressed my fingers into the delicate folds of flesh.

'You're wet again,' I said. 'Naughty.'

She murmured contentedly.

'I ought to smack you again,' I said, 'but I suppose we ought not to allow ourselves to be distracted. However, I do think you're a little overdressed for the forthcoming task. Stand up and take off your knickers.'

I watched her as, red-faced, she stood before me, pulled up the skirt of her dress, and tugged her knickers down until they were free to fall to her ankles.

'I'll look after them,' I said as I rose from the sofa. I stroked her bottom as she bent over to retrieve her knickers, and pressed my hand hard between her buttocks to pull her into my embrace as she straightened her body.

After a while I suggested that we should move to the study. There, between kisses, we discussed where each of us should sit, and what Eloise would say. From time to time I put my hand up Eloise's skirt to assess her condition, and each time I found her wetter and hotter. 'Let's call Anne now,' I said at last.

Eloise made a low noise of frustrated protest.

'The sooner we deal with Anne,' I pointed out, 'the sooner I can deal with you.'

She brushed down her skirt, smoothed her hair, and went to call Anne. I sat in an armchair at the side of the room. I heard Eloise's voice calling in the hall. She returned and took the seat behind the small desk, so that she was facing the door. The afternoon sun cast a pattern of diamonds on the faded Persian carpet. We waited for Anne.

Footsteps, irregular but as loud as gunshots, announced Anne's approach, and stopped suddenly as she appeared in the doorway.

She had followed Eloise's instruction to dress smartly. She was wearing one of her new outfits: a blue-grey shift dress that, as I had anticipated when I chose it, was a perfect match for her eyes. The material, a blend of silk and wool, followed the contours of her body. I guessed that under the dress she was wearing one of the new sets of lingerie, as her breasts were thrusting prominently and, beneath the hem of the short skirt, her legs were clad in grey stockings, which must have been held up by a suspender belt. The stiletto-heeled sandals on her feet explained both the loudness of her footsteps and her unsteady gait: she wasn't used to wearing high heels. But they successfully extended her long, slender legs and accentuated the pertness of her bottom. She had been experimenting with her new make-up, too, and had had the sense to use only a little lipstick, blusher and mascara. She looked spectacular.

'Well?' she said. 'Here I am. Can someone please tell me what I'm here for?'

Eloise glared at her. She was making a good fist of appearing annoyed. 'Come here, Anne. Stand in front of the desk.'

Anne glanced at me – to make sure I was watching her, I'm sure – before taking careful steps across the carpet. Her bottom swung gracefully from side to side.

The top of the desk was clear but for one sheet of paper, which Eloise now indicated.

'Anne, your mother left this letter, to be opened and acted upon on your eighteenth birthday. I intend to proceed entirely according to her wishes.'

'All right.' Anne shrugged. 'So what does it say?'

'We'll come to the precise wording later. There are three matters which we need to address. I will leave until last the question of your continuing education. Before that I will deal with the second item, which is how I intend to respond to your increasingly wilful and ill-mannered conduct. And first of all, in accordance with your mother's letter, I will give you some guidance in a very personal area.'

Anne signed theatrically.

'Pay attention,' Eloise said. 'This morning Michael and I wished to consult a work of reference, and therefore we went to your room to find the relevant book. In our search we came upon this, concealed under your bed.'

Eloise placed on the desk the textbook on human physiology that she and I had discovered in Anne's room. I watched Anne's face closely: as she recognised the book her eyes widened and a pink glow appeared on her cheeks.

'We found that this book falls open at one particular page,' Eloise continued remorselessly. 'It is clear that you have studied one illustration considerably more than any other. This illustration.'

She opened the book and held it up for Anne to see. Even from where I was sitting there could be no mistaking the graphic depiction of female genitalia.

Eloise let the silence lengthen. Anne lowered her head and shuffled her feet.

'Is this picture of particular interest to you, Anne? Well? Yes or no?'

Anne's whole body revealed her acute embarrassment. She kept her gaze fixed on the floor, and her red face was almost hidden behind the curtain of her long blonde hair. Her shoulders were hunched, and she was scuffing the carpet with the pointed toe of her right shoe. 'I suppose so,' she muttered.

Eloise gave her no respite. 'And do you look at this picture when you're lying in bed? Is that it?'

There was a long pause. 'Sometimes,' Anne admitted.

It was time for me, playing the role of conciliator, to come to Anne's rescue.

'There's nothing wrong with looking at pictures like this,' I said. 'It's just that it's rather childish to keep it a secret. One of your mother's wishes is that, now you're an adult, you should be more aware of your body. In her letter she asks Eloise to help you to understand everything about a woman's body.'

'That's right,' Eloise said. 'As Celia wished I've kept you in considerable ignorance of subjects such as sexuality. Now it's time for you to find out everything, and to learn to be proud of your body.'

Anne's demeanour changed considerably as she began to understand the import of our words. Her eyes seemed brighter, and she tossed her head to throw her hair from her face.

'So,' Eloise said, 'take off your dress and let us see that you have the body of a grown woman.'

Anne's pretty pink lips opened in an O of surprise. Her hands flew to her bosom.

Eloise walked casually from behind the desk and put her hands on Anne's shoulders. 'Come along,' she said. 'There's nothing wrong with showing off your body. You're very beautiful, and it's reasonable to let people appreciate you. And don't worry if you feel shy: that's perfectly natural, and it's quite a nice feeling really. It's exciting to be embarrassed, isn't it?'

Anne nodded, and her hands dropped to her sides. She remained still while Eloise unfastened the back of the grey-blue dress. Anne glanced up to catch my eye as the dress slid from her shoulders, caught at her waist, and then fell to create a pool of silk around her high-heeled shoes.

I feasted my gaze on her. Her head was lowered, and once again her face was almost concealed behind her golden hair. However, I could see that she kept glancing towards me.

I made a circular gesture with my hand, and Eloise touched Anne's shoulder to encourage her to take a step towards me, and turn to face me.

I was delighted with the tableau the two women presented. It was as if Eloise, with her bobbed dark hair and simple summer dress, was serving as maidservant to her younger and taller blonde mistress. Anne was wearing the most scandalously flimsy of the sets of lingerie that Eloise and I had bought for her: the bra, knickers and suspenders were made of sheer grey gossamer, edged with grey lace. The cups of the bra drew attention to, rather than obscured, Anne's firm young breasts and little pink nipples; the knickers were so scanty that they consisted almost entirely of lace trimming, and barely covered the prominent mound of her pubes. The suspender belt

75

emphasised the narrowness of her waist, while the taut suspenders made her slender hips appear more rounded.

I looked at her for some time, until she had the confidence to return my gaze and my smile.

I was already sure that she would present no strenuous objections to her mother's wishes. She might protest at each new imposition, for the sake of appearances, but it was clear to me that she enjoyed exhibiting herself and was keen to discover everything she could about sex.

'Anne,' I said, 'you are breathtakingly attractive. It really is a crime to keep yourself covered up.'

Her smile widened as she struck a pose, placing her hands behind her head so that her breasts jutted. Her eyes crinkled at the corners, which made the blue-grey of her irises seem to twinkle. She had the most devastating facial expressions, and I had to cross my legs swiftly to conceal the growing evidence of my desire.

Her hands dropped to her sides as she felt Eloise's fingers touch her back.

'It's all right,' Eloise said. 'I'm just helping you to take off your bra.'

Anne's eyes widened. 'But I shouldn't,' she said. 'Michael's watching.'

Eloise and I both uttered carefree laughter. 'Of course,' Eloise said. 'I'm sure he'd like to see your breasts. That's the whole point.'

'Wouldn't you like to show me your breasts, Anne?' I cajoled. 'Remember, I've already seen you almost naked, when you were trying on your new clothes this morning.'

Anne nodded. 'All right, then,' she said, and allowed Eloise to undo the clasp and pull the straps down her arms.

'Stand as you were a moment ago,' I suggested, 'with your hands behind your head.' She was charmingly bashful, but I didn't want to give her time to become too embarrassed.

Her breasts were as firm and prominent as they had been when supported by her bra. They were large for a woman of her age, and seemed almost to be jostling for space on her narrow ribcage. The skin was paler than that of her shoulders and midriff. The nipples were small and pink, and obviously erect.

A slideshow of imaginings flickered through my mind. There were so many things I wanted to do with her breasts. They would look superb spilling from the top of a tightly laced corset; or bound in black silk cords; or decorated with jewellery dangling from clips on her nipples; or striped with the lines of a lash. And once she had been trained at the Private House, all of my imaginings would be made real. She would be mine, to play with, penetrate and paint.

'Do you like to touch your breasts, Anne?' I asked.

She pouted, and began to let her arms drop, as if she unsure of the correct answer.

'It's all right,' Eloise insisted once again. 'You have lovely breasts. You should enjoy touching them.'

'Hold them for me,' I said. 'No, don't cover them. Cup one hand underneath each, as if you're presenting them to me. That's right. And now touch your nipples with your thumbs. Does that feel nice?'

She nodded, with her head lowered so that she could watch her thumbs catching on the hardness of the pink tips. Then she looked up at me.

'You like playing with yourself,' I said. 'That's excellent. I think you're going to prove to be a very adept student. Next, then, we have to discover how you touch yourself when you're studying your book on female genital anatomy. Take your knickers off, please.'

Anne stared at me for a moment with a horrified expression, but realised that she had already come too far to retreat. She made a few murmurs of protest, but moved her legs apart and lifted her feet as Eloise slid the wisp of fabric downwards.

Now she was naked but for the suspender belt, stockings and shoes. I saw no reason to deprive her of any more of her clothes.

In a last attempt to preserve her modesty she turned her back on me. Her buttocks were as pale as her breasts. They were high, round and firm, and therefore were well separated. I could glimpse the pink rosebud of her anus between them, and could clearly see the gap between the tops of her thighs and the W of her sex which was covered with downy hair. The thought that soon Eloise would rain smacks upon those perfect hemispheres made my breath catch in my throat and my erection convulse.

'Anne,' I called out. She looked over her shoulder. We exchanged smiles. She had no inkling of the punishment that was in store for her.

'Would you sit on the sofa?' I continued.

Eloise took her arm and guided her the few steps to the sofa that stood facing my armchair. She sat Anne in the centre of the seat, and perched herself at one side.

'Sit back,' I said, 'and pull your feet up on to the seat.'

Anne settled her back against the cushions and began to draw her knees towards her. She stopped with the toes of her shoes just touching the carpet. 'But you'll be able to see –' she protested.

'Yes,' I explained in a patient tone that belied the urgency of my feelings. 'I want to see. And now you're a grown woman it's perfectly all right to show me. Lift up your legs, and keep them slightly apart.'

She tossed her head to one side as she placed the heels of her shoes on the seat of the sofa. I could see between her slender ankles the swelling of her sex, decorated with tiny curls of golden hair and divided by a pink slit. Eloise murmured words of encouragement to her, and ran her fingers through her long blonde hair.

'Now, Anne,' I said, 'move your feet as far apart as you can. So that your vulva looks like the illustration in the book.'

Anne looked up at Eloise, who nodded, and then edged her feet towards the arms of the sofa. My gaze alternated between her sex and her face as her movements opened her outer labia and revealed the convoluted membranes of delicate pink flesh. Her face and breasts were flushed with a similar hue.

Eloise leant forward and placed her hands on Anne's knees, gently pushing them apart. 'Have you discovered, Anne,' she said, 'that it feels very good when you touch

78

yourself between your legs? It's something you're allowed to do when you're grown-up.'

Anne gave a murmur of agreement. Her eyelids looked heavy, and I was sure that she was sexually aroused.

'Let's test your knowledge of anatomy,' I said. 'Anne, please show me your inner labia. Touch them with your fingers.'

She turned her head to look straight at me. Her eyes were wide with shock.

I nodded, said nothing, and waited for her to comply.

Sure enough, her right hand crept into her lap and began to slide over her mound. She stopped and looked up at Eloise, who smiled encouragement. Her fingers slipped further down.

'You have been studying that book, haven't you?' I said. 'Now use your fingers to open your labia and show me your vagina.'

With her lips parted, her cheeks red and a delightful frown on her brow, Anne moved her fingers apart. She was too embarrassed to meet my gaze, and too excited to look away. The entrance of her vagina glistened like wet coral between her fingers.

'Use your left hand, too,' I said. 'Put it under your leg, so that you can touch yourself from underneath. Use a finger to touch just inside your vagina.'

Now there was less hesitation. Anne's left hand appeared around her thigh, and the index finger felt for the gap between the forked fingers of her other hand. She touched the place; paused; stared at me almost defiantly; and then the fingertip sank inside her. I saw her body give a brief shudder. Eloise leant forward and kissed the top of her head.

'How would you describe your vagina now?' I asked Anne.

She looked away from me and murmured. 'It's warm,' she said at last, in a low voice. 'And damp. And it feels sort of tingly, right inside.'

Eloise raised her eyebrows and mouthed, 'Mine, too,' for my benefit.

'That's very good,' I told Anne. 'That's exactly right. Now I'm sure you've discovered that you can increase those pleasant sensations by moving your fingers. So move the fingers of your right hand up and down, very gently, so that you're stroking the inner labia, and let your other finger move in and out of your vagina.'

Anne performed as instructed, and began moving her head from side to side as she succumbed to the pleasure she was creating for herself. Eloise slid from the arm of the sofa and curled herself next to Anne. She caressed Anne's neck and shoulders, and then moved her hand down to fondle Anne's breasts.

'I've never touched another woman's breasts before,' Eloise said quietly. 'Yours are lovely, Anne. Big and firm, but with such soft skin. And such pretty little nipples.'

'Thank you, Eloise,' Anne said. Her eyes were closed and she sounded drowsy. As Eloise's fingers teased her nipples she couldn't help arching her back and turning her body; her breasts rolled from side to side.

I cleared my throat. 'Look at me, Anne. Remember that the purpose of this exercise is for you to discover how much you enjoy showing off your sexual arousal. Are your fingers thoroughly wet now?'

Anne murmured that they were, although I didn't need her to tell me: I could see that the movements of her fingers had produced a fluid response, so that her hands, her sex and the insides of her thighs were shiny with her wetness. There was more than enough lubrication for the next stage of the lesson.

'Now then, Anne,' I said, trying to keep my voice businesslike, 'as I'm sure you know from your studies of anatomy, the most sensitive part of your body is your clitoris. Do you know where to find it?'

Anne was clearly finding it even more difficult than I was to concentrate. 'I think so,' she said.

I decided that it was necessary to reduce, temporarily, the amount of stimulation that Anne was experiencing. 'Eloise,' I said, 'stop stroking Anne's breasts for a moment. Sit on the arm of the sofa, facing Anne. Pull your dress up and part your legs. Show her your clitoris.'

Eloise stared at me with her mouth open for a second, and then slowly did as I had instructed.

'Don't stop playing with yourself, Anne,' I said, 'and look at me until Eloise is ready.'

Eloise's face was bright red as she pulled the skirt of her dress up to her waist. Reluctantly she parted her legs until one knee was pressed against the back of the sofa. She gave me a look of mute appeal.

'Use your fingers,' I told her. 'Hold your labia apart so Anne can see.'

She ruched the skirt into her lap and her hands disappeared between her thighs. I saw her body shiver.

'Anne,' I said, 'you can turn your head now to look at Eloise. Don't be shy: Eloise likes to show off, and it's important that you learn what a woman's body looks like. And where her clitoris is.'

Anne glanced between Eloise's legs, averted her eyes, and then looked again. Her fingers moved a little faster against her own vulva.

'As you can see,' I said, 'Eloise isn't wearing any knickers. Adults are allowed to go without underwear if they want to. You'll discover that it feels liberating and exciting. Your mother says that she wants you to become accustomed to being naked.

'Can you see Eloise's clitoris?' I continued. 'It's a large organ, but most of it is inside the body. It's very sensitive, and becomes even more so when you're aroused. All you can see is the tip of it: it peeks out just above your urethra when you're sexually excited. It looks like a little round button. And it's higher than you might expect: not particularly close to the vagina. Can you see it?'

Anne nodded.

'Good,' I said. 'Then you can show me yours. Move your right hand up a bit. Use your fingers to part your labia. And look at me.'

Eloise slid from the arm of the sofa to kneel on the seat. She resumed caressing Anne. I noticed that she kept one hand between her legs.

81

Anne's blue-grey eyes didn't leave mine as she drew her fingers towards her and spread them apart. The glistening inner folds of her labia were a delicate shade of light pink, but her clitoris was clearly visible, a tiny protruding mushroom of paler colour.

'Good,' I said. 'You're very pretty, Anne. Now move your fingers together a little: just enough so that you can feel them pressing very lightly on both sides of your clitoris.'

Anne was so intensely aroused that I began to worry that she would come before she was spanked. She was blinking her eyes, her body was trembling, and she had captured her lower lip between her teeth in her effort to concentrate on my instructions. I gestured to Eloise to stop touching Anne's breasts.

Anne's clitoris was now peeking from between two of her fingers.

'Press your hand down very gently,' I said, 'and then up again.'

Anne's fingers made the slightest of movements. She gasped and cried out.

'Stop!' I said. 'That's enough for now. Anne, look at me again, angel. Have you touched yourself like that before?'

Anne struggled to control her breathing. 'I've touched near there,' she said at last. 'But not as close as that.'

'And do you know what will happen if you continue to touch yourself there?' I asked her.

She had stepped back from the brink now, and was able to think more clearly.

'Well, I know that's not how you become pregnant,' she said. 'Is it something to do with orgasm? It's such a strange word.'

'You've obviously been reading some books that Eloise doesn't know about,' I said. 'Yes, you can give yourself an orgasm by touching the tip of your clitoris. And we'll let you do that, later. It's very appropriate that you should have your first orgasm today, when you come of age, and Eloise and I will be privileged to witness it.'

Anne looked from me to Eloise with an expression of undiluted delight. She was looking forward to her first climax, and she seemed to have no qualms about performing in front of witnesses. I decided to take her exhibitionism one step further before I turned her over to Eloise for her punishment.

'You still have one finger in your vagina,' I reminded her. 'Don't stop moving it in and out.'

Anne's bright face frowned with embarrassment as the movements of her finger produced wet, sucking sounds. She began to make little moans, and was soon once again close to coming.

'I can see that feels pleasant,' I said, 'but in fact your vagina isn't particularly sensitive to touch. Your inner labia are more sensitive to being stroked, and you'll find that your vagina responds more when you put something large inside it. That's because your clitoris, inside you, extends all the way back to all around your vagina. But there is one more part of your body that is very sensitive: more sensitive than the entrance of your vagina, and not very far from it.'

I let Anne play with herself a little longer. She wasn't able to concentrate on my words. 'Where?' she murmured at last.

'Take your finger out of your vagina,' I said, 'and let it slide down slowly. Stop there. That ridge of skin you're touching now is called the perineum. It's quite hard, but also quite sensitive. Now move your finger a little further down. Yes, that's it. It's all right: you can touch yourself there. Press the tip of your finger into the little hollow.'

Anne's eyes were wide with alarm. 'I can't,' she moaned. 'It's rude. It's dirty.'

'Do as I tell you,' I said. 'Play with your anus. Isn't it exciting to do things that are rude and dirty? Feel how sensitive it is. Massage around the hole with your fingertip. Does that feel good?'

Anne lifted her eyes and turned her head to one side. The fingers touching her clitoris moved more quickly. The finger touching her anus began to press rhythmically in and out.

'Does that feel good?' I insisted.

83

'Oh, yes,' Anne sighed.

'You see?' I said. 'It's perfectly all right to touch yourself there. It's a very sensitive area, and you'll find that there are many ways to give yourself pleasure there – and to give pleasure to others. But stop now: we don't want you to come yet.'

I had to tell her several times to remove both hands from her body. It was almost as difficult for me to give the instructions as it was for Anne to obey them: with her face turned to one side, flushed and ecstatic, and her legs parted to provide me with a spectacular view of the delicate movements of her hands, she presented a captivating picture.

At length, however, I coaxed her from the sofa to kneel on the carpet. Eloise occupied Anne's previous position in the centre of the couch. I remained in the armchair, and as Anne was now facing away from me I was able to rest my hand on the uncomfortable hardness of my erection while I admired the perfection of her slim, round buttocks.

I don't know how much of Eloise's lecture penetrated Anne's lust-clouded consciousness. Eloise told her that in recent months she had become more and more badly behaved. She was disrespectful and disobedient. She sulked and complained. She threw tantrums, and was rude to guests. All in all, she needed discipline, and now that she was fully grown she was old enough to be disciplined properly, in the most direct and effective manner. Celia's instructions were at one with Eloise's judgement: Anne was to be spanked.

It was only at this point that Anne became animated. She lifted her head to stare at Eloise; she turned to me with wide eyes, as if expecting me to join in her amazement; she turned back to Eloise.

'What? What are you talking about? You can't spank me. I'm too old.'

'On the contrary,' I said, in a voice I hoped was firm and authoritative. 'You're just old enough. Smacking is a barbaric way to punish a child: it's frightening and painful and simply too overwhelming. But you're no longer a child, Anne. Your mother's clearly stated intention is that you should be punished physically from now on. It's part of growing up. Eloise agrees that you merit punishment. I'm here to assist Eloise administer the spanking, should she need my help, and because you will feel the humiliation all the more if you have an audience. There is no point in objecting. The sooner you receive your spanking the sooner you will be allowed to play with yourself again. Now go and lie across Eloise's knees.'

This was the crucial moment. Anne would either submit, or she would run from the room in a storm of outrage and confusion. I had no way of knowing, then, that Anne would find pleasure in being punished. I judged merely that she was an exhibitionist, and that she might grasp the opportunity to display herself bent across Eloise's lap; I also hoped that the reward of being allowed to play with herself again might induce her to acquiesce in her punishment.

Of course, I had no need to worry. Anne rose to her feet and stood for a moment in the centre of the room. Her golden hair and lightly freckled skin seemed to glow in the sunlight: she was a young goddess in grey stockings and high-heeled shoes. She looked over her shoulder at me. I glared at her, and she lowered her eyes and turned away. She stepped slowly towards the sofa, and I contemplated the firm curves of her bottom, as yet unreddened.

Anne climbed on to the sofa and positioned herself on elbows and knees above Eloise's thighs. Neither of them seemed to know how to proceed.

'Lower the front half of your body,' I instructed Anne. 'Rest your head on the cushions, and press your chest down on to the seat.'

I watched with admiration as her pendant breasts squashed against the upholstery and her bottom rose into the air.

'Now move your knees back a bit, and legs wide apart. Eloise needs to be able to reach the sensitive inner sides of your buttocks, and part of the punishment is to show off your vulva and your arsehole.'

Eloise flinched at my use of coarse vocabulary, but Anne merely followed my instructions. I rose from my chair, collected Celia's letter from the desk, and stood close to the sofa. I wanted a good view of Eloise's hand descending on Anne's firm, quivering buttocks, and I wanted Anne to be aware that I could see everything.

I rustled the sheet of paper so that Anne could be sure that I was consulting her mother's words. 'Celia says that you are to receive eighteen smacks,' I said. 'And I agree that will probably do for now. Although if you don't keep still, Anne, Eloise will start again from the beginning. Thereafter you are to receive a similar spanking every day to remind you to conduct yourself in a grown-up fashion, and other punishments whenever you behave childishly or inappropriately. That seems clear enough. Eloise, I think you can begin now. Stroke her bottom gently for a moment, and then start spanking.'

With my hand on my cock I watched Eloise's hands caress the perfect roundness of Anne's buttocks; the tips of her fingers strayed into the damply shining pinkness between Anne's thighs, and drew little moans from where Anne's head was sunk into cushions and surrounded by the halo of her blonde hair. Then she lifted her hand, and brought it down on Anne's right buttock. The slap resounded in the sunlit room. Anne didn't move. Eloise and I watched the imprint of her hand develop on the pale skin, like a photographic print appearing out of white paper. Eloise lifted her hand again, and I imagine I smiled broadly as, without prompting, Anne hollowed her back and pushed her bottom up a little more to receive the second smack.

As Eloise spanked Anne with hard, well-spaced smacks, I found my gaze moving back and forth between Anne's reddening bottom and Eloise's excited face. After six smacks, and again after twelve, Eloise interrupted the spanking to stroke Anne's bottom, and to allow me to see that juice was seeping from Anne's vagina more freely than ever. We exchanged long, conspiratorial looks: we were imagining the things that we would read next in Celia's journals, and the things that Eloise and I would do together once Anne had been dismissed; and, as far as I was concerned, I was thinking of the many ways in which I intended to take pleasure in Anne once she had spent the summer in training at the Private House.

From the diary of Anne Bright
11 May (continued)
I think I've calmed down enough to be able to write now. I'm back in my room, of course, and if this is difficult to read it's because I'm writing this while lying on my bed. Lying on my front!

My first spanking. And my first orgasm. I suppose I should write about how humiliating and infuriating it was. And it certainly was both. Why on earth did I let them do it? That charming creep Michael has seen everything – and he kept making comments, all the time Eloise was smacking me and all the time I was touching myself, just to remind me that he was watching.

My bottom's so sore. Well, it's already feeling much better, actually. In fact it's hardly even warm any more. It's a bit of a disappointment, really: I expected to be able to feel it for hours afterwards. Still, I'm going to get the same again tomorrow. Maybe Michael will spank me – he'll probably do it harder than Eloise, and the soreness will last longer. I'm afraid he's right about me enjoying it: I'm already looking forward to being smacked again tomorrow. There – I've admitted it.

I just had to stop writing for a moment to look in the mirror again. My bottom's still a bit pink, which I think looks very attractive. Eloise says that when I've been smacked I'm not supposed to wear anything covering my bottom until all the marks have completely faded.

I really, really want to touch myself again, but Eloise says it's selfish and childish to keep things like that to myself. So if I want to play with my genitalia I'm to ask Eloise or Michael to watch me. What else? I'm to keep my breasts uncovered as much as possible, too, because Michael says they're too attractive to be hidden away. I wonder if I'm supposed to show Eloise and Michael what I'm doing every time I play with my breasts? No, that would be ridiculous: I'd be chasing after them all the time to watch me. It's not that I want to deprive Eloise and Michael – I'm happy to let them see me – but it just wouldn't be practical to bother then every time I feel like stroking my nipples. That's settled, then. I can play with my breasts now, at least.

What shall I do? I'll stand in front of the mirror and hold them in my hands, and squeeze them until it almost hurts. That's always good. Then I'll stroke them underneath, and then I'll start touching my nipples very lightly. I find that by the time my nipples are very hard I start to enjoy it when I hurt them – no, that's wrong, because although I pinch them as hard as I would if I wanted to hurt them, it doesn't hurt any more. It just feels like a nice, tingly shock. Very strange. But very enjoyable. So, anyway, I'll pinch my right nipple between my fingers (I always do the right one first) while I use my other hand to do lots of little pinches around the edge of the crinkly skin. And I'll close my eyes and pretend it's Josh doing it to me – no, not Josh; the pirate captain, he'll do. I'm going to enjoy this.

Back again. Oh, that was lovely. I think my breasts are fabulous. I'm glad Michael and Eloise like them. They feel hot and extra big now. I pressed them against the cold glass of the mirror and kissed my reflection. I seem to be getting terribly vain.

But in a way playing with my breasts has only made things worse. I'm very wet between my legs again, and I want to touch myself there even more. And now, of course, I know where all those delicious feeling are going – or should I say coming! Because, of course, I've now had my first orgasm. I've come. And it's fantastic.

It's like you're a balloon, getting bigger and bigger, and closer and closer to exploding. And then you do explode, and then gradually all the pieces of you gather together again, and you feel peaceful. Oh, no, that's just silly. It's indescribable, really.

And now I know about coming, just about everything seems to make me want to do it again. Playing with my breasts; being spanked; just thinking about being spanked, in fact; taking my clothes off, particularly with people watching me, and particularly when they make me show off my breasts and my bottom and my genitalia. I would love to come again before the end of the day. I suppose I'll have to ask Eloise to watch me do it – perhaps after dinner.

Michael says that every time I play with myself in front of him he's going to make me touch my anus. I'm still not sure about that. It does feel exciting, that's undeniable. And if Michael and Eloise say it's all right, I'm sure it is. I expect it's something that grown-ups do all the time. But I think Michael gets a thrill from knowing that I think it's dirty. And – worst of all – I think I get a thrill from knowing that that's what he's thinking.

It certainly made my orgasm today very special. I had a sore bottom, and Michael was watching me press my finger into my bottom-hole while Eloise was stroking my breasts. I hardly had to touch myself near my clitoris before I felt the tidal wave start to bear down on me.

I couldn't help shouting and writhing about when it was close to happening. But what sent me over the edge was Michael: he touched my hand, so that my finger almost went inside my anus, and he whispered, 'Tomorrow, you can play with yourself like this while we're spanking you.' That was it. It took just a second for me to imagine being spanked, and playing with myself at the same time, and my balloon exploded. I think I was screaming. Amazing.

But best of all – and I've been saving this until the last paragraph of today's diary entry – best of all, after Eloise and Michael are sure that I've learnt how to be spanked and how to show off my body and how to come – most of which I already know, I think – I'm going to be allowed to go to away. I'm going to a place called the Private House, where Mummy went years ago. It's some sort of finishing school, I think, and I suppose it might turn out to be very dreary. But it's away from here. I'll be independent at last. A free woman. I'm so thrilled. I can hardly wait.

From the journals of Celia Bright
[Inevitably, these early pages of my notebooks will consist of extracts from my diary. The following entry is significant for two reasons: it records the day on which D, with motives that I misunderstood entirely at the time, encouraged me to maintain my diary; and it was the day on which I first heard of the Private House.]

I have told D that I keep this diary. I have been reluctant to reveal the fact, because I feared that he might consider it indiscreet, or perhaps even a betrayal of my commitment only to him. However, he was pleased, and encouraged me to continue. I suppose it appeals to him to have a permanent record of his mastery of me. He says that he will not insist on seeing what I write; my diary will remain private.

It is curiously difficult to be a slave. It is not that it isn't easy to adore D – on the contrary, I grow ever more devoted to him. And I am becoming more and more accustomed to obeying his instructions, not merely without outward question but entirely without inward hesitation. But the very fact that it is so simple to obey him – so simple and so rewarding – makes me almost forget, at times, that my actions should be purely for his satisfaction. I find myself submitting to him because I know that I will enjoy it, whereas my submission should be for him alone.

I think of D all the time when we are apart. I summon into my imagination the velvet hardness of his cock pushing against my tongue, and his thick, salty, ammonia-fragranced cream splashing, a hot blessing, on my face. I let my hands brush against my breasts, and in my mind I am bound and helpless, and his fingers are at my nipples, touching, teasing, pinching. I hear his voice in my ears, whispering instructions so perverse that I blush; I hear the leathery slither of his belt as he draws it through the loops of his waistband, and wherever I am I become suddenly conscious of my buttocks, always naked now under my outwardly respectable clothes, and I ready myself for the fall of the whip.

At my place of work my colleagues have noticed the change in me. I have become a dreamer, they tell me; they try to discover whether I am in love. I hug my secrets to me. I know that they would not understand, would be horrified to learn the nature of my dreams, and of the gentle, considerate, careful cruelty of my lover.

I live in my own house hardly at all now. I spend most nights at D's house. Usually he allows me to sleep with him, in his bed; sometimes I am tied up, sometimes not. If, by the end of an evening with me, D decides that I have not been sufficiently punished, he carries me up to a cell in the attic, and lets me sleep on the floor. D is also preparing for me a stall in the stables; he has promised that he will have me trained to the bit and the harness. He says that I will be his palomino pony. I am determined to prance and canter well for him.

There is no fixed routine for the evenings and nights that I spend with D – still less so for the weekends – but he has told me that I should use my diary to record every detail of my life of slavery, and so I will attempt to describe a typical morning.

I will suppose that I have spent the night in D's bed, unfettered. He usually wakes before me (his evening activities are usually less strenuous than mine!) and he tries to rise without disturbing me. Sometimes, half awake, I have felt him lift the sheet and stand over me, watching me. Sometimes he kisses me, and runs his fingertips along the stripes he has imprinted on my skin. Without fail, however, he pulls on his silk robe, tiptoes into the bathroom, and takes a shower. Then he pads downstairs and, whether Thomas and Ruth are on duty or not, he prepares two small cups of strong black coffee. These he carries back to the bedroom, where he leans over me and whispers, 'Wake up, slave.'

I awake to the aroma of coffee and the sight of my master. He gazes at me with such fervour, with such concern in his eyes, that I find myself blinking back tears.

I want to throw myself into his arms and cover his body with kisses; I am sure that he, too, wants nothing more than to hold me in his strong hands and make me writhe and moan. However, he insists that we should drink our coffee before it goes cold, and so we sit beside each other in the bed, just like any normal, respectable, decent couple. And then he sends me off to the bathroom, because he likes me to be clean, and because he knows that I get few enough moments of privacy and solitude.

As soon as I step from the bathroom I am entirely his slave. Naked, I stand at the end of the bed and await his commands. Usually he summons me to stand beside him. He inspects the marks of the previous day's punishments. His touch is electric and within seconds of his starting to peruse my body, even if I have not been thinking about him during my ablutions, I realise that I am aroused. He notes the stiffness of my nipples; he makes me part my legs and show him evidence of my excitement.

He spanks me then. Sometimes he makes me crawl on to the bed and across his lap; sometimes he grabs me and hauls me roughly towards him, making me squeal and giggle. Either way, I have next to ask for my punishment. I am by this point desperate to display my bottom to him, and desperate to feel his hand on my buttocks, so my pleadings are entirely genuine. He listens; he keeps me waiting; he makes me beg; but in the end he relents and administers the chastisement.

I kneel beside the bed and thank him. Often he turns on his side, so that I can express my gratitude by taking his cock in my mouth. Sometimes he likes to watch me masturbate, instead. On the rare occasions that neither of us has an early appointment or meeting he takes the trouble to tie me to the bed, and then he whips my bottom or my breasts, or buggers me, or uses one of the artificial phalluses to penetrate me.

There is usually no time in the mornings for me to give him more pleasure. I always fear, when we part at the beginning of the working day, that I have done too little to show him that I belong to him and that I will do anything for him. He fears – I know, because he has told me – that he has done too little to lavish exquisite torments on me as evidence of his passion for me.

We dream about each other all day.

In the evenings, and at weekends, we find more time to devote to our desires. D conceives detailed and complex rituals for me to perform, usually while dressed in revealing, uncomfortable, restraining garb. There is, happily, little routine involved in these activities – except that I undergo ever more painful pleasures, and D permits me to demonstrate the depth of my servility to him before he uses me for his pleasure. Therefore I cannot describe a typical evening, and will continue to write up accounts of particular events.

D is concerned that, as most of our time together is spent immersed in these esoteric rites, I remain largely untrained. I am mortified to think that I lack in any respect the submissiveness I should show to my master; D says that there can be no criticism of my enthusiasm, but that there are skills and techniques that I must learn if I am to be the perfect slave.

He has decided to send me away to be trained. I cannot bear the thought of being parted from him, but he is adamant. He will use the time to equip his house with the specialised furniture and utensils that he requires to discipline me properly. That, at least, is something to look forward to, and a little consolation. I, meanwhile, am to go to an establishment known as the Private House.

Part Two

LEARNING

The Private House
4 June
Dearest Michael

This will be a short report, my darling. Partly this is because it's only a few days since I was staying with you at the studio (the sketch of me tied to your easel seems to be the general favourite – Jem has, of course, insisted that all the drawings be put on display). And partly it's because I returned in time to meet Tess, who was on a flying visit, and as you know I can never hold out for long against Tess's importuning.

I therefore cancelled a few appointments, cleared my diary, and devoted the whole of the day before yesterday to satisfying Tess's wishes. And I spent yesterday recovering.

I know you think you're very cruel and masterful, darling, and that's very endearing and I love you for it. But you're really no match for Tess when she's in a disciplinary mood. I'm sure she saves it all up just for me. She's known in the organisation for her submissiveness. I've seen her being put through her paces, and it's impossible to doubt that she derives considerable pleasure (one orgasm after another, quite frankly) from being led about by her nipple chains, secured in an uncomfortable position, and thoroughly flogged. But however much she now favours that side of her sexuality, with me she likes to be on top. That's all right, of course – I certainly wouldn't want it the other way – and I confess I still get a guilty thrill every time she calls me a 'snooty Pom'. Which is how she addresses me all the time when she has me at her mercy. Suffice to say that by yesterday morning there wasn't a single part of her body that I hadn't licked, and all of my most sensitive parts were very sore indeed.

I think the bit I enjoyed most was being made to demonstrate the use of the beads you gave me. Tess had spread the word that there would be an exhibition at three in the afternoon, and so there was a small audience waiting in the oriental pavilion when Tess led me in. She discarded her robe at the entrance, and as she walked in front of me to the dais she looked majestic in a white corset and white boots. In her high heels and platform soles she towered over me.

She had had me dress in one of my formal suits – one of those sensible, well-tailored combinations of blouse, jacket and skirt that I wear to board meetings and on trips overseas. She likes to be reminded that I'm wealthy and, in her eyes, privileged. And she likes me to remember it, too, before she makes me debase myself.

She had set up a high throne on the dais, so that even when I was standing on the stage, looking down at the audience, she was still above me even when seated. She had me stand in front of her, facing the audience, and then she introduced me.

'This is Amanda,' she announced. (I'll abbreviate this slightly, as she went on for some time!) 'Amanda's one of the richest women in the country. She owns so many companies she can't even remember the names of all of them.' (That isn't true, of course: I know all their names, and most of the figures from their latest management accounts. But I knew better than to try to correct Tess.) 'She's got four houses and a penthouse apartment. I used to be the housekeeper in that apartment. And she used to pay me less in a year than she earns in a day.'

The audience began to get into the spirit of the show. There were cries of 'Shame!' and 'Disgraceful!' They presumed that they were watching a performance; only Tess and I knew that during the time that she had lived in my apartment she had nurtured for me a desperate desire of which I was completely ignorant. Every day, as she watched me dress to go out for business meetings and formal dinners, as she washed my underwear, as she massaged my tired shoulders, she had had to suppress her fantasies of seducing me, enthralling me, and bending me to her pleasure. And as you know, Michael, by the time I discovered how much I enjoy being made to behave disgracefully, Amanda had undergone her own Damascene conversion, and had plunged enthusiastically into a life of servility. So, even though the audience assumed that we were play-acting, I knew the true depth of emotion behind Tess's words. I began to blush, of course, at the things she was saying about me. And, as you will have guessed, I was acutely aware of becoming aroused.

'Even now we're both in the Private House,' Tess went on, 'Amanda gets to travel all over the world, making important deals and swanning about in posh hotels, while I'm usually one of the household slaves. But every now and then the tables are turned, the slave becomes the mistress, and I have Amanda all to myself. And Amanda loves it.'

Every eye was on me. I could feel the audience's attention like the heat from a fire. I knew my face was bright red. I wish you could have been there to see me, my darling. Tess knows precisely how to make me suffer the maximum possible amount of humiliation. And she whips me much more fiercely than you do. I was quivering with that wonderful combination of shame and anticipation. The silk of my knickers was already sopping wet.

Tess ordered me to undress, and as I did so she supplied a commentary on my expensive taste in clothes and underwear. She had me lean forward to show off my breasts, and she explained that she hadn't whipped them yet but would do so later in the day. Then, when I thought I couldn't possibly be any more embarrassed, she made me turn my back on the audience and kneel before her throne with my head between her thighs. I heard the gasps behind me as I bent forward and, impelled by shame as much as by my desire for the taste of Tess's sex, I buried my face in her lap.

Everyone could see my bottom, still scarlet and striped from the punishments Tess had already administered. She made me move my knees apart and, as she buckled around my neck the collar I wear whenever Tess is dominating me, she commented in complimentary but very coarse words on my bottom, my anus and my vulva. As you can imagine, I was by now trembling with pent-up lust, and desperate for more chastisement.

Tess made me show how diligently I lick her. She had clipped a leash to my collar, and kept on calling me a stuck-up bitch as she used the leash to tug my face hard against her sex. I could tell that she was close to coming when she pushed me away. She slapped my face lightly with the leather handle of the leash, and told the audience that I was dirty bitch with a sticky, messy face.

Then she produced the string of beads. She said that they were a present to me from a man (and, as you know, Tess can inject considerable venom into that three-letter word). As she dribbled oil along the string she explained to the audience how the beads were to be used (although I'm sure everyone had seen such things before). She pressed the beads into my hand and told me to start inserting them.

I'm sure you remember that there are seven beads on the thong, and that the largest is the fourth, or middle, bead. My fingers were shaking as I reached behind myself and felt for the damp valley between my sore, heated buttocks. Tess summoned the audience to move closer so that they could see, as she put it, my pretty little arsehole open as I pushed the first bead into it.

You know, Michael, how sensitive my anus is. In fact, that's largely your fault! These days I always touch my anus when I'm playing with myself, and when I'm with you I seem to have something – your penis, or your fingers, or some object – up there all the time. It makes me feel so excited. On my knees, with my face coated with Tess's juices, and showing off my bottom to a room full of my friends and colleagues, I found that having to push the beads into my anus was absolute heaven. I was sure I would come before I had pushed them all in.

Tess, however, didn't intend to let me. As soon as the first bead was lodged inside me she ordered me to stop. The remaining beads hung like a tail from my bottom, and brushed maddeningly against my yearning cunt.

She told me to start licking her again – and she called for a volunteer from the audience to smack my bottom while I did so. I didn't see who was spanking me, but even with Tess's thighs gripping my head I could hear her urging harder smacks.

And so the pattern was set for each of the seven beads: I received a spanking, from a different member of the audience, for each one. By the time only the tail of the thong was dangling from my bottom and the seven beads were coiled and shifting in my rectum, creating the most delightful sensations, my bottom felt as though it was on fire. The pain came in throbbing waves that took my breath away. The juices from my sex were running down the insides of my thighs. I was more than ready.

And now, at last, Tess allowed me to come – seven times. She played with my breasts – quite gently, surprisingly – as I pulled on the thong and, following her instructions, used two fingers to pat lightly against the front of my sex. I felt the first bead begin to press against the inside of my anal sphincter; I felt the delicious sensation of the ring of muscle expanding, and I cried out as I came. Tess's fingers tightened on my nipples.

'And again,' she said. And so it went on.

I think it was the most humiliating experience of my life. I don't think I've ever before had seven orgasms, one after another, and by the end I was so exhausted I could hardly stand. The audience applauded each time I came, and I think Tess came a couple of times, too. She was in a good mood for the rest of the afternoon, and allowed me to rest for a couple of hours before reporting to her again. In the evening she whipped my breasts, as promised, and hung bells from my nipples before taking me with her into dinner. As she had bound me in chains she had to feed me morsels from her plate; she made sure that my striped and swollen breasts were a talking point among the diners, and after dessert she demonstrated that when my breasts are sore I can be made to come just by having my nipples played with. It was all wonderfully shameful, but not as cathartic as the performance I gave in the pavilion.

So. There you are. I've put your present to good use. And that explains why I'm still feeling a little light-headed today.

I'm not so distracted that I've forgotten your request, however. Anne arrived today, and I have met her, introduced myself, and done my best to make her feel at home.

She is very pretty, isn't she? I can see why you're so keen to have her trained here. You're incorrigible, Michael. She's obviously very well developed physically, but her behaviour seems a little young, even for her tender years. She pouts, and flirts, and has little temper tantrums. I suppose men find such things attractive. She's obviously got a lot to learn, and so Jem has appointed two Mentors for her – Matt and Simone. I'll let you know how she gets on (although I must stress that I am already jealous of her, and I insist that when she leaves here you mustn't have too much fun with her).

I'll send this to the studio, even though I recall now that you said something about being there only intermittently during the summer. Have you found a rural retreat? I hope you won't get bored.

I will use the beads again tonight and think of you. And then tomorrow I really must get on with some work.

Ever yours
Amanda.

ONE

The few weeks before Anne left for the Private House were both entertaining and frustrating.

Eloise spanked Anne daily, and whenever I was at the cottage I delighted in increasing Anne's embarrassment by watching her receive her punishment and by helpfully suggesting little ways in which the ritual could be improved. Thus I contrived to witness Anne's first bath-time spanking, with both Eloise and Anne naked, rosy-skinned and glistening with hot water and perfumed bubbles. I was there on the occasion when Anne refused to keep still, so that Eloise had to start the punishment over and over again, and I volunteered to hold Anne's nipples tightly in my fingers so that Eloise could complete the eighteen smacks; thanks to Anne's struggles her poor bottom had received several times its allotted chastisement before I succeeded in restraining her, and she started to come as soon as my fingertips closed about her nipples. And I was there for Anne's first outdoor spanking, on a balmy evening after the servants had been sent home: the loud smacks resounded across the cottage grounds.

I tended to go down to the country when the weather was clement, and therefore I was able to appreciate the fact that Anne had taken to heart her mother's injunction that she was to wear few clothes. During the morning Anne usually slouched about the cottage in one of her new sets of lacy underclothes; in the afternoon, if the sun was out, she would remove everything except her knickers in order to sunbathe and scandalise the gardener; and in the evening, after she had been punished, she would wear nothing at all. I was unable to prevent my gaze returning to rest again and again on Anne's tall, golden, slender form, and she made no secret of appreciating my attention. Eloise seemed driven to compete, and by the end of an evening I would often find myself sitting back on the sofa in the drawing room with a naked woman on each side of me.

Anne's behaviour, however, showed no sign of improvement. She saw no reason to delay by as much as a day her departure from the cottage, and she maintained a continuous muttering of complaint about wanting to be independent. At first I thought that she was under the impression that she would not be punished unless she misbehaved, but when Eloise told her for the fourth or fifth time that she would be spanked every day regardless of her conduct, and that therefore she might as well at least try to be polite, Anne responded, in a fit of temper and at a high volume, with words to the effect that she didn't need to be told.

In fact Anne could be guaranteed to be calm, pleasant and tractable only when summoned for a punishment. When she stood naked before Eloise and me, awaiting instructions the obeying of which she knew would entail at the least exhibiting her private parts and enduring the shame of a spanking, Anne shed the graceless, sulking demeanour of a teenager and was transformed into an elegant, poised and vibrantly excited young woman.

She performed well during her punishments, of course, and whether she was instructed to play with herself or was caressed by Eloise the charming little moans of excitement that issued from her coral-pink lips were as delightful to the ear as the sight of her perfect, round buttocks jumping and blushing under Eloise's increasingly practised hand was to the eye.

And she remained good-natured for some time after each spanking, too: sometimes when Eloise and I were sitting side by side on the sofa Anne would drape herself across our laps and we would pass a long, slow hour watching the sunset and stroking Anne's prone body.

These lacunae of erotic languor, however, hardly compensated for the stress and sheer noise that Anne created most of the time. And because she insisted on sharing with Eloise and me her impatience to be sent away to the Private House, she no longer spent much time locked in her room or stamping about the countryside. This was inconvenient for Eloise and me.

Eloise had begun to read Celia's journals from cover to cover, and each evening that I stayed at the cottage she provided me with a passage from the journals which had particularly appealed to her. Anne's mother and her master had had a commitment to sexual experiment which at times during my reading of their exploits caused even me to raise an eyebrow. Eloise left me in no doubt that she wanted me to take her in hand and introduce her to the forbidden pleasures that Celia had so thoroughly explored. Anne's presence in the cottage was unhelpful. Eloise and I could not find a time or place in which we could be sure that we would be free from Anne's grumpy interruptions. Late at night, or when we found ourselves alone together during the day, we engaged in furtive, watchful fumblings which increased our mutual desires without satisfying them.

Tense with pent-up lust, and leaving Eloise in much the same state, I would return to the city where I would immediately begin again to yearn for both women.

Therefore I was as anxious as Anne was to receive the confirmation that a place was ready for her at the Private House. I wanted time alone with Eloise: time during which I would teach her to endure and enjoy, as Celia had, the cruel lessons of an attentive master. And beyond that, once I had taught Eloise to discover and reveal to me every dark corner of the dungeons of her imagination, Anne would return, trained to serve my every perverse whim.

At last Eloise received the letter for which all three of us had been waiting, and within a day Anne had her new luggage packed and was ready to depart. I returned to the city, which I found was becoming stifling and crowded now that the heat of summer had arrived, and I made arrangements to leave my studio in Stephanie's care. I packed only the bare necessities of my craft, as I didn't anticipate that Eloise's passion for following in Celia's footsteps would leave me with much time for painting, and I fled from the grimy heat and travelled once again to the bosky peace of the cottage in the valley.

From the diary of Anne Bright
4 June
So here I am at the Private House. I think it's a horrible place. Why on earth did Mummy want me to come here?

I suppose it has its points. The main building is a fantastic old mansion. It's vast, and made up of bits from every conceivable style of architecture. Right in the middle, with a Palladian wing on one side and a Gothic wing on the other, there's a huge round tower which must have been the keep of a mediæval castle. The whole place is like Gormenghast.

I'm writing this in the room I've been given. It's on the top floor, right under the battlements (I think they're for decoration rather than defence), so there are sloping ceilings, complete with dark oak beams, and it feels very cosy. The windows are little dormers, with seats built in so that I can sit and look through the leaded panes at the view.

And the surrounding park is absolutely magnificent, with formal gardens full of follies and statues and fountains and pavilions, and beyond them an expanse of countryside that all belongs to the Private House, as far as the eye can see. I haven't had a chance yet to explore even a bit of it, but I'm told there are entire farms within the estate, and lakes, and other, smaller houses. And a maze!

I have to admit that everyone's been very nice to me, as well. They're all very friendly. But I get the feeling that they're all in on some private joke that I don't understand. It's certainly a confusing place. It's not what I expected from a finishing school. The ethos seems to be a combination of the severely formal and the wildly unconventional. For instance, everyone wears the most outrageous costumes: some are flamboyant and colourful, others are downright indecent. I'm sure I caught a glimpse of a young man wearing nothing but a sort of harness made of leather straps. But, on the other hand, they address me, and each other, with exaggerated formality, and there seems to be a rigid hierarchy.

I've had a meeting with a woman called Amanda, who seems to be quite an important person here. She looks like a sort of glamorous version of Eloise, but with a bigger bust and an expensive haircut. She says that she's a friend of Michael's. He obviously goes for slim, dark women with short hair. But then I've got long blonde hair, and I'm sure he's interested in me, too.

I get the impression that there's a lot that I'm going to have to learn here, but they don't want to rush me because this is the first time I've been away from the cottage. And I admit – but only in the pages of this diary! – that I am feeling homesick.

Matt and Simone are friendly, too. They're going to be my Mentors. Amanda says it's unusual to have two Mentors, but an exception has been made for me because I'm to be here only for the summer. And, Amanda says, because I'm young and particularly promising! Matt's a bit of hunk: he's about my height and colouring, and he looks pretty muscular. I like watching him move. He smiles a lot. Simone's a black girl with an exotic accent; she's terribly pretty, and tall and slim, but she's rather aloof. I have to address Matt as 'sir' and Simone as 'miss'. I've already been told dozens of little rules, and I get the impression that there are many more I'll have to learn.

One bit of good news is that Amanda already knew all about the way I've been brought up at the cottage, and specifically that now I'm no longer a child I have to be spanked every day. She says that I'm not to worry: that part of my life, at least, will remain unchanged. I confess I'm relieved: it will be reassuring to continue the routine, and anyway I've come to enjoy being smacked. I didn't dare ask whether I'd be allowed to touch myself and make myself come while I'm being spanked. I needn't have been so coy, as Amanda gave me a thorough grilling and made me tell her every detail of my regular punishment. She didn't seem at all surprised that Michael has taught me to play with my anus. She just smiled in a knowing way that made me feel quite jealous, even though I was so embarrassed I could hardly speak.

They've left me alone here. I think they were worried that I was being overwhelmed by all the rules and information. This afternoon I'm to have an Inspection (it seems appropriate to use Capital Initials in this place), and then a lesson called an Induction. I think that's when I'll be spanked. I'll probably meet Jem Darke, the Mistress of the Private House, this afternoon, too. I expect she's a humourless old crone.

So, all in all, I don't know what to make of it. I'll write more later.

From the notebooks of Celia Bright
D doesn't insist that I wear my collar when I go out alone, to work or to meet old friends. When he isn't with me it doesn't matter to him whether or not other people know that I'm a slave, and the chain through my outer labia is a constant and very intimate reminder to me that I am always his. Nonetheless I often wear the collar anyway, because – well, because it suits my looks, for one thing, and because it gives me a thrill to wonder which of the people I meet understand the significance of the black leather band around my neck. How many of them, on seeing the collar, begin to suspect that under my skirt my buttocks are naked and striped red? Or that under the starched white of my blouse my nipples are pierced with gold rings, to which my master attaches chains so that he can tug on my breasts while he uses my mouth for his pleasure? Or that my unprotected

vulva, its lips chained and sometimes locked together with a weighty padlock, is oozing wetness because I am wondering who can detect that I am a slave?

When we go out together, however, D always has me wear the collar. Sometimes, to emphasise his ownership of me, he clips a leash to the little ring that hangs from the front of the collar, and as we walk side by side the people we meet can see that I am his pet. He tends to put me on the leash when we go for walks in the country, where there are fewer passers-by. When he is sure we're alone, he merely has to pull on the leash and I know that I am to lean forward so that he can lift my skirt and expose my bottom.

We have been shopping today, and D put me on the leash. I wore the collar, of course, but I was also wearing matching cuffs around my wrists, and D clipped the leash to one of these. We were looking for clothes for me, and we set off looking forward to a day filled with opportunities for D to humiliate me in front of shoppers and sales assistants. D had hung a bell from my labial chain: it swung between my thighs and jingled with every movement I made. And shortly before we left his house he caned my bottom hard, to ensure that I had vivid marks, just in case I had occasion to try on clothes in a communal changing room.

I don't need any more clothes, of course. Since I have been D's slave I have had everything made for me by a dressmaker who understands D's requirements. I have wardrobes, at D's house and at mine, full of the most marvellous creations: dresses and suits that look outwardly respectable, for wearing in public, as well as corsets, harnesses, gowns and frivolous costumes, in leather and rubber and silk and lace, for indoors. We go shopping simply so that D can show me off to strangers, and have me try on lots of different outfits. The point is to make me feel embarrassed. I always find the prospect both alarming and exciting, and as I left D's house this morning, tethered by my wrist to D, the stinging lines on my bottom and the jingling weight of the bell under my skirt served only to increase my anticipation.

We went to a busy department store, where D told me that I was to ask for a corsetière to measure my bust. We already knew my size, of course: the point was to undress me so that the woman measuring me couldn't fail to notice the gold rings through my nipples. The corsetière was a straight-backed, middle-aged woman who merely raised an eyebrow when D unclipped the leash from my wrist cuff so that I could remove my coat and blouse. She glanced at my face, then down at the collar round my neck, and then caught my eyes again. D waited, holding my coat, while the corsetière and I disappeared into a changing room. As I removed my jacket and blouse I could feel my nipples stiffening against the sheer material of my bra. D had, of course, told me to wear some of my most transparent underwear.

The corsetière displayed no expression at all as she held the tape measure around my ribcage, and then around my upper chest and my breasts. I was sure, however, that her gaze lingered longer than was necessary on my nipples, which felt as though they were about to burst through the flimsy material covering them. The gold rings must have been clearly visible. I couldn't help my face turning red as she inspected me, and although I did my best to keep still I was feeling so aroused that I found myself shifting from one foot to the other, which caused the bell under my skirt to tinkle suddenly. In the nervous silence of the changing room I heard the sound as loudly as breaking glass.

I gasped and held myself rigid.

'Quite charming,' the corsetière said, and wrote down the measurements for me.

I dressed with trembling fingers and returned to D, who made a show of refastening the leash. He took the paper from my hand and pretended to be interested in my bust size. 'I see,' he said to the corsetière. 'She has attractive breasts, don't you think?'

The stern woman smiled at last. 'Very pretty, sir,' she said. 'And decorated with sophistication, if I may say so.'

I heard D chuckle. He realised that the corsetière would be complicit in extending my embarrassment.

We didn't intend to buy any bras, of course: the shop had nothing that met D's standards. However, D selected three lacy confections, in lurid colours, and asked the corsetière to take me into the changing room again and to help me try them on. He offered no explanation why I needed help to change my underwear, and the woman asked for none. She simply smiled and agreed. D unleashed me, and the woman led me away.

She had understood that D had put me at her disposal. Once we were in the changing room her professional detachment evaporated, and she watched me avidly as once again I removed my blouse. She then moved close to me, brushed my hands aside, and unclasped my bra.

My breasts were, quite literally, in her hands. I knew that D expected me to submit to whatever indignities she chose to inflict on me. As she teased the flimsy cups from my flushed bosom I crossed my hands behind my back in a gesture of submission.

The corsetière stepped back and put down my bra. She looked at me for a long moment, until I could no longer meet her gaze, and lowered my head. My breasts felt very exposed.

'You are a pretty little thing,' she said at last. She extended her hand and touched the metal ring at the front of my collar. 'Your husband looks after you very well.'

'He isn't –' I began, and then I said, 'Yes, I'm very lucky. He knows what I like.'

She walked behind me. I felt her lift my hair from my shoulders. She touched the ring at the back of my collar. D often uses it when he ties me up. Sometimes he chains my wrists to it when he whips my breasts.

She was standing close behind me. I could feel her breath on my neck. She reached around me and stroked the undersides of my breasts.

'I see women's bosoms every day,' she whispered. 'I am a connoisseur. I enjoy my work.'

Suddenly she was businesslike again. She moved away from me to pick up the first of the bras that D had chosen for me to try on. It was blue, with sturdy straps and low, lacy, wired cups.

There was no longer any pretence that this was a fitting. I was there to amuse her and to enjoy the humiliation of being handled. Once the bra was fastened she claimed that my breasts were not sitting correctly in the cups, and she pushed and pulled at my flesh with increasing vigour until my breasts felt hot and sore, and she was at last satisfied with their position. She then took the bra off me, and started stroking my breasts again with her thin, strong fingers.

I could easily believe that she enjoyed working with women's bosoms. She seemed to know how I most like to be touched. Her caresses became firmer. While using the lightest of touches on one breast, she slapped the other with increasingly sharp smacks. Then she caressed the smacked breast, and started to administer delicate pinches around the areola of the other.

At last she touched my nipples. She flicked the little gold rings.

'I don't see many customers with these,' she said. 'Does that feel pleasant?'

Pleasant! I was biting my lip to stop myself babbling with pleasure. The chain brushing against the insides of my thighs was wet with my overflowing juices. I nodded.

She pulled the rings abruptly, making me gasp as a thrilling shock arced from within my breasts to my loins. I was very close to coming.

'Did that hurt?' she asked

'A little,' I stammered. I realised that she wanted to think she was hurting me, and that if I encouraged her she would pull on the rings again.

I closed my eyes and threw back my head as she tugged repeatedly at the rings, increasingly fast and hard. My gasps and moans merged into a panting cry that rose, as I came to a climax, to a shuddering cry that must have been audible throughout the lingerie department of the store.

She released my breasts and stepped back as I recovered my breath.

'Will there be anything else?' she enquired.

I was still too breathless to speak, so she turned, picked up the three bras, and left the room.

I collected myself, dressed, and emerged from the changing room to find D and the corsetière standing together, waiting for me.

D pulled me to stand in front of him, so that we were both facing the corsetière. 'I hear you enjoyed yourself in there,' D whispered in my ear. 'Part your skirt, slave.'

I was wearing one of my pleated skirts that have been made to look as though cut from a continuous length of cloth, but which in fact are split from hem to waist at the back. The split is hidden by a considerable overlap of material and by the cunning of my dressmaker's craft, but all I have to do to reveal my bottom is to reach behind me with both hands and pull the sides of the skirt forward. It takes only a second, and when D is standing behind me any casual onlooker is unlikely to notice my movements. The corsetière, although standing in front of me, clearly understood that I was somehow revealing myself to D. I caught her eye as I reached to grab two handfuls of my skirt; she smiled, and I blushed and looked away.

D likes to make me expose myself in public places. I think he enjoys the sense of control over me, and the fact that I find it so thrilling. I was bent forward slightly, as D has instructed me to whenever I display my bottom. If he had stood aside the shoppers could not have failed to notice me, leaning forward with my skirt open at the back. They would have seen that I was wearing no knickers; that I had been caned; that I had a little bell dangling from a chain attached to my sex. They would have been able to see my anus, my parted labia, and perhaps even the glistening evidence of my arousal. It was so frightening, and so exciting.

D didn't move, however. His body shielded me from prying eyes. I waited, with my heart pattering in my chest. I felt his fingers brush my right buttock, and pushed my bottom a little further back. His fingers, warm and firm, pressed against the gap between my labia. I wriggled with frustration: I wanted to come again. He moved his fingers back and forth until I started moaning. When he was able to produce a loudly liquid sucking noise as his fingers massaged my vulva, he seemed satisfied. I sighed with frustration as his fingers slid away.

'I'm afraid none of these is suitable,' D said to the corsetière. 'I hope we haven't wasted your time.'

'Not at all,' the woman replied. 'It was a pleasure to serve you, sir.'

'Cover yourself,' D said to me, 'and say thank you to the lady.'

I straightened. My skirt fell back into position. 'Thank you for being so attentive,' I said. The corsetière merely looked at me.

'Come along, slave,' D said. He fastened the leash to my wrist. 'Let's go and see if there are communal changing rooms on the next floor. I wonder if you can manage to keep those marks on your bottom hidden when you're trying on dresses?' He brought his hand to his nose and inhaled the smell of my juices from his fingers. Then he pulled me into his arms and kissed me. 'I heard you coming,' he whispered. 'And there's a lake between your legs. It's a good thing your juice smells so delicious: you positively reek of sex.'

In the end, after D had judged that I had endured enough humiliations, we did buy one outfit: a two-piece suit which would have been suitable for me to wear to the office. It was made of very soft moleskin, dyed dark blue. The skirt was a simple sheath, but the jacket was rather special: it was tailored to fit snugly, and we found one, a size too small for me, that I could just get into if I went without my blouse. It was gently constricting, and moulded itself to my body. It had long, narrow sleeves, four buttons at the front and a high collar, and a little peplum waist. D was delighted with it, and had

113

me change into it again as soon as we returned to his house.

I wore only the jacket, of course, with no bra under it, and with stockings and high-heeled shoes: the skirt was superfluous. D admired the contrast between my tightly, softly covered top and my blatant nakedness from the waist down. He took me over his lap and used his fingers to make me come again while he spanked me; then he had me kneel in front of him and he used my mouth.

And then he took photographs of me wearing my new jacket.

It is now two days later. The film has been processed, and D sent me to collect the prints. He had me wear the dark blue jacket again (although with the skirt, of course), so that the shop assistants would not be in any doubt that I was the model in the photographs. Before I left he took delight in telling me that as the photographs were so indecent, and the model in them so pretty, he was sure they would have been passed around all the staff in the shop. He hoped that my bottom looked as pink on the prints as it did through the viewfinder of the camera.

As I had half-feared, half-hoped, the shop was staffed by young men. I could see a couple of scruffily-dressed youths standing behind the counter. I pushed open the door gingerly, hoping to make a discreet entrance, but a bell rang loudly as I crossed the threshold. The youths looked up, and I could tell at once that one of them had recognised me. He stared at me with his mouth open for a moment, and then dug his elbow into his colleague's ribs before sprinting towards the back of the shop.

Within a moment there were four young men jostling at the counter to serve me. Four pairs of eager eyes were staring at me; four fervid imaginations were stripping the clothes from me as I stood, blushing, with the receipt for the film in my hand.

'I've come to collect a film,' I said, as steadily as I could. 'There should be a set of prints.'

'There certainly is,' said the tallest of the lads, taking the slip of paper from me. 'Roger, go and fetch the lady's pictures.' He gestured with his hands, by which I understood him to mean that he didn't want Roger to be in any hurry to perform the task.

Roger sauntered towards the back of the shop, and the other three young men leaned their elbows on the counter and looked at me. I pretended to be interested in a display of camera lenses.

'Very nice jacket, if you don't mind me saying so,' the tall lad ventured. The other youths spluttered with repressed laughter.

'Thank you,' I said. I didn't know where to look. I felt warm and sticky. And, of course, I was beginning to feel more than a little aroused. I just can't help it: I start to feel warm and tingly between my legs as soon as I know that someone is looking at me and knows that I'm responsive to being shamed. I hate feeling embarrassed, but I can't resist the sinking feeling in my stomach as I realise I'm enjoying it. I didn't desire any of these four young men, but I was beginning to feel that if they were to insist, for instance, that they needed to see my bottom to check that the photographs were really mine, I would have gone to the back of the shop and removed my skirt.

'Could you ask your colleague to hurry,' I said. 'I really have to get back.'

'Get a move on, Rog,' the tall youth shouted. He turned back to me. 'We can't have you being late,' he said, with an enormous grin. 'I expect you'd get into trouble. I wonder what might happen to a young lady who was late back with her pictures? Me and the lads don't mind giving you a spanking now, if you like, to save your old man the trouble.'

He was an ungainly fellow with pimples, crooked teeth, and appalling taste in clothes. I imagined the expression that would be on his face as I lay across his lap, presenting my bottom to him, and suddenly a wave of nausea swept over me. If D were to order me to offer myself for punishment I would do so: I would gladly present my body to anyone D appointed, no matter how repugnant, because I would be doing it for D. This was, in truth, just such a case. D had sent me to the shop knowing that I would find the experience pleasurably degrading, and I knew that I should accept whatever humiliations were offered to me, so that I would be able to entertain D with my account. But I simply couldn't do it.

My sense of shame was chased from my body by anger and defiance. I was no longer D's slave: I was the Celia who runs an office with twenty staff, the Celia who risks and wins on the stock market.

I looked at the lad until he averted his eyes. I smiled when he glanced again at me. 'Little boy,' I said, 'I would not let you so much as touch me.'

I could have said much more, but I was sure that brevity increased the authority of my words. The tall youth seemed lost for words. He wouldn't meet my gaze. He started nervously to brush his fingers through his lank hair.

'Now go and find my photographs,' I said. He nodded and went to the back of the shop. The two young men remaining at the counter shuffled their feet, glanced at each other, and ambled after their colleague. Within two more minutes I had collected the pictures, paid for them, and left the shop.

On my way back to D's house my feelings of anger and elation drained away, to be replaced by a realisation that I had, for the first time, defied D's wishes. While it was true that he had not specifically instructed me to seek out any further humiliation than exposing myself to the ridicule of the shop staff, I was sure that he would have wished me to take any opportunity to submit to additional embarrassment. And it was clear that the tall young man had been prepared to spank me, with his colleagues as an audience. I should have let him do as he suggested. D would have wanted me to.

When I arrived at D's house Thomas was standing in the hall. 'Good morning, miss,' he intoned. I was so anxious to find D and confess what I had done that I merely muttered a reply and brushed past him.

He uttered a discreet cough, which pulled me up as effectively as D's leash. I retraced my steps, stood in front of him, and fumbled behind my back for the buttons of my skirt.

I still find it mortifying to undress in front of the servants, and that is precisely why D insists that I do so. I blushed scarlet as I tugged the skirt down my hips, stepped out of it, and handed it to Thomas. But for my shoes and stockings I was now naked from the waist down.

'Thank you, miss,' Thomas said. 'The master is in his study.'

I ran from the hall and found D reading papers in his armchair. I fell to my knees in front of him and without pause and, I suspect, without much coherence, I plunged into an account of everything that had occurred in the shop. I wept as I explained how my anger had swayed me from my duty to accept a punishment from the young men who had been taunting me. I had convinced myself that my crime was so heinous that D might disown me, and I begged him to let me prove my devotion.

D listened in silence until I had run out of words. 'Let me see the photographs,' he said at last.

I knelt before him, sobbing, as he slowly perused the prints.

'These two are the best, I think,' he said at last. 'I will keep this one in my wallet; the other is for you to paste into your journal.'

He passed one of the prints to me. I tried to clear my mind and concentrate on it. In the picture I am standing with one hand touching my hair and the other on my hip. D had taken the shot from the side, so that my bare bottom curves in profile beneath the dark material of the jacket. My upper body is turned towards the camera. I have a slight smile on my lips. It is a very flattering portrait, and looking at it I begin to

117

understand why D is pleased to own me. I will paste the picture on to the page opposite this entry.

D leant forward and stroked my hair. 'You see?' he said. 'You're adorable, Celia. I can't imagine wanting to lose you. We mustn't waste the time we have together. I entirely understand your reasons for acting as you did with those uncouth young men. Had I been with you I probably would have let them punish you, as both you and I would have enjoyed your shame. But as I wasn't there, your misbehaviour was not serious. I'll punish you this evening: as you know I have had a pillory made for you, and I'll lock you into it and whip you a little harder than usual. I'm sure that will suffice.'

I was speechless, and conveyed my gratitude by leaning forward and kissing his feet.

He laughed, and pulled me towards him. 'Come here,' he said. 'Sit with me. I want to kiss you.'

Later that day I found another picture to illustrate this journal. In the afternoon D sent me out on another shopping expedition, this time to one of the specialist bookshops that I have sought out on his instructions. The staff in these bookshops, like those in the retailers of fetters and marital aids that I have found for D, are not used to female customers. Sometimes D accompanies me on these expeditions to secret, perverse shops: he likes to show me off as his slave to the seedy men who staff these places, and as he browses with me through the wares on offer he talks in matter-of-fact terms about whether these manacles would suit me, or whether I would like to be punished while tied up in the manner of the model in that picture. These trips make me feel delightfully wicked.

Going alone is a thrill of a different kind: it is more humiliating to enter such establishments on my own, of my own free will, than it is with D. The staff and the other customers must regard me as utterly depraved, particularly as I have to ask the shopkeeper each time to direct me to the products that are to do with female submission.

Today I was looking for pictures: D wanted me to buy photographs and artworks of women posed or bound in positions that I thought would appeal to him. I was to bring home a selection, and over the next few days I am to choose a few favourites, and write an essay about each one. The essays, which D will read, are to describe how I would feel, and what I would like D to do with me, if I were the women in the pictures.

The pictures that I have bought, and the essays I will write, will appear later in this journal. I will include here, however, a photograph that appealed to me immediately, and which I couldn't wait to show to D.

The model doesn't look like me: she's dark, while I'm fair. However, the position she is in – on her knees and elbows, with her legs widely parted, her head resting on her forearms, her bottom lifted high, and her back arched downwards – is one that D likes me to adopt and which I never tire of. He calls it the presentation position, because I am offering him my bottom, my anus and my sex.

This photograph is, I think, a particularly charming example of a woman presenting herself. The fact that it is in black and white emphasises the contrast between her pale skin and the gleaming blackness of her long, tight boots and gloves. The picture is so sharp that one can see the delicate, crinkled skin of her anus and the glint of liquid between her shaven labia. Her hair lies in shining tresses around her recumbent head, but her face is towards the camera and between the locks of hair one can detect a dark eye, gazing expectantly, and the corner of her mouth curved in a smile.

When I showed it to D he agreed that I should put it here in my journal. He has told me to add that he very much likes me to present myself to him in this position, and that it is convenient for him to perform the following acts: to play with my intimate parts, or to watch me while I put my fingers, or an artificial phallus, into my anus and make myself come; to whip my buttocks or my sex; and to bugger me.

And now, having written those words, and with the photograph in front of me as a very graphic reminder of how I look when I present myself, I'm afraid that I'm becoming too excited to write any more. I must go to D and ask his permission to touch myself.

I had reached the end of the section that Eloise had extracted for me to read. I turned back one page and looked again at the photograph of Celia, caught with a shy smile on her face as she turned towards the camera. With her upper body contained in the soft, tight, dark blue material, her nakedness from the waist down seemed all the more provocative.

The resemblance to her daughter was unmistakable. She was like a petite version of Anne. Celia's hair was curly, while Anne's was almost entirely straight, but their faces were identical. Even the expression on Celia's face recalled the quirky smiles that flitted across Anne's features and caused such havoc to my equanimity.

'She was very pretty,' I said to Eloise. We were sitting side by side on the swing seat that was situated to catch the afternoon sun at the edge of the lawn on the south side of the cottage.

'Yes,' Eloise said. Her voice was wistful. She reached out and let her fingers rest on the photograph. 'She was lovely. Right up until – until the end.'

I closed the folder and placed it on the grass. We sat in silence, enjoying the warm sun on our faces, both lost momentarily in thought.

'Michael,' Eloise whispered. 'Have you noticed that I'm wearing the suit?'

Having seen the photograph of Celia, I had already realised that Eloise had found and dressed in the very dark blue moleskin suit that Celia and her master had bought in the department store. 'How could I have failed to notice?' I said with a smile. Eloise's eyes were glittering, and her cheeks were flushed. It was clear that reading Celia's journal had affected her as it had me.

'I never realised that Celia and I were the same size,' she said. 'While she was alive I would never have dared to wear anything of hers. But I don't think she'd mind me wearing this for you. The jacket is a very tight fit. I'm not wearing anything under it. And no knickers, either. I wanted to find out what Celia felt like wearing this suit.'

I pulled her into my arms and ran a hand across the front of the jacket. The material was softer than velvet, and Eloise's breasts felt like furry creatures as my fingers crushed them. 'And how do you feel?' I asked her.

'Very naughty,' she whispered.

'Really?' I said, pulling away from her. 'I'm surprised. After all, you're not dressed as Celia used to dress. You're wearing the skirt.'

'I know,' she said, 'but I still feel . . .'

She hesitated when she saw the fixed expression on my face. I wanted to see her with the skirt off. She understood.

'Come indoors,' she said. 'Let's go in now.'

I shook my head.

Eloise at last realised that I wanted her to take the skirt off immediately. She turned her head from side to side, anxiously scanning the garden for anyone who could see us. There was very little likelihood of being seen: the gardener and maid had gone home, Eloise almost never had visitors to the cottage, and there were no nearby footpaths. Nonetheless our position, which provided a view across the lawn, into the orchard and on to the tilled hillside fields, felt exposed.

'I can't,' she said. 'Not outside. As I told you, I'm wearing no knickers.'

I deliberately misunderstood her. 'It's a warm day. You won't feel cold. In fact, I'll make sure of it. And of course you're wearing no knickers. I sincerely hope that such is your usual practice these days.'

She stood up, and once again cast her gaze far and wide. Her cheeks were very red now. With a resigned sigh she put her hands behind her back and fumbled for the buttons of the skirt. 'Oh, damn it,' she said. 'Help me, would you?'

I sat back in the seat and allowed it to rock gently. 'Have you already forgotten how to ask properly?'

She looked over her shoulder at me and gave a high-pitched mew of frustration. 'Please,' she said. She looked delightfully agitated.

I leant forward, undid the top button, and sat back again to watch her continue her striptease.

The skirt was a tight fit, and even with all of the buttons undone Eloise had to wiggle her hips and hop from one foot to the other in order to push the garment down her legs. I was afforded an eye-level view of her shapely bottom as it was slowly revealed.

At last she was able to step clear of the skirt. She turned to me and placed her hands on her hips. 'Well?' she demanded. 'Are you satisfied now?'

'Not yet,' I said. 'Walk on to the lawn, and then back again, so that I can see you properly.'

She opened her mouth to protest, but having once more failed to detect any sign of onlookers she turned and very cautiously, with much peering from side to side, she began to walk towards the centre of the lawn.

She had found dark blue stockings to match the suit, and so the pale ovals of her buttocks were fetchingly framed. She was wearing high, thin heels, too, which were not entirely suitable for walking on grass. Her hesitant steps made her buttocks roll slowly against each other as her hips swayed. My penis hardened as I watched her, and I began to find it hard to concentrate on the details of the entertainment I was planning for Eloise and myself.

Eloise was in the middle of the lawn now, an incongruously, erotically indecent figure, isolated in a sea of striped-cut grass. She turned to face me, and stood with her thighs pressed together, and one foot slightly raised, like a bather paddling in water that is not quite warm enough. Her eyes were wide with mute appeal: I knew that she must feel very visible, and even the swing seat would now seem a safe haven.

I waved at her, and made a circle with my arm to indicate that she should return to me not straight across the lawn but by way of the curving flower border. She stared at me from a moment, and then set off with still-hesitant steps towards the border.

Lazily I monitored her progress. I admired her slender thighs and calves. I knew that beneath the direct beams of the sun she would be getting hot in the tight-fitting jacket. I also knew that the longer I made her parade around the garden, anxious that at any moment she might be seen wearing her lewd costume, the more excited she would be by the time she returned to me – and the more ready to undertake whatever I demanded of her.

She reached the path that ran alongside the flower bed, and was able to walk more confidently than on grass. She strolled towards the swing seat where I was waiting for her.

'There,' she said. 'I've allowed every hiker and farm worker within miles to gawp at me. Are you satisfied now? Can we go indoors?'

She was desperate to play some of the games she had read about in Celia's journal, and she assumed that we would have to be indoors to do so. 'No,' I replied. 'I like it out here, in the sun. Anyway, I haven't finished with you. Don't you think it was inconsiderate of you to wear the skirt in the first place? I think that merits a punishment.'

'Oh,' she said, and her face brightened. 'All right, then. What do you want me to do? Where shall we go?'

'I'm not going anywhere,' I said, 'and you're going on to my lap.' I patted my knees.

Eloise pressed her thighs together and wriggled delightfully. 'Here?'

'Yes,' I said sternly. 'Here. And this minute, or I'll spank you harder than you like.'

'But –' was all she said. With a last despairing look over her shoulder, she scrambled on to the seat and positioned herself across my lap. I stroked her bottom until the seat had stopped rocking, and then proceeded to smack her buttocks, making each slap sound as loudly as I could.

Eloise squealed and wriggled on my lap, which did nothing to ease the pressure of my erection. The hardest smacks were loud enough to produce echoes from the distant hills, and I did my best to bring the rest of the spanking up to this resounding level. 'The whole valley must be able to hear this,' I told her as I administered a

123

series of particularly resonant smacks, and she cried out in protest and wriggled more energetically.

Her buttocks grew bright pink, and jiggled very prettily as she writhed on my lap.

My right arm began to tire and, as I had more work for it to do later in the day, I stopped smacking Eloise.

I thrust my hand between her thighs and found, as I had expected, that she was so wet and ready that my fingers slid into her slippery vagina without encountering any resistance.

She gasped, and I felt her body shiver. I moved my fingers in and out of her for a while, as I stroked her heated buttocks with my left hand and enjoyed the moanings and tremblings that the movements of my hands engendered.

When her cries became louder, and I thought she might be about to come, I stopped. Slowly I pulled my fingers from her.

'I think you should show me your spanked bottom,' I said. 'In the manner that Celia used to exhibit herself to her master. Adopt the presentation position, Eloise.'

She looked over her shoulder at me. I thought she might protest, but evidently the punishment had so excited her that she was prepared to overcome her embarrassment. And she was clearly in a mood to emulate Celia in every way she could.

'All right,' she said. 'Here? On the seat?'

'There isn't enough space,' I said. 'And I want to be able to see you properly. On the lawn, in front of me.'

I helped her to her feet. She stood for a moment, looking at me and thinking how best to arrange herself for my benefit. Her light blue eyes were bright. Her breasts rose and fell under their coating of soft blue.

She turned and knelt, with her back to me, just in front of my feet. She looked over her shoulder again, and I saw a mischievous smile half concealed behind a wing of her dark hair. Then she crossed her arms in front of her face and very slowly lowered her torso until her forearms were resting on the grass. She arched her back downwards, so that her chest was pressed to the ground and her bottom

124

was pushed towards me. She inched her knees apart, no doubt ruining the dark blue stockings as she did so, and when she could separate her knees no further she brought her ankles together and crossed one over the other. She then remained completely still.

Her hindquarters, their pale perfection accentuated by the dark blue above and below them, were open for my inspection. The gluteal muscles of her buttocks were taut, and the stretched skin at the centre of each tight curve was glowing pink from the spanking. My right hand flexed involuntarily and I regretted that I had left my riding crop in my room. I made up my mind that before I took my pleasure with Eloise, or permitted her to enjoy a climax, I would have to whip her until her bottom was well marked. She wanted to know how it felt to be Celia; I would help her to find out.

A breeze rustled the branches above my head. The valley was so quiet that I could hear the birds singing in the woods that crowned the far hills. Somewhere in the distance a late cuckoo started to call. Eloise remained motionless, apart from the slight rise and fall of her body as she breathed and, I noticed, a slow seepage of clear fluid from the split of her sex. Occasionally, as if to attract my attention, the muscle of her anus twitched; in truth I needed no incentive to study the funnel of delightfully dark pink skin, and I was lost in considering the several cylindrical objects, both animate and inanimate, with which I intended to penetrate it during the next few weeks.

I extended my right leg and brought my foot up beneath Eloise's vulva. She started as the top of my shoe came into contact with the wet folds of her labia, but otherwise she remained still. I pressed my foot up a little, and watched the lips of her sex open and spread across the polished leather, as if trying to engulf the toe-cap. I moved my foot back and forth a little, and induced in Eloise a rocking movement of her hips. I heard her murmur wordlessly.

I withdrew my foot. The toe-cap of my shoe had a sheen of wetness. Eloise's labia remained parted and slick. She hollowed her back more, thrusting her sex towards me in mute invitation.

I set the seat to swinging gently, and with each forward swing I allowed my foot to touch Eloise. Sometimes I nudged her open vulva with the wetted toe-cap, or her anus with the point of the toe; sometimes I delivered a lazy kick to one or other of her buttocks. After a few little kicks Eloise began to move her hips to the same rhythm.

We continued in this way for some time, as I could think of no more pleasing way in which to while away an afternoon in early summer.

In the end I stopped only because the increasing vigour of Eloise's movements and of the audible gasps she had begun to utter convinced me that once again she was approaching the point of orgasm. I brought the swing seat to an abrupt halt and planted my feet firmly on the grass. I waited until she was still before telling her to turn round and kneel up so that I could address her.

She kept her knees parted and her arms raised above her head. Her eyes were misty, and her lips were parted. The soft cloth covering the mounds of her breasts, impressed with grass cuttings, rose and fell as she brought her breathing under control.

I looked at her enquiringly.

'Wonderful,' she breathed.

'I expect Celia would have enjoyed it,' I said. 'Not merely presenting herself to her master, but also enduring the indignity of getting a good kicking on her arse and her cunt. Just the sort of thing she liked. And so did you.'

Eloise's flushed face turned a deeper shade of red. She muttered her agreement, and then said sulkily, 'You didn't let me finish, you beast. And anyway, you're not my master.'

'No? In that case, you're presumably not interested in any more punishment.'

She looked up at me with wide eyes. Her arms dropped slowly to her sides. 'More?'

'It's what I recommend,' I said airily. 'Celia was accustomed to being whipped regularly. So far you've had no more than a spanking. It's not really in the same league, is it?'

Eloise looked perplexed. Her hands were now together, pressed against her lower belly, and her hips were gyrating gently. She was desperate to experience the climax that she had twice been denied, but she was also clearly tempted to follow in Celia's footsteps further into the realm of forbidden sensations.

'Do you want to whip me, then?' she said. 'You can if you like.'

'Is that what you want?' I was adamant that she would have to ask.

'Yes.' She was suddenly decisive. She leant forward, rested her arms on my thighs, and kissed my knees before looking up at me again. 'I'd like you to whip me. Please.'

'Very well. I can't pretend I won't enjoy it, too. Stand up. We'll go into the cottage.'

She rose to her feet, and extended her hand to pull me up from the swing seat and into her embrace. As we kissed I grasped her naked buttocks and pressed her body against mine. She ground her breasts into my chest. 'No,' she said.

In my surprise I released her from my arms.

She smiled secretively. 'Not in the cottage. Somewhere better. I'll show you.'

Eloise led me around the cottage. I trailed after her, conscious that I had allowed her to overrule my authority, but bewitched by the sight of her stockinged, high-heeled walk and the movement of her buttocks. On the other side of the cottage she paced carefully across the cobbled courtyard towards the outbuildings.

In my previous visits to the cottage I had had little time or inclination to visit this sprawl of storerooms. I now saw, however, that the largest of them – a substantial structure, rendered and whitewashed to match the cottage – had been transformed. The exterior had been washed down, and brilliantly reflected the sunlight. The windows, which had been opaque with grime, were clean, and the drapes that had hung inside then had been drawn back. This was the building to which Eloise was leading me.

Having read some of Celia's journals I should have been prepared for the sight that awaited me as I followed Eloise

127

into the cavernous room. Nonetheless I confess that I simply stopped in the doorway, and was speechless except for a muttered imprecation.

I hadn't seen, outside the walls of premises owned by the Private House, such a comprehensive collection of equipment designed for bondage and punishment. My gaze took in purpose-built furniture, all padded in black leather, with attached chains and straps; metal hooks and eyes and arrangements of pulleys, set into the wooden beams that crossed the ceiling; racks of whips, crops, canes, tawses and other straps; a glass-fronted cabinet containing shiny phallic objects; wardrobes, the costumes in which I could only imagine. This, I realised slowly, was the collection that Celia's master had accumulated. Celia had had everything transported to her new home in the country, and had kept the collection under lock and key.

It occurred to me that perhaps she hoped that her daughter would one day come to delight in the torments to which her master had subjected her when he utilised this equipment. I imagined Anne bound tightly on to the articulated bench in front of me, her long, golden limbs held tautly spread by the black leather straps. I pictured myself, standing beside her with a whip in my hand, ignoring her pleas as I adjusted the bench to raise her hindquarters to greater prominence. Once she had completed her training she would be ready to be used in this room.

I was so taken with the thought, and so suddenly oblivious to the presence of Eloise, that I murmured, 'All this must be for Anne.'

'Perhaps,' Eloise said. 'Celia's will doesn't mention this room and its contents specifically. I suppose it all forms part of the estate, and will therefore pass to Anne. But in the meantime,' she whispered, insinuating an arm around my waist, 'it seems a shame to waste it. We should make sure everything's in working order, don't you think?'

'Of course.' I felt less confident than I hoped I sounded. One or two of the pieces of furniture, embellished with chrome-plated handles and complex systems of gear wheels, and the pulley arrangements on the ceiling, were more sophisticated than anything I had previously seen. I simply didn't know how to operate them. While in the role of Eloise's master I couldn't afford to appear ignorant or indecisive.

'We don't have time to look at everything,' I announced. 'You've already waited long enough for an orgasm, and you still have to wait until you've been properly flogged. We'll keep this simple. Go and sit in that chair.'

The chair in question consisted of a narrow back and a tiny seat that was shaped to hold the lower back of the sitter. Attached to this basic structure were padded arm rests, stirrups, restraining straps, and a host of handles and wheels by means of which every element of the construction could be adjusted. I had no intention of being diverted into an exploration of the chair's controls: I had merely spotted that it was raked slightly backwards, and had a spreader bar suspended from the ceiling above it. It would therefore be a simple matter to secure Eloise in a doubled position.

Eloise perched her bottom on the shaped seat and reclined on the chair. The heels of her shoes barely reached the floor, and she had to cling on to the arm rests in order to prevent herself from sliding off the seat. She had a doubting look on her face. 'This isn't comfortable,' she said. 'And I thought the idea was that you would whip my bottom?'

'I very much doubt that it was designed with comfort in mind,' I said. 'But you'll feel more secure if you put your feet into the stirrups.'

I helped her lift one foot, and then the other, into the gleaming metal D-rings. I didn't need to use the ankle straps to tie Eloise in place as her high-heels prevented her from lifting her feet clear of the stirrups. I stood in front of her. 'That's better already,' I said, making it clear with my gaze that with her feet in the stirrups her legs were raised and held apart. She pouted at me as her cheeks reddened.

'Celia seems to have enjoyed being tied up,' I said, as I ran my hand along the insides of Eloise's thighs. 'I hope you're not going to object.'

'You're going to tie me to the chair?' Eloise asked. Her eyes were shining with excitement.

'Well,' I said, 'it seems a shame not to use all these big leather straps. They must be here for some purpose.'

Luckily the straps proved straightforward in use. Eloise made only token mews of protest as I tightened them across her body. One went around her waist; two others went over her shoulders and around her chest, crossing each other between her breasts. I adjusted the arm rests so that Eloise could place her arms against them when she held her hands up as if in surrender. I then used all three of the straps that were attached to each of the rests, securing her arms just below the shoulder, at the elbow, and at the wrist – not because it was necessary to be so thorough, but because it looked pleasing and would leave Eloise in no doubt that she was completely pinioned.

'Try to move,' I suggested.

She could no more than wriggle. She was secured to the back of the chair, and would be held in place no matter how much she tried to buck and writhe under the lash.

'Now then,' I said, 'I understand you'd like to be whipped on your bottom. Is that right?'

'Yes. Please,' she added, remembering at the last minute that she was occupying Celia's role as a slave. 'But how –'

'Like this,' I said, and turned the handle which lowered the spreader bar.

Eloise watched with trepidation as I secured the stirrups to the metal rings at the ends of the bar. Her feet were now spread as far apart as they had been when she had presented herself to me on the lawn, and even before I began to hoist the bar her vulva, protruding over the edge of the tiny seat, was exposed and open.

I turned the handle in the opposite direction and the bar moved towards the ceiling. I stopped when Eloise's cries of protest became vehement, and I judged that she was beginning to feel real discomfort. By this time her slender, blue-stockinged legs were vertical, her heels were pointing skywards, and the muscles at the backs of her thighs were stretched and taut. She was bent almost double, and was unable to move.

Only the small of her back was still resting on the seat. Her bottom was widely parted and completely vulnerable, as was her sex. I caressed her for a few moments, gently at first and then with increasing roughness, and watched her struggle in her bonds as she lost the fight against the waves of pleasurable sensations. Her vagina was leaking liquid again; her breath came in short gasps.

Once again I left her on the brink of a climax. She swore at me as her vision cleared.

'Don't move,' I said. 'I'll be back before long.'

As I sauntered towards the array of whips and rods, intending to allow Eloise plenty of time in which to appreciate the discomfort and exciting anticipation of waiting for punishment while in bondage, I had time myself to appreciate the design of the room.

Although it was spacious, it had been divided by wooden partitions and carefully placed screens into discrete areas. Only from the doorway could one appreciate the overall extent. The walls had been roughly finished and had exposed beams, creating an antique effect which was augmented by the dark, heavy drapes. These were pulled back, so that the entire room was flooded with daylight, but it was clear that when the drapes were closed each area of the room would feel intimate and enclosed. Grilles set in the floor suggested a system of underfloor heating, and lamps of all kinds – chandeliers, standard lamps, wall lights – would allow a variety of levels of illumination. This was clearly much more than a place to store old artefacts: Celia had designed it to be a functioning dungeon.

I tore myself away from admiring the plethora of sturdy ring bolts set into every beam and at intervals across the floor, and proceeded to be amazed at the panoply of instruments of correction from which I was to choose. What thoughts had gone through Eloise's mind, I wondered, as she had drawn the dust sheet from this cabinet and had seen the dozens of whips that she had uncovered.

I selected a leather strap, a thin wooden rod, and a short whip with half a dozen tails. Each was the smallest and lightest in its class: I intended to punish Eloise thoroughly, but I knew that it would be necessary to start modestly. And there would be, after all, several weeks to experiment with the equipment in the room and to introduce Eloise to sterner chastisements.

I returned to Eloise, who was wriggling very prettily in her bonds, and showed her the three implements.

'Would you like me to choose?' she offered impertinently.

I shook my head and gave her what I hoped was a sinister grin. I ran my hands lightly from her ankles to her hips, and caressed the tender skin between her stocking-tops and her sex. I stroked and then gently smacked her stretched, rounded buttocks. I played with her vagina until she was squirming, and then massaged some of her overflowing juices into the crinkled skin of her anus, which made her squirm even more.

I started with the rod, and administered two firm strokes to each buttock. The rod left fine red lines on her pale skin, and as each stroke landed she yelped.

Next I used the strap, which made a more satisfying sound each time it struck, and drew from Eloise a shuddering gasp of indrawn breath. After only six lashes her buttocks were beginning to glow ruddily.

I then tried the whip. It felt very light in my hand, and it was difficult to put any force behind the blows, but it must have been effective as each time the six thin strands of leather slashed across her flesh Eloise produced a whinnying cry that tailed off into a sob. It was, of course, impossible to ensure that all of the strands landed only on the curves of her buttocks, and in truth I made little effort to prevent the wicked little tails flailing against the tenderest membranes of her exposed sex and anus. This, no doubt, explained the intensity of her cries.

I paused, and allowed Eloise to open her eyes and focus them on the whip I still held in my hand. 'This is the one,' I said cheerfully. 'Does it sting? Yes, it obviously does. Another twenty, I think, and then we'll take a break and decide how many more.'

Eloise made no reply other than a hopeless groan, and I resumed flicking the tails of the whip all over the vulnerable area from her stocking-tops to her anus. As I neared the end of the promised twenty strokes I concentrated on vertical lashes directed down on to her labia and then up, to catch the open furrow between her buttocks. I slowed the pace of the whipping, too, waiting for her to stop writhing and to open her eyes and look at me before I administered another stroke. She was completely helpless to prevent me tormenting the most private and sensitive parts of her body. Her blue eyes with bright with tears, but the liquefaction of her heated sex demonstrated that the punishment was stoking the fire of her desire. I had no doubt that with the merest touch of my finger near the tip of her clitoris she would spiral into a sensational climax.

'I think you need more,' I said. 'Ten? Twenty? Oh, I'll just keep going until I think you've had enough.'

Eloise seemed to have lost the power of speech. She simply moaned now, fairly continuously as I whipped her. She had stopped struggling against her bonds, and merely rolled her head from side to side. I whipped harder, aiming alternately for her buttocks, which were now thoroughly reddened.

By the time I stopped there were drops of liquid falling from her open vagina on to the floor. I stood between her uplifted legs and placed the handle of the whip vertically against her vulva. She gasped, shuddered, shook her head and looked at me. I removed the whip handle.

'I think that's enough,' I said. 'All this corporal punishment has got me quite worked up. I'm going to fuck you.'

'Yes,' she exclaimed. 'Oh, yes, please. Take me to bed.' She turned her head in the direction of the vast iron bedstead that occupied one of the areas of the room.

'That won't be necessary,' I said, unbuttoning my trousers. 'I'm sure Celia's master wouldn't have bothered to untie Celia before using her for his pleasure. You're very conveniently positioned just as you are.'

Eloise's insincere complaints ceased abruptly as I thrust my rigid member into her vagina. It felt like entering a cave of molten lava, and I had to clench my muscles to prevent my seed from spurting forth immediately. When I was in control of myself I began to move in and out with slow, steady strokes, pulling back until only the tip of my glans was touching her inflamed flesh and then sliding forwards until the entire length of my cylinder was enveloped in her wet heat.

Eloise had closed her eyes and turned her head aside. Her lips were parted and she was breathing deeply, with occasional gasping sobs as my penis sank into her. At the extremity of her passion, spanked and whipped and bound and on the point of falling over the precipice of her long-delayed orgasm, she looked beautiful. I let the fingers of my left hand tease through her pubic hair and stray towards the hood of her clitoris. She cried out, and opened her eyes, and turned her head to gaze pleadingly at me. With my right hand I brought the handle of the whip to her buttocks, and rubbed it against the sore skin until she started to moan. Then I placed the rounded end of the handle in the funnel of her anus, and pressed gently until I felt the ring of muscle begin to yield.

It occurred to me that it would be very easy to withdraw my penis from her vagina and to insert it instead in the smaller hole. Celia, in Eloise's situation, would certainly have been buggered by her master. The thought of buggering Eloise, however, added to the irresistible sensations surrounding my thrusting cock, was enough to bring the seed boiling from my balls. I pushed into Eloise as hard as I could, I pressed the tip of the whip handle into her arsehole, and my fingers slid down to surround the bud of her clitoris. Eloise gave a raucous cry, and began to shiver in spasms as my sperm jetted in hot bursts from my penis.

Afterwards, as I untied Eloise and massaged her aching muscles, I relived in my imagination the events of the afternoon. In my thoughts, however, it wasn't Eloise who asked to be spanked, and then presented her body lewdly to me, and then was bound in the dungeon to be whipped and buggered. It was Anne.

'That was very satisfactory,' Eloise said. Her face displayed her contentment. 'I think I'll let you stay for dinner. And then, tomorrow morning, we can read another extract from Celia's journals. She is such an inspirational writer.'

From the diary of Anne Bright
4 June (continued)
It's late in the afternoon now, and at last I've got a moment in which to update my diary. I've been Inspected, I've been Inducted, I've had lessons, and I've been spanked several times. The weather is absolutely glorious, the grounds of this place are beautiful, and I've been stuck indoors all day.

Where to start? Well, there was Inspection first. Matt and Simone came up here to my room to prepare me. They brought several identical sets of the uniform that I'm to wear every day while I'm at the Private House, unless I'm specifically told otherwise. I'm getting quite used to people watching me while I'm changing my clothes, and I'm afraid I took the opportunity to flirt with Matt as I undressed and paraded around the room in my new costume.

As it's summer the uniform is all in white, and doesn't consist of very much: a short skirt which, at least when I'm standing straight, just about conceals the fact that I'm wearing no knickers; sandals with wedge heels; and a halter top made of thin, stretchy cotton through which my nipples are clearly visible. I like it: it's comfortable and it makes me feel more naked than when I'm wearing nothing at all. The thin material stretched across my breasts make me conscious of them all the time, and because the skirt is so short I find myself thinking continually about whether anyone will see underneath it when I walk up stairs or lean forward. It's as if it had been designed to keep me in a state of nervous excitement – which I think is fun, but I have to admit it's not the sort of uniform I expected to wear at my finishing school.

Not that Matt and Simone are very much more dressed. Matt always looks as though he's ready for the gym: he wears a singlet and shorts, both very tight fitting, which show off his muscles. I have to try very hard not to make it obvious that I'm staring at his body. As I was tying up the back of my new top I managed to stand so close to him that my nipples brushed the front of his singlet. 'Don't forget that I'm supposed to be spanked every day,' I reminded him. He just smiled at me, and it was Simone who said that there was no danger of anyone forgetting.

Simone looks amazingly athletic: she's even slimmer than me and her dark brown skin gleams with the curves of her muscles. She wears a halter top and a skirt very like mine, but made of some shiny red material.

They made me walk about the room in my uniform, and seemed satisfied with my appearance. I was allowed to put on a restrained but sophisticated few touches of my new make-up, and a spray of perfume. They made sure that I remembered how to address my superiors and that I knew how to stand, with my hands behind my back, my legs apart, and leaning forward slightly, so as to show off my body to best effect. And then they took me to be Inspected.

We walked along deeply carpeted corridors and down stone stairways, and arrived at last in a small room. One wall had tall windows which were open to let in the sunlight and a summer breeze; the other three walls were hung with vast mirrors, so that wherever you looked you saw yourself reflected. There were a few pieces of antique furniture placed against the walls, and one low couch precisely in the centre of the room. Matt, Simone and I stood in a line behind the couch, and waited.

The door opened and three people came in, making the room rather crowded. Amanda walked in first, and winked at me. She was wearing ordinary clothes – obviously well made and very expensive, but nothing extraordinary – so I was not at all prepared for the appearance of the next two women.

Amanda was followed by a slim woman with long curls of dark hair and flashing dark eyes. She had an ageless, gypsy look, and was very striking, but I found myself staring at her remarkable costume. She was dressed in leather: she had thigh-length boots, gauntlets and a tunic all made of tight, shiny, black leather. The tunic was shaped to accentuate her breasts, but was fastened up to the neck and so covered her upper body completely. The black hide that hugged her torso and her limbs only served to draw attention to the fact that from her waist to her thighs she was naked. I found myself staring at the dark triangle of her pubic hair. I thought I glimpsed a glitter of gold at the junction of her thighs. From the tight waistband of her tunic hung a riding crop and a pair of handcuffs. When I tore my gaze away I found her looking at me and frowning. I shivered: she seemed sinister, and had an air of authority despite her outrageously revealing clothes.

My mind was awhirl with suppositions. Could this woman be the Mistress of the House? Why was she dressed in such menacing clothes? What kind of educational establishment was this to which my mother, Eloise and Michael had conspired to send me?

Now I understand much more about the Private House. It seems silly of me not to have understood by then the nature of the education I was going to receive. I had been trying to rationalise the strange uniforms and behaviour I had seen: it made sense to wear almost nothing, I told myself, because of the summer heat; I reasoned that it wasn't surprising that an old-fashioned school would have lots of petty rules about deportment.

But no finishing school, no matter how liberal or old-fashioned, would think it normal for a member of staff to walk about clad head to toe in black leather and showing off her private parts. With a lurch of my stomach – half of trepidation, half of excitement – I suddenly realised that in the Private House I would learn secrets that are concealed from most of the world. I divined a connection, a common thread that ran between the mysterious black furniture I had discovered under dust sheets in the locked outhouse, my naughty daydreams of being captured by pirates and chained in dungeons, the thrill I feel when people look at my body, and the waves of pleasure that crash over me when I stroke my vulva while Eloise spanks me. Here, in the Private House, I realised I would learn how these things are connected.

There were still more surprises in store for me. The leather-clad woman didn't close the door behind her: she held it open, and a third woman swept into the room.

She was quite the prettiest thing I have ever seen. Slender and petite, with masses of red-brown hair, greeny-blue eyes that seemed to twinkle with intelligence and mischief, a heart-shaped face and the most adorable lips. I knew at once that she was the Mistress of the Private House. She couldn't have looked more different from the dried-up harridan I had imagined in the role, but nonetheless I understood at once that she would inspire both love and respect.

It seemed quite right that she was wearing an even more outrageous and revealing costume than any I had yet seen. She was dressed in no more than a corset, basically – a red satin corset, drawn so tightly around her that her waist appeared impossibly thin. Her breasts, which are as big as mine, were supported but not covered. Apart from the corset she was wearing only black stockings, held up by suspenders from the corset, high-heeled pixie boots, and a short cape. Fine silver chains ran from a necklace up to her earrings and down to the clamps that were pinching her nipples.

My own nipples hardened immediately as I wondered how it would feel to wear jewellery like that. I had no more time to think, however, because I realised that the woman was looking at me as intently as I was staring at her, and I had to look away.

'Mistress,' Amanda said, 'this is Anne. Anne, look up. You are honoured. This is Mistress Julia, the commander of the guards, and Jem, the Supreme Mistress of the Private House.'

It sounds silly now, but I couldn't think of anything to say. I tried to curtsey.

'How charmingly polite,' Mistress Jem said. Her voice was low, like, I imagine, the purr of a leopard, and slightly drawling. 'Stand up, Anne. Things aren't quite that formal around here. Not these days.'

I straightened, and tried to remain calm as she looked at me. I kept my hands behind my back and remembered to push out my bottom. She walked around me, and then turned to Amanda.

'Michael didn't exaggerate,' she said. 'She's completely lovely. Her breasts are already well developed. She appears to be fit, although no doubt there's room for improvement.' She turned to me again. 'Anne, my dear, would you please kneel on the couch.'

I climbed on to the upholstered seat, and remembered to keep my knees apart as I knelt.

'Matt and Simone,' I heard Jem say from behind me. 'Two Mentors?'

'We have Anne for only the summer,' Amanda replied. 'I think we can train her fairly intensively. As you'll see, she's naturally well qualified. Anne, lift your skirt at the back and lean forward.'

I had guessed that I would have to show off my body: after all, at some point these people would, I hoped, get round to spanking me. Even so I had to take a deep breath and nerve myself to reveal my bottom to this small crowd of strangers.

They were all standing behind me. I held my skirt in both hands at the small of my back. There was a silence that seemed endless.

'Eminently punishable,' said a voice I hadn't heard before and which must have been that of the leather-clad Julia.

I started as a hand touched my right buttock. Delicate fingers began to stroke my skin.

'Amanda tells me,' Jem said, 'that recently you've been punished daily. Is that so?'

'Yes, mistress,' I blurted out. 'Since my eighteenth birthday I've been spanked every day. Eighteen smacks. Sometimes more.'

'More?' The fingers seemed to know exactly how to caress me so as to make me feel all tickly and confused. I was already damp inside my vulva, and I was beginning to get very excited.

'Yes, mistress. If Eloise or Michael thought I was behaving childishly they would give me extra smacks. And –'

'Yes, my dear?'

'Well, mistress, it's just that –' I was stammering with embarrassment. 'It's just that whenever I was spanked at home I was allowed to play with myself until I had an orgasm. And I was hoping that I'll be allowed to do the same thing here. Because I like having orgasms.'

It sounded very lame, but I find that when I'm showing off my bottom I become sexually aroused, and the subtle movements of the Mistress's fingers were making me desperate.

'Anne has clearly already undergone some preliminary training,' Jem said dryly.

'You know Michael,' Amanda replied. 'He wouldn't have been able to resist the temptation.'

'Do you want to come now,' Jem asked me in a conspiratorial voice, as if no one else could hear.

'Yes, please, mistress,' I babbled. I expect I sounded like an over-enthusiastic teenager, but everyone was being so nice to me and I really wanted to show them how much I enjoyed being spanked and being allowed to come.

'Julia, I can always rely on you to deliver an effective chastisement. Use only your hand, and go slowly.' Jem spoke again to me. 'How do feel,' she asked, 'here?'

Her fingers fluttered down the inside curve of my buttock and rested lightly on my outer labia.

I said, 'Oh my goodness,' which wasn't very grown-up of me, and then, 'I'm excited, mistress. I feel warm and tingly and wet.'

'Let us see,' Jem told me. 'Use your fingers to open yourself. No – not that way. Your hand will get in the way when Julia spanks you. Put your hand between your thighs from the front.'

It didn't occur to me to do anything other than Jem had told me: after all, I wanted to touch myself and it was exciting to know that the Mistress and everyone else could see inside my private parts. Jem, however, commented to Amanda that I was precociously obedient. 'You'll do well here, Anne,' the Mistress said. 'Obedience is the first principle of the Private House. You must remember always to do as you are told.'

'Yes, mistress,' I replied, but I wasn't concentrating on what she was saying because as I held open my labia I was pressing the palm of my hand against the prepuce of my clitoris, and creating lots of delicious thrills.

I saw the sheen of the Mistress's red corset and realised that she had come to stand in front me. I wondered whether she, like Michael, wanted to watch the expressions on my face as I came.

'I'm going to play with your breasts,' she said. 'Try to keep still.'

Her fingers touched me again, and again set off little tremors of pleasure wherever they caressed my skin, even through the material of my top. My breasts felt heavy and warm, and my nipples seemed very sensitive. I had to stop moving my hand between my legs or I would have started to come immediately.

'Try to hold back until near the end of your spanking,' Jem whispered to me, and held my nipples in her fingers as, behind me, Julia's hand descended.

I'm used to being spanked now, and I always enjoy it, but today's was really rather special. For one thing, Julia's smacks are very hard! I made more noise than usual, although perhaps that was partly because I had a larger than usual audience that I wanted to impress. And whenever I glanced up I could see the Mistress's gorgeous body in its wonderfully rude costume, and reflected in the mirrors Matt and Simone and Amanda watching me, and Julia's black-gloved hand rising and falling, and – above all – I could see myself, kneeling on the couch, offering my bottom to Julia and my breasts to Jem. I wanted the spanking to go on for ever, but with Jem's fingers nipping my breasts and my own fingers sliding back and forth as if they had a will of their own, I was helpless to resist the juggernaut of sexual climax.

I don't know how many smacks I had received, but I remember thinking that my bottom was feeling good and hot just before I lost control and felt my orgasm beginning to roll over me. I must have cried out, because the spanking suddenly became faster and even harder, and that was all I needed to go over the edge. Jem's fingers tightened on my nipples and I shook and trembled as those wonderful lightning bolts zigzagged through my body.

'What do you say?' It was Simone's voice, hissing in my ear as I recovered my wits. 'Anne, what do you say?'

'Thank you, mistress,' I said, and looked up into Jem's green eyes. She was smiling, and seemed pleased with my performance. She leant forward and kissed me – a proper kiss, on the lips. I'd never been kissed like that by a woman. It was swooningly nice.

'I'm told your mother was taught here,' Jem said. 'I'm afraid that was long before my time. Jules, have you checked the records for the reports on Celia Bright?'

'Of course,' Julia replied. I noticed that Julia and Jem spoke to each other almost as equals, without the formality of address to which I was becoming accustomed.

'And?'

Julia made some wordless response which I was unable to see. Whatever it was, it made Jem smile. 'We'll see,' she said. 'We'll see.'

I was left to recover my breath and, as Jem said, to look decorative, while she, Julia and Amanda discussed me with Matt and Simone. After a few minutes I was left alone with my Mentors, who breathed sighs of relief.

'Well done,' Matt said as he helped me from the couch. 'That was brilliant, Anne. Wasn't she good, Simone?'

I didn't understand what all the fuss was about, but I was happy that I'd pleased my Mentors. They led me from the room and on to the next stage of my introduction to the Private House: Induction.

Induction proved to be much less fun than Inspection. It was simply a matter of Matt and Simone lecturing me about what I would be expected to learn. I had to make notes, too.

The curriculum is certainly not what you'd expect at a finishing school. But having been Inspected I wasn't exactly surprised at the subjects I would be taught.

It sounds like there will be plenty of exercise classes and gym work, which I won't mind at all. There will be classes on food, nutrition and cookery, because it's apparently very important that I learn to eat healthily. I can understand that, but I'm not sure I see the reason for learning etiquette. I mean, who cares which way round one passes the port? Matt and Simone were quite shocked by my free-thinking opinions on the subject of table manners, and I had to stand with my skirt up in the corner of the room for quite a long time. And then I had to ask Simone to spank me.

Deportment is apparently considered important here. When I suggested that it wouldn't take long to learn to walk correctly, Simone talked mysteriously about being able to look elegant in all circumstances, no matter how uncomfortable or restrictive. I think I have an idea what she means.

The most interesting subject of all is sexual skills – but I won't be allowed to so much as start the course until I've made satisfactory progress in the other subjects. I complained bitterly that this was unfair, and that I was sure I was ready to learn sexual skills. My 'unhelpful attitude' earned me another spanking from Simone. This time she used a little leather strap which really stung.

Above all, I am to learn obedience. I think if anyone tells me to do as I'm told just once more I'll scream. They all take it so seriously. I mean, it's not as if I don't do as I'm told. I do. Nearly all the time.

After all the boring Induction there was time for only one lesson this afternoon, which turned out to be a

143

session in the gym. Simone had other duties to attend to and so I was alone with Matt, which I didn't mind at all. In my opinion Simone is getting rather too keen on smacking my poor sore bottom, and I was glad of the chance to show off to Matt how fit and lithe I am.

Once we were in the gymnasium, however, Matt turned into a hard taskmaster. He assured me that he would let me do a gentle programme of exercise, just to assess my fitness, and that therefore I needed to change only my shoes. Therefore I found myself surrounded by vaulting horses, horizontal bars, rope ladders, exercise machines, weight training machines and piles of rubber mats and medicine balls, wearing my flimsy halter top, my tiny skirt and a pair of rubber-soled canvas shoes.

Matt's exercise programme was, of course, anything but gentle, and my costume was quite frankly inadequate. I'm sure it amused Matt to watch my breasts bouncing as I ran on the conveyor belt, and to make me do headstands so that my private parts were completely uncovered. And I wouldn't have minded showing off like that, if I hadn't been too out of breath to enjoy it. Matt made me try every piece of equipment at least once, and he had me running and lifting weights until all my limbs felt like jelly. And then he said he wanted me to finish off with a good long cycle ride.

I perked up at that, but I should have known that he didn't mean a real bicycle. No, it was a cycling machine, and he set the controls for a modest distance but with the pedals incredibly stiff, so that I had to push down with all my strength to make the things turn at all.

Obviously my skirt was too short for me to sit on it, so my sore bottom was perched directly on the saddle, which as I laboured and puffed gradually worked its way between my buttocks. If I leant forward the front of the saddle pressed against the sensitive area around my clitoris; if I leant back I could feel my little hole kissing the cool leather. Even though I was cycling so hard I could hardly think, I began to fall into a rhythm of leaning forward and then back, and found the sensations distinctly pleasant.

144

I was conscious, too, of Matt standing next to the machine and watching me. Whenever I glanced at him I found his gaze fixed on my face, or on my breasts, or on the saddle of the machine where, because my skirt had ridden up, he must have been able to see the stiff leather pressing into my vulva.

As I panted and pedalled he told me about the exercise bicycles that were available for use in the park. These were real bicycles, but some of them had been modified so that specially shaped parts of the saddle would move in time with the circulation of the pedals. Each bike could be adjusted to suit the physique of its rider and so that the moving parts would begin to move only after the rider had pedalled a certain distance or achieved a certain speed.

I could see clear blue sky through the narrow windows near the ceiling of the gym, and with much panting I managed to tell Matt that I'd much rather be cycling in the fresh air than indoors.

He leant over, inspected the dials between the handlebars of the machine, and laughed. 'You've a long way to go,' he said. 'I'll let you go cycling outdoors only when I'm confident you can complete a reasonable distance. Still, that's probably enough for today.'

He switched off the machine and I pulled myself from the saddle. As I rested my hands on my shaky knees and drew deep breaths, I hear Matt say, 'Oh dear. That's not what I call considerate use of the equipment.'

I turned to find him looking at the saddle. It was, of course, sticky with the juices from my vulva.

'You've made a mess here,' he said. 'It's not worth getting a towel. Your clothes will need to go in the wash, of course. So take off your skirt and use it to clean the saddle.'

I felt his eyes on me as I dropped the skirt to my ankles, picked it up from the floor, and carefully wiped the black leather until it shone. Now I was wearing only my halter top, which was damp and transparent with my perspiration, and the canvas shoes. I felt very exposed, which did nothing to alleviate the state of arousal that the cycling machine had induced in me. I wondered how many young women before me had been obliged to polish this saddle with their own lubricious emissions.

'That will do, Anne,' Matt said. 'Now, I suppose I'd better think of some way of reinforcing the message that the gym equipment must be kept clean.' He rubbed his chin and cast his gaze about the gym.

I was in for yet another spanking. My own fault, really: having recovered my breath I had been dancing all round the cycling machine as I rubbed the saddle, sticking my bottom out so that Matt couldn't fail to notice it. I had certainly noticed the big bulge in the front of his shorts, and while I don't know much about sex yet I'm pretty sure that an enlarged penis is an indication of male sexual arousal.

'I know,' Matt announced. 'We'll use the horizontal bar. Take off your shoes, Anne, and come and help me lower it and turn it.'

'Yes, sir,' I said happily. I'm incorrigible, I really am. I had already been punished three times, and my bottom was still smarting, but I couldn't wait to feel Matt's big, strong hand smacking me. My vulva was wet and hot, and my nipples felt sort of electric, so I knew I wanted to come again, too. I hoped Matt would let me.

The bar is a long, polished wooden beam, flat and quite wide on one side, and tapering to a narrow edge on the other. It slots into two vertical beams, and it can be turned so that either the wide or narrow side is uppermost. Its height from the floor can be adjusted by moving the pegs which fit into the beams and on which it rests.

I helped Matt turn the bar so that the narrow edge was uppermost, and to adjust the height so that it was at the level of my waist. Then, with a delightful feeling of anticipation in my tummy, I bent forward over the bar and spread my legs.

I heard Matt chuckle. 'Are you quite comfortable, Anne?' he said.

'Yes, thanks, sir,' I replied, and looked over my shoulder to encourage him to get on with it.

'It's not much of a punishment if you're comfortable,' he said. 'That's not the idea at all. Now stand up and put one leg over the bar. I want you standing astride it.'

I stepped back from the bar and considered its height. I began to lift my right leg over it when I realised that it was set too high, and would have to be lowered.

'It's too high,' I said.

'That's another ten smacks for failing to address me properly,' Matt said. 'The bar is not too high. Now get astride it or I'll pick you up and put you on it.'

I liked the idea of being picked up in Matt's strong arms, but I wanted to find out slowly just how high the bar was. By placing both hands on the narrow top of it and sort of lying along it I supported my weight while I lifted my right leg over the bar.

I was balanced precariously along the narrow top edge of the bar. I lowered my feet towards the floor, and found to my consternation that the floor was too far away. My feet didn't reach it. As I extended my toes I felt myself wobbling, and although it wouldn't have been far to fall I didn't want to look undignified in front of Matt. I turned my head until I could see him, and did my best to look alarmed and helpless.

'Come along, Anne,' he said sharply. 'Get into position. Stretch your toes as far as they will go, and stand up straight: that will give your legs a longer reach.'

I pointed my toes and stretched my leg muscles as hard as I could – and the tips of my big toes touched the floor. Reassured, I straightened my body, and found that doing so gave me just enough extra reach to be able to stand on tiptoe.

But the narrow edge of the bar was pressing right up against my vulva. It was inside me, in fact. If I relaxed my leg muscles for just a moment the weight of my body was supported entirely by the bar, which wedged itself between my outer labia and made me cry out in pain. I

147

stood on tiptoe again, and without my weight on it the bar became once again merely an uncomfortable intrusion in my private parts.

'That's more like it,' Matt said. 'Now lean forward a little, so that you can rest your hands on the top of the bar, and push your bottom backwards.'

I did as he advised, and found that by pressing down with my hands on the bar I could relieve some of the strain on the muscles of my legs. Leaning forward had the effect not only of making my bottom look more prominent, but also of pressing the front of my sex against the top of the bar. The tip of my poor little clitoris was crushed against the hard wooden surface. The pain was sharp but also sweet. I realised that if Matt spanked me hard enough to press my body even more on to the bar, the pain would be excruciating but I would be unable to prevent myself having an orgasm.

I managed to turn my head to look at Matt, and saw that I was in no danger of receiving a mild chastisement. He was flexing one of my rubber-soled shoes in his hands as he advanced towards me.

'That's better,' he said, and without further ado he lifted my shoe high into the air and swung it in a low arc that ended with a loud crash on my left buttock.

I had extended every muscle in my arms and legs in an attempt to minimise the effect of the blow, but even so I couldn't help the force of the impact nudging me a little further on to the cruelly narrow edge of the bar. I managed to confine my audible reaction to a loud grunt, followed by a long murmur as I felt the sting of the smack merge with the aftershocks of the jolt of sensation between my legs. As I waited for the next stroke I realised that I was as helpless and immobile as I would be if bound or chained in position.

'Ten for failing to keep the gym equipment clean,' Matt said, 'and ten for failing to address me correctly. I think you'd better ask for them, don't you?'

'Please give me twenty smacks, sir,' I said quickly. I wanted him to get on with it. 'And please, sir, would be all right to have an orgasm?'

148

Matt considered the question for a frustratingly long time. 'Yes,' he said, 'I don't see why not. But don't come until the end. If you come too soon I'll start again from the beginning.'

I heard the shoe swishing through the air and tensed my limbs again. Now I knew what to expect, and I was able to appreciate the combination of raw pain and searing pleasure. I gave up trying to remain silent, and kept up a continuous stream of cries, gasps and groans as the rubber sole splatted again and again against one buttock and then the other.

The punishment was about half-way through when I began to feel the unmistakable sensations of an approaching orgasm. Each smack was like a hammer-blow, driving a spike of pleasure deeper and deeper into my body from the point where my clitoris was pressed against the unforgiving hardness of the bar. Pulses of sensation, like explosions of sparks from a firework, radiated from that little agonised bud and electrified every nerve in my body. My toes lost their precarious purchase on the floor, but I almost failed to notice. I began to ride the bar as if it was a horse that I was urging to a faster gallop.

Matt struck faster and even harder, and my cries rose to a crescendo that echoed around the gym. As he delivered the final few strokes I was coming. I have no idea whether I received the correct number of smacks, or whether Matt simply kept going until I was finished. I just threw back my head and screamed until the shuddering jolts and shocks stopped reverberating inside me. And then I fell forward on to the bar, utterly exhausted.

I felt Matt's hand on my bottom.

'Very red indeed,' he said. 'That's what I call a properly chastised rear end. I can even see the pattern of the treads, imprinted on your skin. I don't think that's a lesson you'll forget.'

'No, sir,' I replied. My voice sounded feeble. 'That was fantastic. There's just one problem.'

With a gasp of pain I pushed down with my hands and lifted my divided vulva from the apex of the bar. I swung a leg up and managed to tumble gracelessly from my perch. 'You see,' I said. 'There. I've already reoffended. I just can't seem to stop making the gym equipment wet.'

Matt looked at the bar and laughed. 'You're running out of clothes to use as cleaning cloths,' he said. 'You'd better use your top this time. And then get yourself bent over the vaulting horse for another spanking. But this really will have to be the last, Anne. At least for the time being.'

So now it's the evening, and I'm back in my room. It's been a hectic day, in the end. It's a real shame I haven't been allowed outdoors yet, but then on the other hand I have been permitted to have two orgasms, both of them hugely enjoyable. And my bottom is indescribably sore. So I'm feeling very satisfied and languorous.

In a while Matt and Simone are going to come up and help me dress for dinner. I'm going to share a table with them in the main dining hall, and Matt says that if I behave myself and remember all the rules of etiquette, I'll be allowed to play with the slaves who wait on the tables. I don't quite know what he means, but it sounds exciting. I think perhaps I do like this place, after all.

TWO

From the diary of Anne Bright
10 July
At last! I've started the sex lessons. I'm not really complaining: Matt and Simone have been very good at making sure I get spanked properly at least once every day, and every time I'm spanked I'm allowed to touch myself and I've had some pretty spectacular orgasms. Matt says my bottom's had so much attention that it's getting noticeably bigger. He's just teasing, but secretly I hope it's true.

I know my way around the House now, and most days Matt and Simone show me another part of the estate – it's even bigger than I'd imagined in my wildest. I'm totally enjoying myself here: I know lots of the people by name now, and in my free time I'm allowed to roam wherever I want to.

The only thing is, it was getting frustrating being able to see other people doing all sorts of amazing things with each other, and not being allowed to do any of them myself.

But apparently at long last Matt and Simone are satisfied with my progress in all the other subjects – deportment, and fitness, and obedience, and nutrition, and so on – and today I started on sexual skills.

I had my first lesson this morning. And it was fantastic. I'll have to write down all the details. It's so exciting. I was doing sexual things – and with Simone!

Yes, it's true. I've been learning all about lesbianism – which isn't what I expected at all. Certainly not as an introductory lesson, anyway. But Matt says that as I'm a woman, and I'm not averse to the idea of sex with other women, then I should start by exploring a body that's similar to mine, with similar responses, before progressing to men's bodies. I suppose it makes sense.

At first I was a bit disappointed: I've been looking forward so much to getting my hands on Matt. But Simone's all right, when you get to know her, and she's very beautiful. That gleaming black skin! The lesson took place right here in my bedroom. Matt and Simone brought me breakfast in bed, and the three of us ate together.

It's always good when they come up to my room first thing in the morning: it's as if it's a bit too early for the formal rules, and they let me call them Matt and Simone instead of sir and miss. We've become close friends, and I ask them loads of questions about the things I've seen in the House. We sit on the bed and gossip and giggle – it's as if they're as teenage as I am.

Of course, I'm still completely naked, and I let the bedclothes slip off me as we eat and chatter. I know they both like looking at me, and I like to feel their eyes on me – particularly Matt's.

This morning, as happens whenever my Mentors come to my room early, I flirted shamelessly with Matt. I use him as a back-rest while I'm eating, I goad him into a pillow-fight – that sort of thing. As usual Simone became more and more disapproving until, of course, she decided that I was being just too provoking and deserved a spanking. This has become a sort of game now, and it's one of my all-time favourites. I pretend to be un-cooperative, so that Matt has to wrestle with me – it's heavenly. He's so big and strong that it doesn't take him long – unfortunately – to subdue me, and then he holds my hands and head down on the bed so that Simone can punish me. I can't begin to describe how wonderful it feels. I just melt, and surrender to Matt's muscular arms.

152

I wonder if I'm falling in love with him? I don't know. What I do know is that my insides go all shivery when he tells me to push my bottom up and move my legs apart. And then Simone starts to smack me, and my consciousness sort of curls up on itself so that I'm not really aware of anything except the feelings: Matt's hands holding me, and Simone's hands building a fiery blaze on my bottom, and my orgasm beginning deep inside me.

Simone's wicked: I always keep still, but she claims that she can see me move, and therefore she has to start the spanking again from the beginning. I usually get lots more than my eighteen smacks.

Today they didn't let me touch myself while I was being spanked: Matt held me tightly until Simone had finished. Usually I love to touch myself, and feel myself getting wetter and wetter, while the smacks are actually landing on my bottom, so that I can have an orgasm when the stinging pain is still increasing, but there's something special about being held down by Matt so that I'm completely helpless. It's almost more exciting. When Simone stopped smacking me, and Matt released me and told me to kneel and start playing with myself, I wasn't at all surprised to find that I was as wet as if I'd been stroking myself all the time.

Matt and Simone sat on the bed, curled up together in front of me, and watched me. They told me to stroke my breasts and my bottom for a while, and said that I was adorable and a model student. I really couldn't hope for kinder and friendlier Mentors. They say such nice things about me. And they're both keen on spanking my bottom! Eventually they let me put my hand between my legs. I was so close to my orgasm that I yelped when I touched my clitoris. I put my other hand behind my back and pressed a finger into the entrance of my anus, and I started to come straight away.

Until today I would have said that there was nothing in the world I liked better than being spanked and then giving myself an orgasm. Since my birthday I've done it at least once a day, and it's always terrific. But now I would have to say that it's merely one of my favourite things. Because today I started to learn about sex with women.

After my orgasm Matt and Simone hugged and kissed me, and told me all over again how pretty I am, and tucked me up in bed. They told me to rest for a while, and then to get dressed in my uniform and to wait for them to return.

I didn't sleep again. In fact I couldn't even rest, because I was so excited at the thought of starting my sex lessons. I got up and had a bath; I put on some perfume and make-up; I tried to read. I kept wandering over to the long mirror and peering over my shoulder at the reflection of my bottom. Each time I looked the redness had faded a little more. I was disappointed, because I thought Simone had smacked me quite hard. In the end I knelt on the floor, with my bottom towards the mirror, and I spanked myself. My bottom was still sore, and it took only a few smacks to bring the colour back and to get me ready for another orgasm.

But that only made me feel even more frustrated: I couldn't actually have an orgasm, because there was nobody to watch me. And there are very strict rules about that. So I had to put on my top and my skirt, sit – gingerly – on the bed, and wait.

Matt and Simone returned soon, thankfully – and after that I spent most of the morning on the bed with Simone. Matt said he was there 'as an observer', but I noticed that he had brought with him a black attaché case, which looked very incongruous with his white singlet and shorts. I asked him what was in it, but he just sat himself in the armchair and said I must wait and see. Which I thought sounded promising – and I was right!

At first, though, I was a bit nervous. I know what it feels like to touch my own body, of course, and I was fairly sure that I'd like touching Simone – she's so

154

strikingly attractive, and her dark skin looks like velvet. But I didn't know what it would be like to feel her touching me – I mean, a cuddle is one thing, but my breasts and my vulva are very sensitive, and Simone can be quite brusque at times. I didn't know what to expect, and it seemed like ages since the days at the cottage when Eloise used to hug and kiss me after she'd punished me.

This morning, though, Simone was all smiles. I think she had been looking forward to starting the sex lessons with me as much as I had. She walked around me as I stood between the bed and Matt's chair. I felt her lift the back of my skirt, and then she pressed a hand against my right buttock.

'Still sore?' she said.

I nodded, and said, 'Yes, thank you, miss.'

She stood in front of me. 'We'll take this slowly,' she said. 'You can undress me. Start with my blouse.'

Today Simone was wearing red, as usual: a little top, held together in front with only two buttons, and a short skirt, both of soft, shiny material. I know it's silly, but I found that my fingers were trembling as I reached for the upper button.

'Feel the material,' Simone suggested. 'Rub it against my breasts.'

I let my hand rest on the front of her blouse. It was so thin and delicate that I wanted to stroke it, and I was caressing her left breast before I really knew what I was doing.

I think breasts are lovely. We women are so lucky. They're firm and soft at the same time, and the best of it is that when you're touching someone else's you know that you're giving them all those nice tingly feelings. I could feel Simone's nipple getting harder under my fingers, and she made a little purring noise in the back of her throat.

I brought my other hand up, and started stroking the material of Simone's top across both of her breasts. And of course I knew exactly what to do, because I know what I like to do to myself. So I made circles with my hands, spiralling in towards Simone's nipples; I raked my fingertips up the undersides of her breasts, from her ribcage to her nipples; I caught the stiff little tips between my fingers, and squeezed them gently before releasing them.

All the time I watched Simone's face, in case I was doing anything wrong. But she seemed very pleased with me: her big dark eyes were shining, and her wide smile faltered only when I did something she particularly liked, so that she couldn't help drawing in a breath.

At last I remembered to undo the second button, and pulled open Simone's blouse.

Now that I've been in the Private House for a month I'm used to seeing people naked. Even so, I hadn't seen Simone unclothed, and there is something very special about undressing one of your Mentors. I actually glanced up at Simone's face to make sure she didn't mind me looking at her. She instils that sort of respect. But she was still smiling, and I let my gaze and my hands return to her exposed breasts.

They're smaller than mine: perfectly round mounds that I can cover with my hands. Warm and soft, and the skin feels as smooth as butter. Her nipples are very dark – almost black, even darker than her skin. I had a sudden ridiculous thought: chocolate puddings, each topped with a roasted coffee bean. I giggled, and couldn't resist leaning forward and kissing one of them. I kissed her right on the nipple: I put my lips around the hard point and flicked it with my tongue. I didn't really expect Simone to taste of chocolate, and I don't suppose she does, but her skin did smell wonderful: vanilla is the nearest scent I can think of. And I think I did sense hints of coffee and, yes, chocolate.

I suddenly realised that I hadn't been given permission to kiss her, and that I might have gone too far. I drew back, but Simone just whispered, 'It's all right. Don't stop.' So I kissed her again, and licked her nipple, and felt the softness of her breast tremble against my lips.

'That's very good, Anne,' Simone said after a while, 'but you still have to take off my skirt. So stop now, and kneel in front of me.'

I have to admit I was reluctant to move: Simone's breasts were so warm and comfortable pressed against my face, and my tongue was quite happy playing with her stiff little nipples. But kissing her was making me very damp in my private parts, and I hoped it was having the same effect on her. I wasn't going to be able to find out unless I took her skirt off, so with a final peck of my lips I said goodbye to Simone's breasts and sank to my knees.

I suppose it was forward of me, but I didn't wait to be told what to do next. I put hands on Simone's slim hips and pressed my face against the silky material of her skirt. The scent of her was stronger here, and I inhaled deeply the sweet and spicy aroma. Simone seemed content to let me do as I wished, and I held her close against my face as my fingers fumbled for the fastening of her skirt.

I pulled myself away from her to let the skirt fall to the floor, and I found myself looking at her smooth, flat stomach, the swelling of her pubes, and the black wiry triangle of hair. I leant forward and planted little kisses all over the place. I already knew, from watching the activities in the House, that I liked the appearance of women's bodies. But to be so close to, and to be able to touch and kiss, Simone's delectable skin, I found almost overwhelming. I can't explain it – perhaps it was Simone's scent, or the smoothness of her skin, or the fact that she is my Mentor, or knowing that Matt was watching me, or a combination of all of those things – but I wanted just to kiss and kiss and kiss her.

I looked up to find her gazing down at me. 'Please, miss,' I said, 'move your legs apart.'

She did, and the black curls tickled my face as I pushed forward, trying to kiss and lick her labia. She was so aroused that her wetness had covered the outer membranes of her vulva. She tasted of honey and musk. As my tongue searched deeper into her I felt her hands on my head. Her whole body was shivering, and I knew that she must be getting close to an orgasm. I so wanted to feel her come while I was licking her!

But she didn't let me. She stepped back, and held my head to stop me lunging after her.

'What a very precocious student,' Matt said.

I was looking up at Simone, who was breathing deeply and gazing down at me with dilated eyes. 'Please,' I said. 'Please, miss.'

Simone recovered her breath. 'Not yet,' she said. 'I don't want to come yet. And you're still dressed, Anne. Stand up and I'll take your clothes off.'

I leapt to my feet, because I'd suddenly realised that Simone was going to do to me all the things I'd been doing to her. And I wanted her to, very badly. As I stood she pulled me into her arms.

'Don't worry,' she whispered, 'I'll let you carry on later. You're very good. But that doesn't mean you're not going to get lots of training.' And then she kissed me – a proper kiss, on the lips.

I'd only once before been kissed by a woman – I mean a proper kiss. That had been the lovely Jem Darke, and now this was a naked woman with vanilla-scented skin and nipples so hard that I could feel them pressing into my breasts.

I'm so wanton – it took me all of about a second to get used to the idea, and then Simone and I were kissing each other as if we were new lovers. Which, in a way, we were. And still are.

What have I said? I thought I was in love with Matt. And I am, I think. But now I'm a bit in love with Simone, too. And I think she's in love with me. We were both laughing and crying while we were kissing, even though I know it sounds impossible, and saying silly things to each other. I wanted to hold Simone tight but also run my hands all over her body. She was trying to pull my halter top off without interrupting our kissing. 'I want to see your tits,' she murmured. 'I want to hold them and squeeze them so tightly.'

And she did, when she'd finally succeeded in removing my top. Now, I always like stroking my own breasts, and sometimes I like to pinch them a bit, too. But no matter how wonderful it feels, it's just not as good as when someone else does it. Particularly someone as loveable and strict as Simone.

She has such strong fingers, and she can use them to touch like feathers one moment, and then really squeeze hard the next. I hardly had time to appreciate each sensation before I was suddenly in the midst of the next. I must have sounded ridiculous, because I couldn't help crying out 'Oh!', over and over again, each time Simone did something different. She kissed me, and whispered lovely things in my ear, and stroked my breasts so gently; and she squeezed and pinched and pulled. She couldn't leave my poor little nipples alone.

Of course, I loved every minute. My mind couldn't keep track of all the things Simone was doing, but my nerve endings knew exactly what was going on, and my vulva was soon dripping wet. And that was before Simone leant forward and started to lick me.

I've had so many new experiences today. And having my breasts kissed was one of the best. I knew, as soon as Simone's lips touched my nipple, and I felt a surge of energy like an electric shock from my breasts all the way to my toes, that if she carried on for long enough I would have an orgasm. Kissing was wonderful; licking was even better; and when she started to suck on my nipples, going from one to the other and drawing them abruptly into her mouth, I put my arms around her head to stop her from moving away. I could feel the rising swell of a climax building inside me.

But I wanted something else, and suddenly I realised what I needed. I opened my eyes and turned to Matt. 'Please, sir,' I said, 'please spank me. Just a little.'

I must have looked desperate, as Matt jumped from the chair and was at my side in an instant. He stroked my hair, lifted up the back of my skirt, and began to apply gentle slaps to my bottom.

I was in heaven. My bottom was still sore from the previous spankings, so Matt's light smacks were all that were needed to rekindle the aching heat. I began to move in what must have been a very undignified fashion, thrusting my breasts against Simone's face and my bottom backwards to meet Matt's spanking. Simone's lips were encircling my left nipple and, having realised what Matt was doing, she was sucking fiercely in time with the smacks that were landing on my bottom. My orgasm came in pulses of unbearably sweet sensation, shoving me inexorably up to the edge of the cliff – and then with a shout I was there, and flying over the abyss, and then drifting slowly downwards.

Matt and Simone were very pleased with me, but didn't give me much time to recover. Simone knelt in front of me, removed my skirt, and began stroking me, working her hands ever closer to the wetness between my thighs.

I didn't think I would be able to have another orgasm immediately, but Simone has magic fingers, I'm sure of it. She was very gentle, and when she held my vulva in her cupped palm, and just sort of rubbed very softly, I began to feel those unmistakable sensations that you know will just keep on growing until you have an orgasm – unless the person stops touching you.

But Simone didn't stop. She ran her fingers along the edges of my labia; she circled the tip of my clitoris with a fingertip, and then she put her face against my groin and started to kiss me and lick me. And she has a wickedly skilful tongue.

Even so I didn't actually have another orgasm until she suddenly turned me round, pressed her face into the crack between my buttocks, and did something very rude and very, very wonderful.

She licked my anus. And then she pushed the tip of her tongue into the hole, like I do with my finger when I'm touching myself after a spanking. It was the most amazing sensation I'd had, in a morning full of amazing sensations, and I started to have my orgasm immediately. Simone didn't really need to put a hand between my

160

legs and press upwards until her fingertips were touching my clitoris, but when she did it felt like a dam bursting inside me, and I shouted and shouted as I came.

After that I had to lie down for a while. Simone came with me on to the bed, and for a while we just lay cuddled together. She stroked my arms and legs, and kissed me, while I dozed. It felt very warm and cosy. I don't see how anything can be more enjoyable than being licked until you have an orgasm, and then doing lots of lazy cuddling and kissing with a woman you're in love with. It just has to be the best thing in the world.

Simone and I were lying together on our sides. Simone was behind me, with her firm nipples pressing into my back. We were curled up, so that my bottom was nestling in her lap. She had brushed aside my hair and was kissing the nape of my neck as she ran her hand back and forth from my shoulder to my hip. Gradually I became more wide awake, and I turned my head so that she could kiss my face. Her lips still carried the scent of my wetness.

I remember precisely what I whispered to her. 'I think you're lovely, miss. I've never been happier in my life. And do you know: I'm afraid I'm getting excited all over again.'

Simone chuckled. I felt her hand caress its way from my hip, down between our bodies, and press into the gap between my thighs. I felt a shock of pleasure, and gasped. Simone said, 'Yes, you're ready again. Would you like to see what we look like together?' She kissed me again, and then looked up at Matt. 'Bring the mirror,' she said.

I know I've said it before, but I do like to watch Matt moving. He's so strong and lithe. So I particularly enjoyed lying on the bed while Simone toyed with my labia and Matt exerted his muscles to pull the big mirror across the floor until I could see the entire surface of the bed reflected on it – and Simone and I curled in the middle like a pair of spoons.

We looked ever so sexy. I think anyone would have thought so. Even if I had been alone on the bed I definitely think I would have been thought of as desirable: the sheets were crisply white, and my skin and hair had a golden sheen, and the way I was lying on my side emphasised the curves of my waist and hip. With Simone lying behind me the effect was, I'm sure, absolutely stunning. Matt certainly couldn't keep his eyes off us. Simone's dark skin contrasted with mine and with the sheets: as she moved her hands across my body, she rested her head on my shoulder so that both of us could watch what she was doing.

'Let's show Matt everything,' Simone whispered in my ear. 'Lift up your leg, like this.'

Simone raised her leg into the air and I copied her movement, so that our legs parted simultaneously. It was such a rude position to adopt! With one of my legs resting on the bed and the other bent at the knee and lifted up, I had a clear view in the mirror of my private parts: my widely parted outer labia, and the pubic hair on them slicked down and darkened with my wetness; the pink petals of my inner labia, glistening and moist; even the little button of my clitoris was visible.

Simone's dark thighs were pressing against mine, and holding mine apart. And behind my vulva, touching my bottom, Simone's parts were just as visible as mine. Her black curls were as wet as my blonde ones, and glistened against her dark skin. The inner folds of her labia made a vivid pink gash, like the surprising red interior that you reveal when you peel back the skin of a ripe fig.

She manoeuvred an arm under my torso: I watched in the mirror her long-fingered hand appear from beneath my body and curl around my breast. I saw her face, peering over my shoulder, grin wickedly as she squeezed the nipple. I groaned and pressed my bottom back against her body. Her other hand appeared between her parted thighs. It covered her gaping sex, and she smiled lasciviously as she pressed the heel of her hand against her vagina. The fingers reached forward

162

and rested on my inner labia. Her other hand continued to torment my nipple. I closed my eyes as I began to lose myself in the sensations, and whenever my lids fluttered open I could see myself in the mirror, a picture of abandoned lust.

Instead of returning to his seat Matt had remained by the mirror, seemingly unable to move his eyes from Simone and me on the bed. At last, however, when our two bodies were writhing in the same rhythm and I think both of us were nor very far from reaching an orgasm, Simone drew a deep breath and spoke to Matt.

'Matt,' she said hoarsely, 'get the strap, would you?'

I seem to have an inability to ignore any reference to smacking, and even lost in the mists of sensual pleasure I heard and understood Simone's request.

I turned my face upwards, and Simone's lips were immediately on mine. 'Is Matt going to whip me?' I asked excitedly, between kisses.

'Not this time, Anne. Me first.'

I turned away from her and saw that Matt, having opened the attaché case, had taken from it a short, narrow length of leather which he was now bringing towards the bed.

'Behind us,' Simone instructed him. 'So that we can see you and ourselves in the mirror.'

Matt went to the far side of the bed and sat on it behind Simone. He drew the leather strap through his fingers, and then let the tongue rest across Simone's raised thigh.

Simone moved her knees, and mine with them, closer to my chest, so that our private parts were even more exposed. She put her arms around my body and held me tightly. I could feel her breasts pressing into my back as she took a series of long, deep breaths, as if readying herself for an ordeal.

'Now?' Matt said.

'Look in the mirror, Anne,' Simone whispered, and then she lifted her head from my shoulder and said, 'Now.'

163

I saw Matt lift his hand, and with it the strap. I saw his hand sweep down. And then I gasped almost as loudly as Simone as I saw the strap land with a loud crack not on her bottom but along the very centre of her split fig. Her arms tightened around me, and then with a shudder she relaxed.

Matt's face was expressionless as he delivered the next stroke. Simone's vulva was pressed so closely to mine that I felt the draught of displaced air as the strap lashed again at her most vulnerable and sensitive tissues. She gripped me tightly again, and uttered a short cry of pain.

I turned my head towards hers. 'Does it hurt very much?' I asked. A bit of a silly question, really, but I wanted to know what it felt like.

Simone's body convulsed as the third blow landed, and she released a shuddering sigh. 'Oh, yes,' she said with, to my surprise, a contented smile. 'Yes, yes, yes. Oh, how it hurts.'

Well, of course, I wasn't prepared to let Simone have all the attention. I watched in the mirror for a while as Matt continued to snap the leather down into the soft membranes between Simone's parted thighs. As Simone began to ride the waves of pain her little cries became more and more like gasps of pleasure, and she began to make small thrusting movements of her hips – which I liked because they pushed her pubic mound into my bottom.

But however arousing it was to feel Simone being whipped while she held my naked body against hers – and it certainly was arousing – I still wanted to know what she was experiencing. So, during one of the pauses that Matt allowed between strokes, I caught his eye in the mirror and said, 'Please, sir, please do it to me too. I want to find out what it's like.'

Matt looked doubtful. 'You're supposed to be smacked only on your bottom, for the time being,' he told me. 'I shouldn't whip you yet. It's more painful than you imagine, I'm sure. Simone, what do you think?'

Simone let out a wailing groan of frustration. 'I'm almost there,' she pleaded. 'Don't stop now. I don't mind sharing with Anne. Just be gentle with her.'

Simone tightened the grip of her arms about my body. I turned my head so that we could kiss each other while we were being whipped. She tucked her raised knee under mine, and said, 'Keep your legs wide apart, Anne, so that Matt can see where he's striking. Kiss me until I come.'

I kept my lips pressed against Simone's. Matt's next blow was for Simone, and she uttered into my mouth her ragged gasp of enjoyment.

Then it was my turn. I heard, or sensed, the descent of the strap, and then knew nothing except for an all-encompassing wave of stomach-lurching agony. It made me want to curl up into a ball and sob. I was dimly aware of having cried out, and then of Simone's lips kissing mine. And then I felt a flood of heat spreading across my private parts – as though I was on fire from my vagina to my clitoris.

I had expected it to feel like being spanked on my bottom. It was completely different. Everything about being spanked is wonderful, from the moment you have to show off your bottom, to the sting of the first slap, to the lovely warmth that spreads through you as the spanking continues. Being whipped on your vulva is nasty: the initial pain is sickening, and you feel horribly violated, and after that it's not warm but really, really hot, as if you're burnt. And I know that sounds awful, and it is at the time, but the trouble is that as the anguish recedes there's just something inside you that wants another stroke of the whip.

I think it's something to do with the fact that it's such an intimate place to be punished: to hold your legs apart and offer yourself so openly makes you sort of proud of the pain. And then, at least as far I'm concerned, it's an inescapable fact that having anything done to my vulva arouses me. The strap is hot and harsh and biting, but as soon as the first stab of pain had ebbed away I

165

realised that I had taken a great big step on the path to my next orgasm. And, of course, I was being held and kissed by the lovely Simone, and the strap was being wielded by the gorgeous Matt.

All in all, by the time I had felt Simone judder under the next stroke, and moan into my mouth, I was ready for another. And then the leather splatted into me again, and I convulsed with the sudden pain, but it wasn't as unbearable as the first one, and I knew that if Matt kept on whipping me I would reach an orgasm.

Matt continued to alternate the strokes of the strap between Simone's vulva and mine. Sometimes he managed to catch both with one stroke, and Simone and I would crush our bodies together as we drank in each other's guttural cries. Soon, before I had become so wrapped up in my own impending orgasm that I had no idea of anything else, I realised that Simone was reaching the brink of hers. Her body was trembling continuously against mine, and she was planting hurried, desperate kisses on my lips between a crescendo of gasping breaths.

'Matt,' I cried out, 'do Simone now.'

I ground my bottom against her pubes as Matt ignored my open legs and concentrated on increasing the rapidity of his lashes, all of which now landed between Simone's thighs.

Simone bucked her hips back and forth, and began panting wildly. Then she pulled her lips from mine, threw back her head, and began to utter, more and more loudly, wordless cries from the back of her throat. Her body went rigid, and she expelled all her breath in one long, keening wail. Then she shook herself, hugged me tightly, and rolled on to her back with her eyes closed and a broad smile on her lips.

Matt and I sat on the bed and looked at her.

'Wonderful,' she said at last, without opening her eyes, and as if speaking in a dream. 'When I'm in the mood for it, that feels like the best way to come. And now I'm so sore.' She pressed her thighs together and rolled her bottom on the sheets.

I leant forward and kissed her forehead. A naughty idea had occurred to me. 'I could kiss it better if you like,' I said. 'And lick it, too.'

Simone opened her eyes then, and propped herself on one elbow. 'Would you like to?' she said.

'Of course,' I replied. 'You taste lovely.'

Simone chuckled. 'I'm not ready yet,' she said, 'unfortunately. Maybe later. Anyway, it's your turn now. Come here.'

Simone pulled herself to the head of the bed and rested, half sitting and half lying, on the pillows. She was on her back with her arms stretched wide and her knees drawn up, showing off her punished and sore private parts. I thought she looked splendidly wanton.

'Come here,' she said again. 'Kneel astride me, and I'll suck your nipples.'

I didn't need a second invitation: I knew exactly how cleverly Simone could use her mouth.

I was so excited by now that I was afraid I was going to drip wetness from my vagina on to Simone's body as I straddled her. But there was no possibility that she was going to do anything other than get me even more aroused. I crouched down so that my body was pressed against hers, and we kissed each other's face, neck and lips for a while. By moving my hips I could brush my labia back and forth against Simone's bushy pubes, and of course in so doing I was giving Matt a fine view of my vagina and anus.

I wonder if that's what gave him the idea to use the strap in the valley between my buttocks? He's supposed to confine himself to spanking me. Anyway, he asked me if it was all right to whip my anus, and of course I said it was.

I lifted my body away from Simone's so that my breasts were close to her mouth and my bottom was raised. Simone took my right nipple between her lips, and started caressing my buttocks with her hands. I curved my back downwards, pushing my breasts against Simone's face and my bottom towards Matt. If either of them had so much as touched my clitoris I would have had an orgasm there and then, but I was glad they didn't: Simone was doing wonderful things to my nipple – sucking on it hard and then gently, and then nibbling and licking, and then sucking again – and I could feel an orgasm building inside me.

And then Matt stood beside us and started to use the strap. He didn't whip me hard, but even so it stung – my anus is very sensitive, after all – and it felt wonderful as the heat spread through me. Simone's hands gripped my buttocks and kept them widely parted so that Matt had a clear view of his target.

He slowed his strokes when it became obvious that I was close to coming, and Simone slipped a hand between my thighs and just pressed upwards very softly. She had my left nipple in her mouth, and she held it between her teeth as she flicked it with her tongue. I was shivering with frustrated desire, because I was right on the edge, but neither Matt nor Simone did anything to tip me over. They just kept licking, and smacking with the strap, and pressing close to my clitoris. It was unbearable.

And, just when I thought I'd never come, the orgasm began inside me. This time it wasn't like exploding, or flying off a cliff. It was like a flower opening its petals, only the flower was me and I was sort of turning inside-out and becoming a weightless creature made of waves of light and energy. Something like that, anyway.

It was the best possible way to end my first sex lesson, that's certain. It's back to ordinary classes tomorrow, but the day after that I'll have my first lesson on sex with men – and that means with the gorgeous Matt.

Although I can't imagine how anything could be better than the things I've enjoyed today. Perhaps sex with women is just more fun than sex with men. I'll find out soon!

From the notebooks of Celia Bright
I haven't told many of my friends and colleagues about D. They know that there is a man in my life, but D has

made it clear that, other than on specific occasions when he instructs me to demonstrate my devotion to him in front of particular people, I am to decide for myself to whom I reveal my secret love. And, in the main, I deter questions about my personal life. I think I have always been a private person, in part perhaps because I have always known that my desires are beyond the boundaries that most people consider normal.

Therefore my friends are not surprised by my reticence when discussing what I've done during a weekend away, for instance, or where I'm going to spend an evening after work. I may discuss the concert I've attended, and imply that I didn't go alone, but I don't mention D by name, and I certainly don't volunteer the information that I sat through the recital with my nipple rings chained to my collar and a carved ivory phallus in my anus. I let my colleagues know that I have spent my week's holiday at a retreat in the countryside, but I give them no hint that I have been receiving another instalment of training in the Private House.

The more perceptive of my friends are aware that I have undergone changes, however. I have become more self-contained since meeting D and, as a result of my education at the House, I think I have also become even more self-confident. And I was never exactly unassertive. And so Gillian and Eliza, in particular, my oldest friends, have been gently persistent in their enquiries, and I have allowed each of them a few insights into the nature of my life with D.

I haven't revealed that he owns me: I think that they would find this too difficult to comprehend, particularly as they know more than most people how much I value my independence. I have, however, given them hints that my new lover is immeasurably more important to me than any previous man I've known, and that his sexual tastes require me to submit to physical discipline. On one occasion, when Eliza happened to call at my house shortly after I had returned from D's, I showed her the marks on my bottom.

I am fortunate in my friends: neither Gillian nor Eliza
has expressed disgust or disappointment, although I can
tell that neither understands why I enjoy being used as
D uses me.

Where D's friends are concerned the situation is
different. To most of his colleagues and acquaintances,
and to his family, I am simply his lover. They seem
pleased that he has at last formed a relationship that has
lasted more than a few weeks. He doesn't, thank
goodness, insist that I accompany him to every formal
dinner and cocktail party which his position requires
him to attend, but I have appeared alongside him at
enough to be known as his consort. I wear the
appropriate outer garments – the evening gown, the
little black dress – and only D and I know that I am
naked underneath, and that both of us are fretting with
impatience for the moment when we can escape from
society and withdraw into our private paradise of
mastery and submission.

And then there are D's other friends: a small,
carefully selected, trusted group with whom D shares his
desires, his secrets and, sometimes, me.

I have described in previous essays the first time that
D offered me to another man, and the first time that I
was required to exhibit myself, in the presentation
position, to a meeting of D's like-minded friends, and
submit to being punished before an audience.

I knew that during my most recent residence at the
Private House D intended to organise a gathering, to be
held shortly after my return, at which I would once
again be presented to a small audience. I had become
accustomed to displaying myself for D's friends, and
while I have never entirely overcome the sense of shame
I feel at performing such intimate and perverse acts in
public, I confess that I had come to look forward to D's
soirées: it satisfies some deep longing of mine to be the
plaything of several powerful men. And, of course, I can
be sure of being thoroughly punished and frequently
penetrated. The photograph on the opposite page was

170

taken at one such event: it is dark and indistinct, but I feel that it captures the atmosphere of the evening. It is strange to see, as if as a distanced observer, my pale body bound with black bands and fenced in by the darkly clothed bodies and avid faces of those predatory men and women. That shadowy blur is the whistling whip, towards whose kiss my buttocks are lifted; the grimacing man with his hand in my hair had no sinister intention, but has been caught by the camera at the moment when my lips and tongue have coaxed the hot seed to spurt from his member.

On my return from the Private House D informed me that he had something special in mind for his next gathering, but I was unable to prise from him any details. As it transpired, however, the evening proved to be memorable. I will describe it in full.

On the day in question I went directly from my office to D's house. By the time I had taken a shower, dusted and perfumed myself, and put on my slave collar, D had arrived home. Thomas and Ruth had prepared the house for D's guests and had left the premises, but there were still things to be done and therefore there was little time for me to please D. He permitted me to kiss him, and to caress his penis. He rewarded me with compliments and with a brief spanking, after which he penetrated my anus with his finger and watched me play with my clitoris until I came.

We went together into the dining room, checked the provision of food and drink, and ate a little ourselves. Then D disappeared into the playroom – the room in which he has set up the ingenious pieces of equipment that he collects – having told me to go to my room and put on my make-up, a pair of stockings, my wrist cuffs and ankle cuffs, and a chain between my nipple rings. I was to remove the studs from my labial piercings: tonight my sex would be undecorated.

I was ready within fifteen minutes, and no matter how many times I looked in the mirror I couldn't see how I could be improved. I try not to be vain, but D is lavish in his praise of my appearance, and the accoutrements of a slave really do become my slight body and fair complexion. The collar and cuffs make me more than usually pretty.

I waited. I heard D come upstairs, and enter his room. I was trembling with trepidation and anticipation. I was nervous – I was, after all, about to be paraded in front of a room full of people and made to perform the most degrading acts – but whenever I stopped pacing back and forth and sat down on the bed I could feel that my vulva was hot and moist as it kissed the coverlet.

I started when I heard the knock on the front door. I heard D striding to meet the first arrival. There were murmuring, indistinct voices; more knocks on the door; more voices, sometimes raised in greeting or laughter. D answered the door seven times, by my reckoning. At least seven guests, then; perhaps as many as fourteen, or even more.

It fell silent downstairs. The guests must be dining, I assumed. I was too excited to be hungry now. I expected D to come to my room, or to summon me, at any moment, but the minutes crawled by in continuing silence.

At last I heard footsteps on the stairs. The door opened, and I leapt into D's arms. He kissed me, held me at arm's length, checked that I was wearing a suitable chain between my nipples, and pronounced me ravishing. He clipped a leash to my collar and led me away.

As we entered the playroom I felt my nervousness melt away. This room had been the scene of the most exquisite hours I had spent with D: hours of devotion, of exquisite torments and delights, of explosive passion. The drapes had been pulled shut, and to a stranger it would have appeared gloomy, mysterious, full of disturbing shadows and enigmatic structures. I felt comfortable there, even though I was surrounded by imposing figures, dressed expensively and strangely. The warm air swirled with fashionable perfume and cologne, the smell of polished wood and leather, and the unmistakable scent of arousal.

The crowd parted before us, and D led me to one end of the room, where he had set up lamps to illuminate the whipping post. I assumed that I was to be flogged for the entertainment of D's guests, and I felt the pulse of excitement begin to throb in my loins.

D stopped in the circle of light next to the post, and I knelt beside him with my hands behind my back and my knees parted. The guests ceased their conversations and formed a semicircle around us.

'Ladies and gentlemen,' he said. 'Masters, mistresses and slaves. Some of you have already seen and enjoyed Celia. She is going to entertain us again this evening, and I have devised a scheme which will, I think, provide us with a unique experience.'

He stroked my hair as he talked, and I turned my head to kiss his hand.

'I intend to hold an auction, my friends. Celia is the sole lot, and I will accept bids until nine o'clock. Don't reach for your wallets and your cheque books: this is to be a rather special auction, and your money will not win her. This will be what is known as a Dutch auction: bids are to be made to me in writing, and after the bidding closes at nine I will decide which bid is the winner. The successful bid will be that which proposes a use for Celia which in my opinion will most successfully entertain us and humiliate my slave. I am hoping for suggestions that are inventive, that make best use of Celia's talents, and that will test her endurance. The winner's prize, of course, will be to enact his or her proposal – here, this evening.'

D's guests exclaimed and whispered to each other. They were intrigued by D's auction, and I confess that I, too, was delighted with the elegance of his scheme. The guests would compete to devise the most unusual and amusing ordeal for me to undergo: the result was bound to be interesting, to say the least.

'I will chain Celia to the post so that each of you has a chance to examine her while you're considering how to bid,' D went on, 'but before I secure her I will, for the benefit of those of you who haven't seen her before, provide a brief introduction.'

He moved away from me, adjusted the lamps so that their light was concentrated on me, and continued to speak from the shadows. I knew that everyone in the room was looking at me, and was assailed once again by the exciting combination of fear, pride and yearning lust.

'Celia has, of course, a very submissive nature. Her body is naturally very responsive, but is particularly so if she is, or even merely expects to be, whipped or tied up or sexually humiliated. As you'll see shortly, simply being displayed as she is now is more than enough to make her aroused. Celia, push your breasts forward.'

As I complied I felt my vulva splitting open. When the time came for D to instruct me to display it, as I knew he would, his guests would be able to see clearly the wetness there. I simply revel in being shown off by D to new people: he is so proud of me.

'Celia's breasts are very sensitive,' D told his audience. 'With the right caresses she can be brought to a climax by stimulation of her breasts alone. I have known her to come while I've been whipping her breasts, and in fact some of her most intense orgasms have occurred while I have been carrying out very precise torturing of her nipples – which, as you can see, have become very hard at the memory of that particularly painful punishment.'

It was true: my nipples had become erect so swiftly that the chain between them jingled. I have become almost addicted to having my breasts punished, and each time I return from the Private House I bring new ideas for D to experiment with.

'As you can see Celia's nipples are pierced. At the moment she is wearing simple rings and a chain, but we have a number of other attachments and items of jewellery that you can suggest are used when you compose your bid.'

D fell silent for a while to allow his guests to watch me. And I, from under lowered lids, watched them.

I recognised some of them. Master Godfrey, a thick-set, muscular man with cropped hair and sharp eyes, had used my mouth at the last gathering: he knew that my breasts were sensitive, as he had stroked and slapped and pinched them mercilessly, while I licked and sucked his cock, until I had shuddered into coming. As soon as he saw that I was enjoying an orgasm he pulled his erection from my mouth, pumped it with his hand, and directed streams of his sperm on to my face while I was still trembling with the aftershocks. 'Your slave's nothing but a slut,' he had shouted to D. 'Very lovely, though.'

I saw that this evening he had a young man with him: a blond youth, goggle-eyed with amazement at what he was witnessing. I wondered whether the young man was Master Godfrey's slave. He was fully dressed, however, which argued against the possibility: a few of the masters and mistresses had brought slaves with them, and the slaves were all naked or nearly so.

I recognised Master James, whom I knew to be as skilful as D with the whip and the riding crop. I saw Mistress Danielle, whom I knew liked to kiss the private parts of any slave, male or female, who was being sodomised.

None of these guests I recognised caused me any disquiet. I knew that D would not allow anyone to harm me, and in any case now that I have been schooled in the Private House I am aware that most of this circle of D's friends are, quite frankly, amateurs compared with the devotees of depravity who have taught me. Master James, I suspected, might have had the benefit of the House's training.

D's voice interrupted my thoughts. 'Turn around now, Celia,' he said. 'Show everyone your bottom.'

I stood up, bowed my head briefly to the audience, and turned. With my legs widely parted and my hands still crossed behind my back I sank slowly to my knees. I crossed one ankle over the other, arched my back inwards, and gradually bent forward from my waist until I could feel my breasts hanging clear of my ribs and the furrow between my buttocks fully open. One learns how to position oneself correctly in the Private House, and the elegance of my movements – or perhaps merely the displaying of my private parts – earned me a polite burst of applause.

'As I told you,' D said, 'Celia becomes aroused very easily. As you can see, she is already very wet. For the purposes of your proposed bids you should be aware that although she is not, strictly speaking, multi-orgasmic, in that she doesn't have series of climaxes that merge together, she will often have several orgasms within one punishment session, for instance, and if she's very aroused she can after having an orgasm be stimulated into coming again with almost no interval.'

I felt D's hand, suddenly, cupping my sex. I started, and couldn't restrain a judder of lust.

'Celia's clitoris is not particularly pronounced,' D said, 'but it is clearly visible and, of course, extremely sensitive. However, Celia can also be brought to a climax through stimulation of her labia and, thanks to some intensive training and practice, through manipulation of her anus. In short, therefore, there are plenty of ways in which you can make Celia come, and come often. The difficulty might be, in fact, preventing her from coming, if your proposal doesn't require her to.'

D squeezed with his fingers, and the pulses of pleasure came so strongly that I started to move my sex back and forth against the pressure of his hand. When he withdrew his fingers I couldn't hold in groan of disappointment, which to my embarrassment caused a ripple of comment among the audience.

'I don't whip Celia every day,' D began, and was interrupted by cries of 'Shame!' I could tell from the sound of his voice that he was smiling as he continued. 'However, I do make sure that her bottom is never

176

without the marks of punishment. As you can see, these lines are now quite faded, and her breasts are unmarked: therefore your bid can certainly include virtually any punishment that you choose to inflict. Don't be misled by Celia's delicate manners and petite form: she finds all forms of chastisement stimulating, and if she is kept aroused she can take lengthy punishment, particularly on her bottom.'

To emphasise his point D slapped my right buttock hard with his hand, and I wiggled my hips in agreement.

'Finally,' D announced, 'there are just one or two things that I would like you to exclude from the activities you propose in your bids. I am happy for Celia to be penetrated vaginally or anally with inanimate objects, but I'm afraid I can't allow any form of sexual congress. Her vagina is, quite simply, out of bounds: I don't permit her to have sex that way. And her arsehole is reserved for me.'

I heard ribald, good-humoured cries of complaint from some of the male guests.

'I'm sorry,' D said, 'but those are the rules. After all, I am expecting you to be inventive in your bids. And remember, Celia's mouth is available for those of you, men or women, who want to include your own orgasm in your proposal. Celia is an accomplished fellatrix. I'll secure her to the post now. Feel free to come and ask her questions, touch her, taste her. And remember: I want your bids, in writing, by nine.'

D helped me to my feet and placed me facing the whipping post. I rested my cheek against the polished wood as he unclipped the chain from one of my nipple rings. He adjusted the height of the narrow, leather-covered saddle that extends horizontally from the post and, taking my hips in his strong hands he placed me on the cool promontory. I gasped as my sex settled and spread on the leather. By standing on tiptoe I could reach the floor with my feet. He tugged on the chain to make me lean towards the post, and when my chest was pressed against it, and my breasts were protruding on either side of it, he refastened the chain to my nipple so that I was unable to move. Then he lifted my arms above my head and secured my wrist cuffs to a metal ring near the top of the post.

For the next hour I was the centre of attention. I think every one of D's guests took the opportunity to play with my nipple rings, or smack my bottom, or test the resilience of my anus. I could feel the leather saddle becoming slippery with my juices. Many of them asked me questions about my experiences, I imagine in the hope of discovering some practice with which I was unfamiliar and which they could include in a winning bid. Most of these questioners went away disappointed – I had to confess that few of their ideas were new to me – but also, I like to think, excited and impressed.

'Your breasts caned when bound tightly?' Yes, sir.

'Vibrating phalluses? In your anus as well?' Yes, madam.

'Heated needles? Just here, just below your nipples? Or here?' Yes, sir.

I began to wonder, as I'm sure all the guests did, what novel combination of punishment and pleasure could possibly be sufficiently inventive to win the auction.

One of the guests asked no questions. I hadn't seen her at any of D's previous gatherings. She was tall and slender, approaching her middle years but still possessed of an elegant beauty. Her hair and eyes were dark; her nose was thin and sharp, but her lips, painted glossy purple, were full. She was wearing a costume that appeared at first sight appropriate for a slave: no more than a satin corset that matched her lips, stockings and high-heeled shoes, and a short, tight skirt. However, it was clear that she was a mistress: she had an air of authority and, at the end of the chain she held in her left hand, she had a slave.

She approached me during one of the brief periods during which I wasn't surrounded by other guests. She touched my face and smiled at me, and spent some time caressing my breasts and my bottom until I began to squirm with pleasure.

'Celia,' she said, as if experimenting with the sound of my name. 'Quite charming. D is very fortunate to own you. I am Judith, by the way. I intend to win the auction. I have something very special in mind for you.'

As she spoke she continued to stroke me, and I could only murmur 'Yes, mistress,' from time to time, and 'Thank you, mistress.'

'I'm confident that I'll be able to compose the most interesting bid,' Mistress Judith went on, 'but I also have a substantial bribe to offer the referee. Do you think D will be able to resist my slave? Say hello to Celia, Kate.'

I had been so immersed in enjoying the touch of Mistress Judith's hands that my eyes were closed. I blinked them open, and saw her slave standing before me.

Kate was naked, and astonishingly pretty. She had the body of a Renaissance woman – plump hips and round breasts – and the face of a girl. It was the shyest, sweetest, most innocent face I had ever seen. It was impossible not to be drawn to Kate: her eyes were wide and trusting and downcast, and her lips were slightly pouting. She looked as though she needed comforting; she would make the hardest heart swell with compassion.

Like me, she was wearing a collar. Her plump breasts were criss-crossed with fine red lines.

'Hello, Celia,' she said. Her voice was soft and childish; her accent indicated an educated and cultured upbringing.

'Kate,' Mistress Judith said, 'tell Celia why you were punished this afternoon.'

Kate looked at her mistress with eyes wide with surprise, and then said, 'Oh. Yes, mistress.' She turned to me again. Her eyes were bright with incipient tears. 'I was a bad girl,' she whispered. 'I didn't lick fast enough, and I didn't play with my arsehole enough. So my mistress whipped my breasts until I started crying. After that I was a good girl and I licked my mistress

179

again. I need to be whipped rather frequently, I'm afraid.'

She smiled shyly as she finished her account. I wished I could give her a kiss. She looked utterly vulnerable and innocent, and yet her secretive smile hinted at the dark pleasure she experienced in putting herself into the hands of a cruel mistress.

'Come along, Kate,' Mistress Judith said. 'I have to find pen and paper. I intend to have Celia.'

At length all the guests had quizzed me, and those who had conceived of suitably original ways to please themselves with me had submitted their written bids to D. He stood next to me, under the lights, as he read them. The hubbub of conversation among the guests dwindled to silence as they realised that D had finished reading and had made his selection.

'There is a runner-up,' he announced, 'whose bid merits a public airing. It wasn't quite good enough to win, but I found it intriguing and I think you might as well. And I expect that Celia and I will find out at a later date whether it's practical and enjoyable.

'This proposal requires two helpers and a minimum of special equipment. Celia would be tied up very tightly, in ropes, in the oriental style: in other words not only with her arms and legs immobilised but also with ropes binding her breasts and her genitalia, and with knots positioned to press against her clitoris, her vagina and her anus. She would then be placed face down on a table, with an A-frame under her to lift her bottom, and instructed to have an orgasm. She would be unable to touch herself, of course: she would have to excite her erogenous areas by writhing against the knots and ropes. This would probably take some time, and would provide considerable entertainment for those watching. Then, when she is getting close to coming, one of the helpers would begin to whip her bottom, to encourage her to writhe more urgently, while the second would, quite simply, put his penis in her mouth and fuck her until he comes. Celia would probably also have a

180

climax, but that isn't the point of the exercise: as I understand it the pleasure is to be found in the way that the meticulous positioning and tying of the ropes and the spectacle of Celia's slow, tortuous struggle towards orgasm contrast with the brief but intense delight of coming in her mouth as she's being flogged. I think it sounds a capital idea, and I'll make sure Celia tries it.'

There was a ripple of applause. I pressed myself against the saddle in frustration: I could imagine all too easily how I would have to wriggle and squirm against the intrusive knots and tight ropes until D judged that I was ready to receive his cock in my mouth.

'I won't read out a description of the winning bid,' D told his guests, 'because you'll see it performed as soon as we have the equipment set up. Please be patient for a few moments.'

I had been won, of course, by Mistress Judith. I could hear her giving instructions to some of the slaves as they arranged furniture and chains in the shadowy depths of the room. D stayed beside me, stroking and kissing my face. 'This will be a challenge for you, Celia,' he whispered. 'Don't disappoint me.'

I was desperate to find out what Judith had planned for me, and very excited. And I was determined to show D's guests that he had an obedient and responsive slave. I was nervous, too: I like performing with women because I know D enjoys watching me, but I prefer being punished and made to come by men. And I was sure that Mistress Judith would be cruel.

The lamps were removed from around me and were set up to illuminate the equipment that Judith had arranged. As D released me from the whipping post I saw in the circle of light a narrow couch and, hanging from the ceiling above it, a metal bar suspended on chains.

I was dizzy with desire and apprehension, but I did not have to discover whether my tremulous legs would support me: D lifted me into his arms and carried me across the room, and laid me on my back on the couch.

My legs were lifted into the air and my ankle cuffs were secured to the ends of the hanging bar, so that my legs were held wide apart. Two leather straps, hanging from the ceiling a little way from the bar, were looped under my knees and pulled upwards so that my knees were bent and my rounded bottom was lifted up. Only my shoulders and upper back were now resting on the black upholstery. The cuffs around my wrists were clipped to rings set into the sides of the couch. The back of my head was cradled in a depression that seemed to be padded with soft cloths. I could hardly move, but I wasn't uncomfortable.

I assumed that I was being positioned so that my bottom could be whipped. But then I realised that Mistress Judith would have proposed nothing so mundane. The fact that my legs were stretched so far apart made my vulva very exposed and vulnerable.

By turning my head to the side I could see D and his guests standing at a little distance from the couch. The slaves were being caressed and aroused by their owners. I noticed with a pang of foreboding that Judith's slave Kate was standing next to D, who appeared to have his hand on her bottom. He caught my eye and smiled encouragingly.

Judith was standing at the end of the couch, and I couldn't see her. She was addressing the audience.

'Celia is in the correct position, but she still needs a little more preparation. The next stage is rather delicate, so I'll perform the operation in a seated position. And to be really comfortable I think I'll dispense with this.'

I heard a susurration of silk, an approving shout from the audience, and then the click of Judith's heels. She moved to the side of the couch and, as my eyes were at the same level as her thighs, I saw immediately that she had removed her skirt. She was naked from her constricted waist to the tops of her stockings.

She leant forward, which movement must have provided the onlookers with a fine view of her bottom, and kissed my lips.

'I need to sit down, Celia,' she said. 'But you're occupying the whole of the couch. We'll have to share. I hope you like the taste of a woman.'

Before I had grasped the meaning of her words she had straddled the couch and her vulva, glistening pinkly and fringed with dark curls, was descending on to my face.

Her sex smelt of the spicy perfume she was wearing, and of the bitter musk of her arousal. She held it a mere finger's-width above my face.

'Lift your head and kiss me, Celia,' she said. 'A good slave knows how to please her mistress. I wonder whether you're as good as my Kate. Come now: reach up and kiss.'

I lifted my head and pressed my lips against the folds of moist flesh. I like the taste of a woman's juices, and I was happy to kiss Judith for as long as she required. I felt her tugging gently on my nipple rings, and kissed her more fervently as the darts of sensation began to flash through my body.

'Very good,' she said, and then lowered her bottom on to the couch. Because my head was resting in a depression I was not smothered. However, my forehead was pressed against her buttocks, the tip of my nose was between her outer labia, and I could extend my tongue to lick her clitoris. As I could see and hear very little, the scent of her overwhelmed my senses. Her wetness trickled down the sides of my nose and on to my cheeks.

She moved her hips, and for a moment my nose was pressed into the well of her anus and her hot sex-lips were on my mouth. She resumed her previous position.

'Oh yes,' I heard her say. 'I'll have some fun riding you, later. But now let's see to your cunt.'

She leant forward, and the front of her slit was pressed against my mouth. Suddenly I became aware of something other than her smell and her taste and the texture of her sex: her hands were stroking the insides of my thighs. Just as suddenly I felt a stab of arousal, and I extended my tongue to lick her. I heard her laugh.

183

Her fingers were on my vulva now, plucking at and pinching my labia and making me writhe on the couch.

'Keep still, Celia,' she said. 'And Kate, bring me the clips.'

Her hands were on the insides of my thighs again: she was touching the tops of my stockings – attaching something to them.

'Come closer, everyone,' Judith called out. 'I want you all to see what I'm doing here. You see? I'm clipping these four short chains to the slave's stockings – two to each leg. And then I take the first chain, and I attach the clip at the other end – like this.'

I gasped as she gripped one of my outer labia in her fingers and pulled it, and then almost cried out as the pinching of her fingers was replaced by an even sharper bite.

I moaned and groaned into Judith's vulva as she continued to torture mine. She had attached two clips to each of my stockings, and she proceeded to clip the other end of all four of them to my labia.

Dimly I heard her commenting on my reactions. 'I distinctly remember telling Celia to keep still,' she said, 'and as she certainly isn't doing so I'll have to punish her. And do you see how wet she is? It's just as well that the jaws of these clips have strong springs; anything less could easily slip off. Even my Kate rarely gets this excited when I put clips on her labia.'

My sex lips were being held apart by the four clips. The sharp pinching of the jaws faded, to be replaced by a dull, pulsing ache that merged with the deep throbbing of my arousal. I could feel, too, the constant pull of the taut chains that connected the clips to my stocking-tops: I could relieve the pressure by flexing the muscles in my thighs and thus lifting my bottom higher, but I couldn't maintain the position for long.

'Now then,' Judith said to her audience, 'Celia needs to be punished, doesn't she? I'm sure you'd all like to see that. Celia isn't used to being whipped by a woman. Only a mistress really knows how to chastise a female slave in the most intimate ways. Kate, would you bring me the whip now? The smaller one: Celia isn't as accustomed as you are to my methods.'

Judith was going to whip the inside of my cunt. I couldn't move: my arms were chained at my sides, my legs were held apart, my head was surrounded by Judith's sex, and the tender lips that should have shielded my most delicate membranes were cruelly gripped and stretched wide. My insides fluttered with trepidation and yet I couldn't help wondering what the punishment would feel like. And I was so sexually excited that I craved more sensations, however painful.

'Thank you, Kate,' Judith said. 'As you can see, the whip is only a little thing: the handle is conveniently shaped to resemble a phallus, and there are just two thin strands of leather. It hardly hurts at all.'

There was no warning: just a stinging pain in the very centre of my being that made me buck and writhe in my bonds. As I jerked my head up I buried my face in the moist wetness of Judith's sex.

'That was very pleasant, Celia,' Judith said. 'I do hope you can keep that up all the way through your punishment. But wait! I'm forgetting something. I'm not entirely comfortable. In all the excitement of the bidding, I simply forgot all about such mundane things. But Celia is supposed to be humiliated as well as punished, so I think I'll just do it here and now.'

She lifted her sex from my face and moved back a little, so that I had a brief glimpse of my suspended legs and the gleaming pinkness of my stretched, gaping vulva. I heard her laugh, and saw her hand descend to press against her belly just above the mass of dark pubic curls.

Suddenly I realised what she was about to do, and I closed my eyes. I heard a hiss from inside her body, and a collective gasp from the audience, and then the stream of her urine struck my face. The hot, acrid-smelling liquid jetted on to my chin, my nose, and my forehead. I screwed up my mouth and eyes. I heard the audience shouting their approval as Judith directed the stream of her piss all over my face.

There seemed no end to the cascade of urine. I breathed it into my nose, and when I gasped the bitter liquid flooded into my mouth. My hair was sodden, as were the cloths on which my head was resting. I was drenched in the warm liquid, and choking and spluttering in its pungent miasma – and then Judith lowered herself once more on to my face.

'That feels much better,' she announced to D's guests. 'And I think it never does any harm to let a slave know her place. Now, where was I? Ah yes, of course. Let us proceed.'

Never had I felt so dirtied and degraded. D had let Judith use me as her toilet. I was stained with her effluent. And now, as she rocked back and forth, she was using my face for her sexual pleasure, sliding my nose between her labia, grinding her pubes against my mouth. The smell and taste of her piss mingled with the smell and taste of her arousal. A dozen of D's friends were witnesses to my humiliation. I could not imagine being more thoroughly abused.

And my whole body was tingling with expectant desire.

I felt a sudden jolt of lust. Both of my nipples were being tugged upwards. I realised that Judith had taken in her hand the chain that connected my nipple rings. I pictured her astride me, riding me as if she were riding a horse, holding my chain as if it were the reins.

'I'll whip the insides of her labia first,' Judith said, 'and then the entrance of her vagina.'

I no longer cared what she did – or, rather, I was so aroused that I didn't care what she did, as long as she did something. I craved sensation – and Judith provided it.

The whipping did not last long. The area to be punished was not large, and even with a small whip Judith was able to chastise my vulva thoroughly with a couple of dozen strokes. The later lashes, in any case, produced diminishing returns: as I became accustomed to the penetrating, toe-curling agony of being whipped in such a private place my bucking and moaning lessened. I was able to enjoy the feeling of the tendrils of pain spreading through my body, firing my clitoris, merging with the pulling on my nipples, and bringing me closer and closer to a climax. I was able to match with my tongue the movements of Judith's hips, so that we cooperated in a complex rhythm: she would slide forward, and tug on my nipple chain; I would insert my tongue between her labia; the whip would strike my cunt and, momentarily witless with pain, I would jerk my mouth upwards against her sex; she would slide back, and I would lick her clitoris.

Judith was becoming as aroused as I was. Having drowned in her piss I was now being smothered in her sex juice.

'That's enough,' she announced breathlessly. I heard the whip fall to the floor. Judith continued to rock on my face, and I continued to lick her. 'Celia is a dedicated slave, D,' she said. 'I'll give her full marks for diligence.' Her voice was slightly hoarse, and I assumed that the audience could be in little doubt about her state of excitement.

She leant forward, and my tongue found the engorged tip of her clitoris. At the same moment I felt her breath on my burning, exposed membranes: she was blowing gently across the stretched, punished skin.

And then she lowered herself a little further, and her lips touched my sex.

'Let me kiss it better,' she whispered, and after that I heard nothing because her tongue found my clitoris and we set out to lift each other on to a plane of ecstasy.

Judith started to come first, but as soon as I felt her body start to shudder against mine I felt my own climax overwhelm me like an avalanche. She lapped at my opened vulva as if she were a cat drinking cream, while I sank my teeth into the soft flesh of her sex and thrust the tip of my tongue like a drill against her clitoris.

At last we stopped bucking against each other, and I became aware of the applause of the crowd. Judith kissed the insides of my thighs, pulled herself upright, and dismounted from the couch.

'Thank you,' she said. 'That was most pleasant. I hope you all enjoyed it as much as I did – although I think that's unlikely, in fact. I must go and make myself respectable again. Celia, being a slave, doesn't need to look respectable, so I'll leave her here for your inspection. Now, where's Kate?'

I, too, was scanning the faces in the room. I wanted to see D. I needed to know whether my performance had pleased him.

Kate was with D. When she heard her mistress's voice, she pulled away from him and started to come towards the circle of illumination.

Judith stopped her. 'No, I don't require you, Kate. I've promised you to D, and you must let him have his way with you. I understand he's going to bind you, cane your bottom and then bugger you. That's perfectly all right as far as I'm concerned. You can return to me when he's finished with you.'

My euphoria dissolved. I felt suddenly and completely wretched. I wanted to be with D. I didn't want to be exposed to the examination of his friends while he enjoyed Judith's pretty slave.

I should not have doubted my master. Before the tears that had gathered in my eyes could begin to roll down my face he was kneeling at my side. His eyes were full of adoration.

'You were wonderful, Celia,' he said. His fingers caressed my sodden hair, and he leant to kiss my smudged and soiled face. 'I couldn't wish for a more delightful and obedient slave. I'm going to deal with Kate in the study – but I want you to come too.'

He began to unfasten my wrists from the couch. 'Can you imagine the expressions that will cross Kate's angelic face as she feels the cane on her bottom? As she feels me entering her arse? Would you like to see?'

I nodded. 'I like to see your face, too,' I told him. 'I don't often have the chance to watch you, and I love to see you come.'

D laughed. 'Very well,' he said, 'you shall stand in front of Kate while I punish her. You will take the mirror from above the fireplace and hold it, so that I can see your face, and Kate's reflected in the mirror. And you will be able to see both hers and mine.'

'That sounds perfect,' I said. And it was.

At the end of my last visit to the cottage, at the beginning of July, Eloise had given me a long extract from the notebooks that Anne's mother had left. She seemed to want me to keep up with her researches into Celia's past. And it was reading the pages from Celia's journal that gave me the idea of taking Stephanie with me the next time I visited Eloise.

It was proving to be a long, hot summer. I couldn't concentrate on my work: my models, even Stephanie, perspired and fidgeted in the heat; the studio was, it must be said, a sultry and stifling place. My mind was, in any case, elsewhere: I couldn't stop thinking about Anne.

Amanda's reports were as infrequent as ever and, when I received one and tore it open, or even when she came to the city and I was able to interrogate her at my leisure, she had little to say about Anne and seemed put out that I was so interested in her. 'She's doing well, Michael,' she insisted. 'Now will you please untie me and make me do something naughty?'

But I couldn't put Anne out of my mind. I tried to imagine the lessons she was being taught at the Private House; I made scores of different plans for how best to enjoy her when she returned.

And so it was futile to stay in the city. Instead I went with increasing frequency out into the country, and naturally I chose to stay with Eloise in the cottage. She was pretty, she was keen to try every strange contraption she found in Celia's dungeon and every perverse practice she found described in Celia's journals and, of course, she was my link with Anne. I had the opportunity to debauch and deprave her while cementing myself into place as part of the household. By the time Anne returned to the cottage I would be a fixture. And Anne, newly trained in the ways of submission, would be mine.

While I was away from the cottage Eloise and I corresponded daily. Had the operatives of the postal service been aware of the contents of the envelopes that passed between us, I am sure that none of the letters would have been delivered and some would have been reported to the authorities. But the envelopes appeared innocuous, and Eloise and I were able to discuss in extreme detail our opinions about Celia's experiences and our plans for my next visit.

On this occasion I had suggested, in the correspondence that preceded my visit, that it was time for Eloise to endure and enjoy one of the several uncomfortable acts to which Celia, according to her journals, had become entirely accustomed. I had told Eloise that instead of chastising her on her bottom, as had become my usual practice, I would whip her breasts. As an alternative I suggested that, now that she was familiar with the sensations caused by having my fingers, and indeed various other similarly shaped objects, inserted into her anus, it would be appropriate for her to experience the uniquely excruciating pleasure of being buggered.

In her reply she responded enthusiastically to both suggestions, and insisted that she wished to try both of them as soon as possible. In my next letter to her I prevaricated, as I was not at all sure that she would find either experience to her liking, let alone both. However, as I sweltered in the humid air that hung in my flat and began to plan for the forthcoming escape into the countryside, it occurred to me that if Eloise wanted to have her breasts whipped and her arsehole fucked, then I had no right to deny her. And it seemed to me, as I read and re-read the extracts from Celia's journals that Eloise had lent to me, that it would be even more enjoyable if the two experiences could be simultaneous, and shared with at least one third party.

And thus was born the conceit of taking Stephanie with me to the cottage.

I have mentioned before that Stephanie is the most shameless and wanton hussy I have met. She was, of course, perfectly content to go along with my suggestion of spending a few days in the country, provided that she was sure that there was a sexual experience to be enjoyed, that I would pay for her train ticket, and that she wouldn't be required to go on any long rural walks.

And so I found myself once again being bounced along the single-track branch line towards Eloise and the cottage, this time in the company of Stephanie.

The train consisted of two carriages, and we had one to ourselves. The paucity of passengers was not, I knew, unusual, but I fancy that on this occasion the few country people who boarded the train had taken one look at Stephanie and had decided to sit in the other carriage.

It's not that Stephanie is unattractive: on the contrary, she is a tall, slender young woman with a curvaceous figure and a vivacious smile. However, her mode of dress is sufficiently outrageous to get her noticed even in the city, and on this particular day, in view of the high temperature, she wasn't wearing much at all: a bikini top, a short skirt, and a pair of sandals with high heels and platform soles which elevated her to above my height. As she seemed to equate a few days in the countryside with going on safari, the little clothing she had on was all made of material with a loud leopard-skin pattern. She had dyed her hair a dramatic and entirely unnatural shade of red, and had painted her lips and nails to match. She looked stunning but, I must admit, rather daunting.

In view of the stares and whispered comments that Stephanie's appearance generated at each dusty station, I reluctantly decided that it would be unwise to have her pose for me on the train. I put away my sketch pad and spent the journey gazing out of the windows at parched fields and shady woodlands. I gave Stephanie the extracts from Celia's journals, which she read avidly, and I had to remind her only occasionally that she should not touch herself quite so intimately while we were travelling.

As we walked through the orchard towards the front door of the cottage I began, too late, to consider whether it had been wise to bring Stephanie. Eloise had, I supposed, a right to some privacy as she submitted herself to forms of punishment and sexual intercourse which were new to her and liable to be painful.

But it was too late to worry about such matters now. We were at the door.

Eloise appeared in the doorway looking as fresh and pretty as ever in a simple, thin dress which showed off her slender curves and through which I could discern that she was wearing nothing else.

The smile on her face faded for only a moment when she saw Stephanie. It was restored automatically by her sense of etiquette, and she remained smiling and chatty as she led us into the drawing room and offered us iced tea. I performed the necessary introductions, but felt that the time was not yet right to explain the part I intended Stephanie to play in the day's activities. Eloise managed once or twice to catch my eye and give me quizzical glares, as if to say that she expected an explanation of Stephanie's unheralded appearance just as soon as she and I were alone together. She also kept glancing down at her dress and up at Stephanie's hair, as if making comparisons between her understated attire and the ostentation of the tall, unexpected guest.

'I'm afraid I haven't prepared a room for you,' Eloise told Stephanie. 'Michael didn't warn me you were coming.'

Stephanie stepped towards Eloise and placed a hand on her arm. 'It's all right,' she said. 'I'll help you sort something out. Michael can be an inconsiderate bastard sometimes.'

I had expected Stephanie to say something less diplomatic – perhaps a comment along the lines that we wouldn't be needing very many beds anyway. I took my glass of tea into the garden and let the two women become acquainted. A little later I heard them, through an open window under the thatch, chatting animatedly as they unfolded fresh sheets and towels.

192

When I had an opportunity to speak with Eloise, as she prepared a salad in the kitchen, it soon became clear that she was still intent on undergoing the trials we had planned for her. In showing Stephanie round the house she had included a tour of the dungeon outhouse, and it seemed that the two of them, sharing an interest in the more arcane aspects of sexual behaviour, had become firm friends as they discussed the relative merits of the specialised furniture and equipment.

'So you'll let me whip these,' I whispered, pulling her back against me and cradling her breasts in my hands. 'First the small whip, and then the cane, as we agreed.' Her nipples were as hard as pebbles. She pressed her bottom against my groin.

'Stephanie wants to do that,' Eloise said, turning her head to kiss me. 'I want you to hold me while she does it. I'd enjoy that.'

I slid a hand down the front of her body and curled my fingers into the gap between her thighs. I pressed inwards, crushing her bottom against the rising hardness of my erection and eliciting from her a moan and a shiver of pleasure. Through the thin material of her dress I could feel that her sex was wet.

'This evening,' I whispered. 'After dinner.'

Eloise murmured her agreement. 'We'll eat early,' she said, suddenly businesslike. 'It's too hot for anything much. Come to the dungeon at eight. I'll be ready.'

All three of us spent the afternoon in languid anticipation. I made a sketch of Eloise and Stephanie, and as the temperature climbed they were happy to remain naked. I sat and worked on the composition of a painting, content to bask in the sunlight and to catch glimpses of the two women strolling arm in arm about the garden. Each time I saw them I imagined the forthcoming entertainment in the dungeon: I planned how I would dress them, how I would bind Eloise, at what point I would instruct Stephanie to join in.

By seven o'clock we had eaten what little of Eloise's salad the heat and our increasing impatience would allow.

Across the lawn the shadows of the trees were beginning to lengthen at last, and the faintest zephyr tempered the warmth and brought the scents of the orchards into the cottage.

I suggested that we should bring forward the appointed time for proceedings to begin in the outhouse, but Eloise wouldn't hear of it.

'It'll be worth waiting for,' she said. 'Don't you dare make an appearance before eight.'

We retired to our separate rooms: we all wanted to take showers and change our clothes. I dressed in soft, cream linen – shirt and trousers – and padded barefoot about the guest bedroom I had been allocated. I took as long as I could checking the things I had brought with me: a small whip with a single narrow tongue of leather, a flexible lath of wood that was so slender that I had to grasp it as if it were one of my paintbrushes, and several lengths of soft cotton rope. The rope was to bind up Eloise's breasts before caning them. I looked at the bedside clock. There was still more than half an hour to go.

I wandered downstairs and into the garden. I had become used to the relative cool inside the cottage, and I felt perspiration break out on my chest as I stood in the rays of the declining sun. I was carrying the whip, the cane and the ropes in a briefcase. Just thinking about the pleasure of having Eloise before me, offering me her breasts and her arsehole, was enough to make my penis rigid.

I couldn't wait. I would get Stephanie to lick me and make me come in her mouth. It would take the edge off my appetite, and I would be able to enjoy the evening in a leisurely fashion. I returned to the cool shade of the cottage.

Stephanie wasn't in her room. I searched the cottage, and couldn't find her or Eloise. The latter, I assumed, had gone to the outhouse to draw the curtains, adjust the lamps, and in general transform it into the dungeon that Celia had conceived it as. And I thought that Stephanie, like me, had grown bored and had set off for a walk

194

through the cottage's gardens and orchards. Although, in retrospect, I realise I should have remembered that Stephanie doesn't understand the concept of taking exercise outdoors.

I couldn't find Stephanie in the garden, either, and by the time I had expanded my search to include the orchards and the meadows beyond them, I was feeling hot and tired. And it was almost eight o'clock. The sun was still above the horizon, but the sky surrounding it was turning from blue to shades of vivid pink. There was going to be a spectacular sunset.

I made for the outhouse. The drapes had been drawn across the windows, and I could see the glimmer of lamplight at their edges. Above the pitched roof the heavens were creating a display of light and colour; inside, the outhouse would seem like a nighted dungeon, buried beneath the ground.

As I opened the door I saw that Eloise had provided illumination in only one corner of the labyrinth. As I made my way towards the lamplight, trying to remember in the gloom the twists and turns I had to make between the partitions and screens, I almost bumped into Stephanie.

'You're here already,' I said, and immediately felt irritated with myself. I hate stating the obvious. 'I was looking for you.'

Stephanie had changed into a costume I hadn't seen before. I wondered whether it had come from Celia's wardrobe. She had on a basque of red satin and lace that matched the colour of her nails, lips and hair. It consisted of a bodice that, to judge from the constriction of Stephanie's waist, was at least on the way to being an effective corset, and two lacy cups of such gossamer transparency that her breasts might almost have been uncovered. Suspenders supported red stockings, and red shoes with thin heels completed the outfit.

I was intrigued to see that she had a bush of pubic hair as red as the hair on her head. This surprised me, as I knew from watching her sitting with her legs parted, during the train journey, that her entire pubic area was freshly shaved.

195

I bent down to investigate, and found that the red hair was in fact a heart-shaped pad of fake fur.

'I've been in here,' she said. 'I've been getting changed, and helping Eloise to get ready.' She noticed that I was carrying a briefcase. 'What have you got in there? You look like a bloke setting off for a day at the office.'

'The whip and the cane, of course,' I said. 'And some ropes. You know that I always think that only the very smallest breasts should be caned without being supported in some way.'

'You needn't have bothered,' Stephanie said. 'Eloise has got everything we need here. The equipment in this place is just amazing. Come on: I'll show you.'

Stephanie led me towards the illuminated chamber. As we rounded the last partition I stopped in my tracks and, a moment later, I threw aside my briefcase with a theatrical gesture. Eloise and Stephanie had indeed arranged everything.

Eloise was naked from the waist down. The upper half of her body was clad in a long-sleeved garment that appeared to be made up of panels of leather laced together. That was all that I could see at first, as she was facing away from me and could not turn because she was bound on to a wooden frame.

'We thought your first view should be from behind,' Stephanie said, 'seeing as you're going to have Eloise's arsehole this evening.'

Eloise's bottom could hardly have been more prominently displayed. The wooden frame to which she was bound consisted of a rectangle of beams with three padded cross-members. It was fixed in a horizontal position, but I noticed that it was supported clear of the floor on a heavy base with triangular uprights that would permit the entire rectangle, with Eloise on it, to be angled. Eloise's ankles were chained to the bottom corners of the frame, so that her legs were held far apart. Her knees were bent, and just above them the backs of her thighs were pressed against the lowest of the three padded cross-pieces. The middle bar was not straight: it bowed out from the back of the frame

196

and into the front of Eloise's hips, so that she was held with her bottom pushed out and splayed open. This effect was emphasised by the fact that her upper body was bent forward from the waist, with the topmost cross-piece running behind the middle of her back, thrusting her torso forwards. Her arms were stretched upwards, and her wrists were chained to the top corners of the frame. In sum, Eloise's legs and body were secured in a zig-zag shape with her bottom and her breasts at the most prominent points. It was a simple, elegant design, that with only four chains held Eloise immovably in the most delightfully obscene position.

I was, for once, lost for words. I think I probably said something like, 'Wow!' I have considerable experience of putting women into bondage, but I think I had never before seen anyone so perfectly secured for both punishment and penetration. Eloise's dusky, crinkled hole was an almost irresistible temptation, and the insistent hardness of my cock indicated that it, at least, wanted to plunge in without any further prevarication. The fact that Eloise was completely helpless to prevent any such occurrence only fuelled my desire, as did the rosy imprints on Eloise's buttocks that indicated to me that Stephanie had been unable to resist administering a spanking once she had Eloise's bottom at her mercy.

I stepped forward and ran my hands over Eloise's buttocks. She recognised my touch, and looked at me over her shoulder. 'Michael,' she said, 'what do you think? I hope you like it: it's jolly uncomfortable.'

'You look wonderful,' I said. 'And very, very inviting.'

'Good,' she said. She seemed utterly carefree. 'I think Celia would have approved, too.'

It was true that Eloise was looking particularly desirable. Her blue eyes were bright with excitement, her cheeks were flushed, and she seemed almost aglow with sensual warmth. The fact that her upper body was clothed only added to the appeal of her exposed hindquarters, and I was also affected by the fact that she had volunteered to be secured and held available for my pleasure.

I realised, as my fingers wandered round the lower curves of her buttocks and encountered the parted lips of her sex, that the pleasure was not to be all mine. I didn't know which had aroused her more – the bondage, the spanking, or the anticipation of what was to come – but she was so wet that drops of her juices were hanging from her labia.

'I don't need to enquire whether you're ready to start,' I said, and kissed the back of her neck before moving to the front of the frame.

I saw at once that Stephanie and Eloise had indeed thought of everything. The bizarre leather tunic did not entirely cover Eloise's torso: her naked breasts protruded through two circular openings. The fit was tight, and Eloise's breasts were squeezed into firm spheres from which her nipples jutted proudly. Sewn into the hem of each round opening was a leather drawstring, by which means the openings could be drawn even tighter. The curvature of Eloise's back pushed her chest forward: her breasts could not have been rendered more prominent, more accessible, or more vulnerable.

'Congratulations,' I said to Stephanie. 'This costume could have been designed for what we have in mind.'

'I expect it was,' Stephanie replied carelessly. 'Celia's master seems to have thought of all the details. I knew you'd like it: I know how you like to operate.'

I ran my hands over the warm, distended globes, and toyed with the nipples. 'The idea, I take it, is to tighten the strings after the whipping, before using the cane?' My fingers pinched and twisted, and Eloise moaned.

'I assumed that's what you'd want me to do,' Stephanie said. 'Here are the things.'

I leant forward, kissed Eloise's nipples, and turned towards the table on which Stephanie had arranged a selection of implements. There were three whips, none of them heavy or capable of inflicting serious hurt. I picked up one with a single lash, which I ran through my fingers. I saw that it was made of several very thin strands of leather, plaited together so tightly that they seemed to make one thin, round, cord.

'Stephanie,' I said. 'Stand in front of Eloise and bend over, please.'

Stephanie has no sense of modesty, let alone shame, and is therefore about as submissive as a drill sergeant. However, she has an utterly depraved imagination and a craving for all kinds of sensation, and so happily acquiesces in whatever I demand of her, as long as there is the prospect of a sexual thrill.

Without hesitation she turned, leant forward, and presented her bare bottom to me and to Eloise. She had her legs parted and she tilted her hips upwards, partly, no doubt, in order to afford me a view of her shaven pudenda, but also, I'm sure, in the hope that the whip would reach those sensitive parts.

Tempting as the sight was, and despite the pulsing insistence of my upright member, I managed to remember that my priority was to punish Eloise, and I delivered just one hard stroke across Stephanie's buttocks.

She started, and a vivid line appeared at once on her tanned skin. She remained in her bending position.

'Too severe, I think,' I said. 'And the marks would be too similar to those of the cane. I'll try the whip with the double tongue.'

This was more suitable for use on Eloise's breasts. The single stroke I administered to Stephanie's bottom didn't leave any clearly defined lines, but produced two indistinct stripes that coloured prettily. However, I formed the impression that it would be difficult to ensure that both tongues landed with the same force, and so I replaced the second whip on the table and tried the third.

The lightest of the three, this had a relatively long handle and about half a dozen short thongs, like leather bootlaces. I took aim at the lower half of Stephanie's left buttock, lifted my arm, and struck.

I had found the instrument I wanted. Stephanie squeaked with surprise as the leather thongs, splayed out as they descended through the air, kissed the inward curve of her buttock.

'That's amazing,' she said. 'It stings a bit, but mainly it sort of tingles. And then it feels very warm.'

The effect was precisely that which I had hoped for. Moreover there were no marks at all: just a slow pinkening of the exact area on which the lashes had fallen. Stephanie would be able thoroughly to inflame Eloise's breasts and yet they would remain a blank canvas for the stripes I intended to have painted on them subsequently with the cane. The long handle and short lashes would enable Stephanie to aim the strokes with precision and to reach the sensitive undersides and inner slopes.

'This is the one,' I announced, and swung the whip again, a little further to the right, so that Stephanie was rewarded with a patch of stinging sensation that included the hairless sex lips she was so keen to exhibit.

Stephanie and Eloise had given me no choice of cane: on the table there was just one, a thin wooden ferule, circular in section, set into a handle. I picked it up and flicked it in the air: it was light, very flexible, and whistled sharply. I brought it down on Stephanie's right buttock, around which it curved. She gasped, and a thin streak appeared on the rounded flesh. I leant forward and touched the line of pale redness: the cane hadn't cut or bruised the skin, and the weal was hardly raised. This particular cane wouldn't be suitable for administering a memorable chastisement on the bottom, but it would be perfect for Stephanie to use on Eloise's smarting breasts. I looked from Stephanie's bottom to Eloise's bosom, and pictured Stephanie laying down a grid of stinging lines on those swollen globes as I thrust into Eloise's anus. My cock chafed against the inside of my trousers.

I thought of delaying Eloise's punishment and taking the time to tilt forward the framework to which she was bound, so that I could insert my erection into her mouth and bring myself to a climax. Stephanie could use the whip on her bottom at the same time. The idea was appealing and it would relieve the unrelenting sense of urgency that I felt because of the pressure in my loins. But I couldn't be sure that I would be ready to come again while Stephanie was caning Eloise's breasts, and I was determined to have her arsehole that evening.

So, having elicited a moan of disappointment from Stephanie by telling her she was to receive no more lashes, I contented myself with kissing Eloise's lips while I caressed her rounded, outthrust, starkly naked globes.

'So,' I whispered to her, 'it will be the whip first, and then when these lovely titties are sore and swollen we'll tighten the laces around them, and then they'll get the cane while I bugger you. I hope that's still what you want. It's too late to back out now.'

Eloise stretched her arms and moved, the little that she could, in her bonds. 'It's just what I want,' she said. 'Do it now, please. And please touch me all the time.'

I stepped back from her and indicated to Stephanie that she should proceed with the first part of the punishment. I stood to one side and watched the first few strokes: Eloise could move enough to toss her head each time the short strands of leather flicked on to one or other of her vulnerable orbs, and as I hadn't wanted to gag her she was able to gasp, groan and cry out. Her breasts jiggled delightfully, and began to take on a roseate hue, as Stephanie, with an expression of utmost seriousness on her face, plied the whip.

I tore myself away from the pleasing sight and wandered behind Eloise. Her legs and splayed buttocks, held open and pushed out by the crossbars of the frame, were an unmoving contrast to the writhing and dancing of her upper body. I saw at once that the whipping had done nothing to suppress her state of arousal: quite the contrary, in fact. Her outer labia were distended and widely parted, and from the quivering mouth of her vagina her juice was seeping so readily that I could see it trickling down the furrow of her vulva and forming droplets on her labia.

My erection was simply too stiff and upright to be contained any longer within my trousers. I undid the buttons and released it. The helmet was huge and inflamed, and slick with the clear fluid that had spread from its gaping slit.

I reached out and cupped the palm of my hand against Eloise's dripping sex. She let out a shuddering moan which

201

was cut short, and transformed into a breathy cry, as the whip descended again on to the peak of her right breast.

'Yes!' she shouted. 'Yes, touch me, please.'

I moved my hand back and forth between her thighs; I used her juice to anoint her anus; I stroked my fingertips across the smooth, stretched skin of her buttocks. Her moans were entirely of pleasure now, and I knew that unless I was niggardly with my caresses she would have an orgasm.

I didn't want her to come until well into the second part of her punishment, so I stepped back from her. Her body was so open, however, so inviting and so obviously ready to be used, that I could no longer resist starting to take my pleasure.

The two things I needed had been left within reach. The first was a prophylactic, which with shaking fingers I managed to open and roll down the thick, hard, straining, sensitive shaft of my penis. I always use a prophylactic when I penetrate a woman's anus. It's not just a matter of hygiene and disease prevention, although these are by no means unimportant. The thin rubber skin, with lubrication, makes it easier to skewer one's erection through the tiny, muscled orifice. And I find that, because an anus is so tight and a rectum is so warm and snug, it's useful to have around my penis a barrier which slightly lessens the sensations. Once I've chivvied and thrust myself inside I like to have time to enjoy the feelings, rather than come immediately, and the additional skin of thin rubber helps to prolong the pleasure.

I once again stood behind Eloise's rounded bottom. She was already in exactly the right position to be sodomised: I merely had to move forward and the blunt tip of my erection would nestle in the furrowed funnel of her arsehole. But I had to restrain myself a little longer, and so I lowered my body slightly so that when I thrust forwards my upstanding shaft slid in one swift motion into the sheath of Eloise's vagina.

Once again it was like entering a cavern of molten lava. I had entered Eloise several times already during that summer, but I had seldom known her to be so hot and open. She and I cried out in unison, and I'm sure that like me she almost came at that moment of sudden penetration. The interior of her vagina rippled against my cock.

I held myself still, with my stomach pressed against Eloise's buttocks, and gestured to Stephanie to stop whipping Eloise's breasts. Gradually my heartbeat slowed and I felt that I would be able to move my penis without risk of having an immediate orgasm. Experimentally I pulled back and thrust in again. My cock, drowning in waves of pleasure, twitched and yearned for release, but I was able to suppress to a simmer the bubbling cauldron in my balls. My groping hand reached for and grasped the nearby tub of lotion.

'I can't wait much longer,' I said to Stephanie. With an effort I kept my voice light and controlled. 'Feel her breasts. Are they ready?'

Eloise gasped again as Stephanie's cool hands explored her punished globes. 'They're very warm,' Stephanie reported. 'A good, even colour, all over. You chose the right whip. Nipples hard, and I should think quite sore.' Her voice was calm, but I could see in her face that she was excited.

'Tighten the laces,' I said. 'I want her breasts to be kept swollen and sensitive. I'm going to get her arsehole ready now, so be careful not to play with her too much: I don't want her to come yet.'

I scooped a dollop of the lotion from the tub and pulled my body back slightly so that I could see and reach the little scalloped ring between Eloise's parted buttocks.

During the preceding weeks I had become very familiar with all parts of Eloise's body. While it had been her trim, oval buttocks that had first attracted my attention and the various punishments that Eloise enjoyed experiencing at least as much as I enjoyed administering, I had promised myself the very first time that I spanked her that I would one day use her anus for my pleasure. It had around it only the finest, downy outskirts of Eloise's dark pubic hair, but the skin itself between her arse cheeks darkened and led the eye towards the little, perfect circle of brown, puckered skin.

I had made Eloise tell me every detail of every pleasurable experience to do with her arsehole that she had had. She had become very embarrassed and very excited when recounting her tales, but in fact there was little to tell: years ago a boyfriend had touched her there when they made love; more recently she sometimes touched her anus when masturbating. She admitted that she had never had her arse fucked: I insisted that she use those coarse terms. I told her that I would be prepared to fuck her arse if she asked me politely: she immediately begged me to do it.

Even now, though in my visits to my cottage during the past few weeks I had made sure to prepare her for being buggered, her anus looked small, virginal and vulnerable. I knew, through empirical experimentation, that it could accommodate one finger; then two fingers; then a small artificial phallus; then a larger one. Eloise confessed, shamefacedly, to enjoying each of these invasions of her most intimate orifice. I made sure that she had an orgasm, either at my hands or her own, every time we indulged in anal play: I wanted her to associate sexual pleasure with the feelings of the opening of her anal sphincter and the filling of her rectum.

Eloise had learnt the lesson well. As my fingers circled the crinkled well, spreading the lotion around the little hole and pressing into it, she began to mew like a kitten. My rigid cock, still half inside her, could feel the spasmodic contractions of her vagina.

'Isn't she lovely, though?' Stephanie exclaimed as she tugged on the laces that encircled Eloise's breasts. 'She's so close. She's almost there. I want to give her a big hug and a kiss.'

I had by now worked two fingers and a considerable amount of lotion into Eloise's anus. The ring of muscle was still tight around my digits, but I was able to move them in and out with increasing ease. Eloise's arsehole was as ready as it would ever be to lose its virginity.

'You've got to cane them, not kiss them,' I told Stephanie. I was abrupt with her: the strain of reining in

my exuberant lust was beginning to tell on me. 'Are they
tied up tightly?'

Stephanie's hands closed around Eloise's bound breasts.
She pushed her face into the space between Eloise's head
and raised left arm, and whispered to me. 'They're as hard
as bowling balls,' she said. 'I'll start caning them now.'

I heard Eloise whimper. I could only imagine the
concatenation of sensations and emotions that must have
been clamouring in her mind and body. Underlying
everything, no doubt, there must still have been a keen
anticipation: of having her anus fucked for the first time,
of her imminent orgasm, of the sharp sting of the cane on
her tender breasts. Then the sense of shame: at being so
blatantly displayed, at becoming aroused by such depraved
treatment, at helplessly exhibiting the lubriciousness and
uttering the wild cries caused by her arousal. There would
be the discomfort of being bound on the frame as a
constant reminder of her position. The sting of the whip on
her breasts would by now be no more than a memory, but
she would not be able to ignore the fact that her breasts
were sore, blazing hot and tightly tied, and these sensations
would merge with the throbbing insistence of the sexual
thrills that had built almost to the point of no return within
her.

I suppose I envied her the variety of her feelings. All of
mine were being rapidly obliterated by the urgent demands
of my erection for the release of an orgasm.

Stephanie stepped back from Eloise. The ferule was in
her hand.

Clenching my muscles in concentration I withdrew my
sheathed hardness from Eloise's vagina and immediately
pressed the tip into the anointed funnel of her anus. My
hardness throbbed and I bit my lip as I held back the rising
sperm.

Stephanie's arm was extended, and then swept in again.
The thin wooden rod whistled as it flew, but made hardly
any sound as it landed across Eloise's bound breasts.
Eloise cried out, however, and at that moment I pushed my
hips forward.

Preoccupied, no doubt, with the line of fire that the cane had inscribed on her breasts, Eloise put up little resistance at the rear. The hole was tight, but I had inserted into it the head and a little of the shaft of my penis before Eloise felt the intrusion, and uttered a hoarse shout of pain, and squeezed the sphincter like a lamprey's mouth around the unyielding hardness of my erection.

Her rectum was hot, and tight around the helmet of my cock. It was like pushing into an oven full of baking dough. I kept on pushing forwards, and thrust a little further in each time Eloise relaxed the grip of her anus – which was whenever the cane laid another stripe on her tender, distended breasts.

A feeling of triumph overwhelmed all my remaining restraint. I was about to come, and the thrusts of my hips became more and more urgent. I reached with my right hand below the curving crossbeam, and curled my fingers into the gaping wetness of Eloise's sex. Like a fire flaring into life when blown upon with bellows, Eloise's desire ignited immediately and she began to shudder violently as she was gripped by the tremors of her long-delayed orgasm. Her cries of pain and her shouts of protest at being penetrated were joined by shrieks of ecstasy, so that the dungeon echoed with her continuous wordless vocalisations. She bellowed and screamed.

The shuddering of Eloise's body, surrounding my confined erection with the most sensational vibrations, was the trigger that finally sent my seed shooting and sizzling up the length of my penis. I looked up, and saw that Stephanie had not ceased to wield the cane, but was now applying shorter, faster strokes. And then the seed came spurting out of me, and I closed my eyes to savour the brief moment.

Afterwards I staggered into the bathroom to dispose of the prophylactic, wash my penis, and splash cold water over my body. I returned to find Stephanie releasing Eloise from the frame, and I assisted her.

We spoke hardly at all. Eloise and I were exhausted: I kissed her and we mumbled tearful thanks to each other.

Stephanie knew better than to chatter in such circumstances: she helped Eloise to stretch her cramped limbs, and gave her a drink of water, and led her to the nearest bed. They lay down together, and Stephanie cradled Eloise in her arms.

I went to join them, but as I approached Stephanie said, 'Bring me the lotion, Michael. Eloise needs some soothing attention.'

When I returned with the tub I found the two women wrapped in each other's arms, kissing, and oblivious to my presence. I cleared my throat and left the lotion on the bed. Stephanie opened one eye to acknowledge that she was aware of me, but didn't remove her lips from Eloise's.

I retreated to a nearby chair and watched them for a while. The embrace was erotic, but my recent exertions prevented my limp member from so much as twitching in appreciation.

Having returned to the cottage to fetch my materials, I sat and sketched the scene as Stephanie smoothed lotion into Eloise's sore, striped breasts. I saw and heard Eloise come again, as Stephanie's lubricated fingers explored more of her body. Later they roused themselves to a mock-fight, and half-heartedly took turns to spank each other's bottom. Then Stephanie straddled Eloise's face, and let Eloise lick her until she, too, at last had an orgasm.

I was able to make sketches for what promised to be several interesting paintings.

From the diary of Anne Bright
12 July
Hurrah! At last! Today I was allowed to get my hands on Matt's lovely penis. And my lips and my tongue. It was heavenly.

It's lunchtime now, and I can't write very much because there's going to be another lesson this afternoon: Matt's going to teach me how to use my breasts to give him an orgasm. I can't wait. I want to feel that big, warm, solid hardness between my breasts, and watch him getting all excited. I've had something to eat, but there isn't much time because Simone's going to come up to my room in a minute. I think she was feeling left out this morning, and she wants to play with me on the bed before the afternoon lessons. So I'll write more later.

I had Matt's body all to myself. I undressed him, following Simone's instructions, and then I was allowed to touch him all over – except for his private parts, which were reserved for special attention at the end. He's got a scrumptious body: big and tanned and muscular, with little blond hairs on his chest and his thighs. I stroked his skin, and played with his nipples, and dug my fingers into his muscles until he yelped. Simone stopped making suggestions about what I should do next and just let me get on with it. I took my clothes off – it's still very warm, so I wasn't wearing much anyway – and lay down next to him and we kissed (proper kissing with tongues) while my hands went all over his chest and tummy. Then I started kissing his neck, and then his chest.

And that's when I saw that his penis had become erect.

I've seen men's erect penises before, of course: you can't really avoid them in the Private House, although I think my Mentors have tried to shield me from close encounters. But I've never seen one this close before. And this one belonged to the gorgeous Matt.

I suppose I shouldn't have been surprised at the size. I've read books about anatomy, even before my birthday, and since I've been here I've seen lots of pictures when I've been doing private studies in the library. I know all about the theory: the engorgement with blood, and the rigidity, and the expansion in size.

But all the same when I lifted my face from licking Matt's nipple and I saw how big his penis had grown, I must have looked quite comical. I froze, and said, 'Oh my goodness!'

And then I said, 'Can I touch it now, please?'

I wriggled down the bed and stared at it. An erect penis isn't a very pretty thing, what with all the veins and the angry red and purple colours, but it's impressive. The thought that this one was entirely for me to play with and become accustomed to – that I was about to touch it, and hold it – gave me even more of that familiar tingly feeling inside (which I was already feeling, just because of being naked with Matt and having done all that kissing with him).

'Touch the shaft first, Anne,' Matt said, 'not the head.'

It was warm and, although I had known it would be hard, the unyielding stiffness of it surprised me. It was like a heated rod of metal inside the softest covering.

'Kneel next to Matt,' Simone suggested, 'while you touch him. Remember that you must try to please him, too. And I'm sure he'd like to look at your intimate parts. So present yourself properly.'

Simone was right. I knelt alongside Matt, and when I leant forward to touch his penis I pushed my bottom out so that he could see my anus and my vulva. It felt much better to know that I was pleasing him while I was studying his erect member.

I put my fingers around the shaft: it was so thick I could only just close my fist round it. I squeezed, and heard Matt gasp.

'Very good,' he said. 'Now I'll explain how to touch the head – the smooth bulb at the top. It's very sensitive – almost as much as the tip of your clitoris, in places – so you must be very careful.'

Simone has arrived. I'll have to stop writing now. I learnt the names of all the parts of the penis, anyway, and how to touch them in order to give pleasure to Matt. And then I kissed all the bits, and then I licked them. Licking's best, Matt said, but he also told me that that's his personal opinion, and other men might prefer me to do other things – sucking hard, and even nibbling!

Matt's penis tastes delectable – musky and utterly male. I was quite happy kissing and licking him until he was ready to come, and when he did it was awesome. A fountain of creamy stuff, coming out of his upright

209

erection in big spurts. I licked some of it off his tummy: delicious! Creamy and salty – a bit like seafood soup.

Simone's getting impatient. I must just write that we did it again, with me kneeling between Matt's legs while Simone gave me my daily spanking. This time Matt came in my mouth – although not as much as the first time, which was a disappointment – and as Simone was playing with me while she spanked me I came too, with my mouth full of Matt's sperm, and some of it trickling down my chin. Heavenly!

Simone's given up trying to stop me writing. She's trying to distract me, instead. She's taken off her top and she's sitting on the bed, playing with her breasts. I'm afraid I can't resist her any longer. I'm glad that I like men, and their penises. But perhaps I still like women better. I'm not sure. I suppose I'll just have to do lots and lots of research.

THREE

From the diary of Anne Bright
9 August

Another memorable morning. Another big step on the way to becoming what Simone calls 'a complete sexual being'.

Ever since I started learning how to do sex with other people, as well as by myself, there has been one aspect of life in the Private House that has become more and more frustrating. Wherever I go – tiptoeing through the dungeons, or peering into the pleasure pavilions in the formal gardens, or even just strolling in the woods – I come across people who are obviously having a wonderful time tied up tightly in ropes, and chained to pillars, and rendered helpless in all sorts of exciting ways. For as long as I can remember my favourite daydreams have entailed being kidnapped or captured, and then being tied up so that I'm at the mercy of my implacable captors. I've tried and tried to persuade Matt and Simone to tie me up, but they've always said that I've got to wait, and that it's as important to learn patience and obedience as it is to learn about pleasure.

But today they decided it was time to teach me about bondage. And so, dear diary, I have had the most marvellous time.

Matt and Simone took me down to the dungeons. I've been there before, just to have a look at the place and, I must admit, to enjoy thinking about what it would be like to be kept a prisoner down there, at the beck and call of Mistress Julia's guards. They look so daunting in their shiny black leather tunics. I wander through the stone corridors, peering through the bars of the cells to see what punishments are being inflicted on the prisoners, and I imagine what it would be like to be chained up, naked of course, against one of the hard, rough walls, and to spend my days being fondled by the sinister-looking jailers, and to receive my daily spanking from Mistress Julia.

So, all in all, I became very excited when I realised that Matt and Simone were leading me down to the ground floor, and then even further down, into the vaults below the remains of the mediæval castle.

We had a cell to ourselves. It was bigger than most of the cells I'd peeked into: Simone said it was a slave training chamber, in fact. Still, its walls, floor and ceiling were of stone blocks, and it was lit by yellow lamps and flaming cressets that created a suitably Gothic atmosphere. The wall opposite the door was lined with cabinets, each of which was fronted with a long mirror in a carved frame. You wouldn't have known that above ground the sun was shining in a cloudless sky: down in the dungeon all was gloom and shadow (although, as Matt pointed out, there was underfloor heating to ward off the subterranean chill – there was, he said, a reasonable limit to the reproduction of mediaeval privations).

I immediately felt very much at home, even though I admit I was also a bit nervous. There's something intimidating about darkness, and being underground – particularly when you're in a room that's equipped with huge iron rings set into the walls, the floor and the ceiling, and whose heavy wooden furniture has straps and chains hanging off all over the place.

I wanted to try everything. I hadn't yet been spanked, and I hoped that I would be strapped down on the prisoner's cot for today's punishment. Just looking at the heavy leather fastenings made my insides feel all fluttery.

'Kneel on the bed, Anne,' Simone said, 'and take off your uniform.'

I suppose I must be very naughty, because I find that merely being told to undress is enough to make me wet, these days. Although today I was already excited. I love the little details of the ritual: removing the top with one precise movement, folding it and placing it beside me, posing with my hands behind my head for a moment, to present my breasts, before starting to undo my skirt, and so on. Matt and Simone watch me intently, in silence unless I do something wrong, and I get more and more excited as I slowly reveal the private parts of my body to their steady gaze. Of course, taking off my uniform is usually the prelude to a spanking, at the very least, so there's the thrill of anticipation, too.

'She's so pretty,' Matt said to Simone once I was naked and kneeling on the rough bed with my thighs parted and my hands behind my back. 'She looks so vulnerable. Don't worry, Anne,' he added, 'we're not going to hurt you.'

That, I thought, was rather rich from the man who ensured that I got a sore bottom at least once a day, but I knew better than to speak without invitation while I was presenting myself. Matt's become a bit soppy about me these days: I think it's ever since I became so practised at using my mouth to give him orgasms.

'We're not going to hurt you much,' Simone said, by way of correcting Matt. 'I'm sure you'd be disappointed if we didn't torment you a little bit.'

I smiled, and felt myself blushing. Simone seems to know exactly what I like.

She went to one of the cabinets, opened the mirrored door, and took out several bands of black leather. I recognised them: they were like the collars and cuffs that the slaves here wear.

Simone came to stand behind me. I leant forward a little, as I have been taught to do. She stroked my bottom for a moment, and then I felt her hands brushing my hair from my shoulders. She was putting the collar around my neck.

213

I shivered as the soft leather collar tightened. It was a symbolic moment. In the Private House collars are worn by those who choose to act as slaves, or those who have been disobedient and are to be punished. And, of course, sometimes, by people who, like me, are learning the ropes (ha ha!). As Simone buckled the collar so that it fitted snugly, I became a slave.

'Thank you, miss,' I whispered.

Simone landed a stinging slap on my right buttock. 'Don't speak unless you're invited to,' she said sharply. We were both, it was clear, aware of our new roles.

Stout leather cuffs were fastened around my ankles and wrists. Like the collar, each of the cuffs had four metal rings, set into the leather equidistantly around the circumference. I knew from the expression on Matt's face that I looked pretty; nonetheless I felt small and defenceless.

'We'll put you in chains this morning, Anne,' Matt said. 'And this afternoon we'll introduce you to rope bondage. You'll pick up the basic principles today, and then in subsequent lessons we'll add new techniques, and you'll have a chance to wear constrictive clothing. Simone is sure that you're going to enjoy playing the part of our victim. I hope you do, but try to concentrate on the details of what we do to you, and bear in mind that you're supposed to be learning how to act as dominant or submissive. Is that understood?'

I nodded. 'Yes, sir,' I said happily.

'Good,' he said. 'Come and stand in the centre of the room.'

I stepped from the bed and went to where Matt was running a chain through one of the iron rings that were bolted to the ceiling.

'Hands together, in front,' he said, and when I obeyed he passed the chain through rings on my wrist cuffs. When he pulled on the chain my wrists were lifted above my head, and with a final heave he had me standing on my toes with my arms stretched up towards the ceiling.

I teetered on my toes as I tried to keep my balance. Once I felt reasonably secure I looked at Matt. He was holding the ends of the chain in his fist, and looking beyond me. I turned carefully, and saw Simone taking off her red blouse and skirt. Dressed only in scarlet high-heeled boots she came to stand in front of me. As I was standing on tiptoe we were almost exactly the same height.

She stared into my eyes until I had to look away. She studied my body. A worryingly cruel smile was lurking on her lips.

'We're both naked,' she said. 'And being naked makes one feel ashamed and vulnerable. But when one of us is chained – just one simple chain – everything changes. I'm in charge, Anne. I'm powerful. And what about you? How do you feel?'

'Vulnerable, miss. Helpless. Afraid.' It was what she wanted me to say, and in any case it was true.

'That's right, slave,' she said, and started to stroke my breasts with her right hand. 'Very, very vulnerable.'

I realised that I was powerless to prevent her inflicting any torture that she wanted to on my defenceless breasts. The very thought made them feel super-sensitive. As her caresses became rougher, and she started to slap my nipples with her fingers, I felt a jolt of pleasure arc from my breasts to my loins. I hadn't realised how aroused I had become. Each slap set off a tremor inside me.

I had closed my eyes the better to enjoy the sensations. Simone's hands left my breasts, and when I looked for her she had gone. Then I felt her hands at my ankles, and I looked down to see her using a spring clip to fasten together my ankle cuffs.

She stood back to look at me. I could no longer move my feet: with my arms stretched above my head the only movement I could make was to sway from side to side. The muscles in my shoulders and calves were beginning to ache.

'Very attractive,' Simone said as she turned away. I found myself twisting, and could do nothing to stop the movement. The room circled in front of me. When

215

Simone came into view again she was carrying a thin cane.

'Don't worry, Anne,' she said. 'I'm not going to give you your eighteen smacks with this. I'm saving your spanking for later. But I thought you should be made to appreciate what it feels like to be punished while in chains. Your inability to avoid the strokes will, you'll find, add a whole extra dimension to the experience.'

I was swaying away from her again. I heard the cane hiss through the air, and jumped when a line of fire ignited across my bottom.

But I didn't jump. I tried to, but my body hardly moved. All that happened was that I almost lost my balance, and for a split second I was taking all my weight on my arms as my toes strained to reach the floor. I quite forgot about the cane – and then the second stroke lashed across my bottom.

This time I succeeded in restricting my reaction to an undignified wriggle and a cry of 'Ouch!' I'm used to being punished with my legs apart, and as I squeezed my thighs together – about the only movement I could make with my legs – I felt again how hot and wet my vulva was. Now, I don't want to cover up my bottom while I'm being smacked, of course – what would be the point of that? – but the knowledge that there was nothing I could do to protect myself from the strokes of Simone's cane made my bottom feel extra exposed and extra sensitive. I was beginning to understand the strange pleasures involved in being tied up for punishment. It was even better than my daydreams.

I stopped trying to prevent myself pivoting slowly as I hung from the chains. Instead I did my best to curve my back inwards and push my bottom out so that it made an attractive target for Simone. I waited for the next stroke of the cane.

But Simone said, 'That's enough, I think, to give you the idea. Now we'll try something else.'

Matt allowed a length of the chain to rattle through the iron ring, and suddenly the tension in my shoulders eased. I was able to stand properly again, although my ankles were still held together and I could lower my wrists only enough to rest them on the top of my head.

I caught Matt's eye. He winked at me and blew me a kiss. I was gratified to see that the bulge in the front of his shorts was so pronounced that I could easily discern the contours of his confined erection. I'm afraid I couldn't resist opening my mouth and running the tip of my tongue around my lips in what I hoped was a blatant hint of fellatio. I know it was rude, but I was getting very aroused and I so wanted to feel his penis in my mouth again.

Simone had made another visit to the cabinet, and this time she had brought back two long rods of polished metal, each with several rings set near both ends. With one of the rods in her hands she knelt behind me and unfastened my ankles. 'Legs wide apart,' she said, and I immediately obeyed.

The purpose of the rod soon became clear, as Simone clipped one of my ankle cuffs to one end of it, and then slapped the insides of my thighs to make me spread my legs still wider, until she could clip the cuff on my other ankle to the other end of the rod. I couldn't move my legs together at all. I didn't even dare to try to shuffle my feet or turn my body, for fear of falling over.

I felt her lips on my bottom. She was kissing along the lines she had made with the cane. 'Now you're even more exposed and helpless,' she said. I shivered, and felt my labia unfurling. To prove just how helpless I was Simone slapped her fingers up against my open sex, and then stroked me there while she resumed kissing my bottom. I could do nothing to evade her caresses but, luckily, I didn't want to. I pushed my bottom back, and Simone rewarded me with a kiss and a lick on my anus, which made me shiver again. She's a very naughty person.

Once again, however, she stopped before I could even begin to think about surrendering to an orgasm. I uttered an 'Ooh!' of disappointment when she stood up.

Matt laughed as he let the rest of the chain run through the iron ring.

I waited patiently while Simone brought the second rod. I had no alternative: my feet were secured far apart, and my wrists were still clipped together.

Simone passed the rod to Matt, who was behind me. I felt him place the cold metal cylinder horizontally across my back. Simone, in front of me, unfastened my wrist cuffs. She lifted my hands to her lips and kissed the palms, very gently, and then pushed my arms wide apart.

'Tuck your arms under the rod,' she said. 'Hold it tightly in the crook of your elbows.'

I did so, and as the pressure of my arms against the rod pushed out my chest I at once understood the purpose of this second rod. It obliged me to present my breasts, just as the first one held open my sex and my buttocks.

Matt busied himself once again with the chains. He ran one through the ring at the back of my collar, and clipped the two tails to rings at the ends of the rod. Simone, meanwhile, attached a short length of chain to each end of the rod and then clipped the other ends of the chains to my wrist cuffs.

They stood back to admire their work. I tried to move. I could turn my head; I could twist my body from side to side, with care; I could bend forward, but only at the risk of overbalancing. And that was all. My breasts felt like two cones of sensitivity thrust out in front of me, and the damp membranes of my vulva felt every little draught of air in the room.

'Should we chain the two rods together?' Simone asked Matt. 'If we pull them together a bit we can keep her bent over. You know how she likes to show off her bottom.'

'I don't know,' Matt replied from behind me. 'It would make it more difficult for her to keep her balance. And she looks very good as she is.'

Simone laughed. 'You're too soft on her. But all right. Now: you do her bottom, and I'll play with her tits.'

And that's what they did. Perhaps because he didn't like being accused of being soft on me, Matt used his strong hands all over my bottom to squeeze and smack. He kept on brushing closer and closer to my anus, and then pushing against it, until I was desperate to feel his fingers inside me.

Simone was no more gentle: she squeezed my breasts and pinched my nipples. Before long I was writhing and squirming, and could not have been more aware of my inability to protect myself or avoid the marauding hands. I was continually conscious of the rods and chains that held me available for my Mentors to treat me as they wished.

I know I've written this before, about other things I've learnt here, but it's true all over again: I don't think I have ever experienced such a fantastic feeling. The shocks of pleasure in my body were like an endless firework display.

I began to make moaning noises, and then Simone let go of my nipples and instead pressed her breasts against mine as she stopped my mouth with kisses. Matt's fingers abandoned my anus, and he started to give my bottom gentle smacks. For a little while the only sounds in the slave training room were the sighing breaths that Simone and I exchanged as we kissed, and the slap of Matt's hand against my buttocks. Chained up, and sandwiched between my adorable Mentors, I felt myself relax as my imminent orgasm began to recede. It was one of those glorious moments that you know you'll remember for the rest of your life.

'We'll do one more position before lunch,' Simone announced at last. She and Matt began to unfasten my wrists and ankles from the metal rods.

'Are you happy to be chained up again, Anne?' Matt asked.

Honestly, he can be so silly sometimes. 'Of course, sir,' I said. Was he mad? The way I was feeling I wanted to spend the whole day in chains, as long as he and Simone were there to play with me.

219

'Would you like to have your spanking, too?' Simone said, running her hand across my bottom. 'I thought I'd use the cane today.'

This was getting better and better. 'Yes, please, miss,' I said. 'And, miss, will I be allowed to have an orgasm? I do so want one.'

Simone's fingers slipped down from my buttocks and into the wet heat of my sex. 'You're incorrigible,' she said, and pinched my labia until I squirmed. 'We'll see. Yes, all right then, if you behave yourself. Is there anything else you'd like?'

She was teasing me. I love her so much. I turned my head and kissed her lips. 'You know what I like, miss.' I widened my eyes and fluttered my lashes and looked as innocent as I could. 'I like you to punish me, miss, and I like Matt's penis. I want him to come in my mouth while you're caning my bottom.'

Simone smiled, and we held each other's gaze for a moment. Then we both looked at Matt.

'Is that all right with you?' Simone asked him.

Matt looked taken aback. 'Well, yes,' he said. 'But, Anne, you'll be chained up again, you know. You won't be able to move. Are you sure you want –'

'Yes,' I said. I was determined to shock him. 'I just love the taste and the smell and the feel of your big hard cock in my mouth. All you'll have to do is go in and out until you're ready, and then fill my mouth with lots and lots of your lovely sperm.' He seemed to need me to spell it out for him in monosyllabic words.

I looked from his face to his groin and then back to his face. His erection was threatening to burst from the front of his shorts. There was no doubt that, however much he voiced his hesitation, his manhood liked the idea.

It suddenly occurred to me that Simone would be rather left out of the fun. 'What about you?' I whispered to her as she arranged me in a kneeling position on the cot.

'Siesta,' she murmured in reply.

I sighed happily. I knew what she had in mind. She and I have developed this sort of secret code, because sometimes we do things without Matt. Today, I knew, she will come to my room and we will spend an hour or so in bed before the afternoon lessons. I'm writing this as I wait for her to arrive – and I'm obviously getting excited at the thought, because my handwriting's gone all wobbly. I expect she'll kiss my bottom better (it's still smarting), and I'll use my fingers and my tongue to make her come. I'm getting very good at it.

Oh dear. Simone and I are so in love. And we can't tell anyone. It's against the rules, I think, for a Mentor and a student to become involved. But she kisses me so tenderly, even when she's doing terrible and cruel things with her fingers. I like siesta with Simone even more than I like doing fellatio for Matt.

Soon, because we were all three impatient, my ankle cuffs were secured to the sides of the bed, so that my legs were kept wide apart. I was bent forward, resting on my elbows and forearms. My wrist cuffs, and a short chain running from the ring at the front of my collar, were clipped to the top end of the bedstead. A wide leather belt was buckled across the small of my back, to keep my spine curved downward and my bottom well rounded. I could move my head a bit, and wiggle my hips, but apart from that I was immobilised.

Matt and Simone stood at the head of the bed and looked at me. I couldn't lift my head enough to see their faces: instead I was able to see Simone's hands flexing the slender cane, and Matt's impressive erection springing free as he pulled down his shorts.

They were ready to begin. And so was I!

Of course, I'm already quite used to having Matt's penis in my mouth while Simone spanks me. All three of us enjoy it, and these days when it's time for my punishment we tend to gravitate to the necessary positions, unless there is something else specific that Matt and Simone want to teach me. Until today I thought that nothing really could improve on lying between my Mentors and suckling Matt's velvety hardness while having my bottom heated by my beloved Simone – but now I know I was wrong.

It's even better when I'm chained up and can't move.

Simone started the caning very gently, for her. I've had the cane a few times now, and Simone can really make it sting. But today, from the very first stroke, I knew I was about to experience something special.

The thing is, it's impossible not to be aware of the chains. Even when I'm being very good, and keeping completely still while I'm being punished, I do move a little bit: involuntary starts and wriggles that I'm not even conscious of doing. But when I'm chained up, every little attempted movement reminds me that movement is impossible. My poor little bottom can't avoid the swishing cane: it can't react in any way to the sudden, stinging lines. It just has to stay there, fixed in position, bent over and wide open to the onslaught. I can vouch for the fact that being chained up makes a caning a much more intense experience.

So I was already gasping and mewling, and getting so wet between my thighs that Simone could see the drops forming (and of course she just had to mention it), and generally making an exhibition of myself – and I felt the musky warmth of the head of Matt's penis against my lips, and I opened my mouth to accept him.

I was grateful for the distraction: I had started to become lost in the intense sensations that Simone was generating with her increasingly wicked strokes of the cane. And with my mouth full of Matt's penis I couldn't make any more of the silly little cries and groans I utter when I'm being spanked and getting very excited.

When it's erect Matt's penis fits perfectly into my mouth. When he pushes in my lips encircle the shaft, and the smooth bulb goes snugly between my palate and my tongue; when he pulls back I tighten my lips around the rim of the glans, and lick round the tip and into the little hole.

I like the way that after a while Matt can't really control himself any more, and goes in and out faster and faster. I realised that because I was chained up I wouldn't be able to pull my head back, as I usually do from time to time, to give him opportunities to cool off: I was looking forward to finding out what it would be like to be completely at his mercy. But he was being very considerate, and maintained a steady to and fro which was very pleasant but a bit frustrating.

And, as Simone was clearly not going to stop at eighteen strokes but intended to continue caning my bottom until Matt was ready to come, I knew I was in for a long session of punishment. It's just as well that I like having a sore bottom!

So I had plenty of time to give the end of Matt's penis a very thorough licking while I endured a chastisement that I think is probably the most severe I've had yet. I tried to imagine what Simone must have been looking at: my buttocks getting redder and redder as the marks of the cane overlaid each other, and my sex getting wetter and wetter. The heat all over my bottom was so intense that it must have been glowing like hot embers; I gave myself up to the burning pain, and felt my body ripping with tremors of pleasure. If Matt didn't come soon, I'd have an orgasm before he did.

At last I detected an acceleration in the pace of his thrusts, and heard him begin to pant and gasp. Simone, too, realised that he was becoming more excited, and she began to use the cane more quickly but with gentler smacks – which made me even more excited!

Matt abandoned his resolution to be careful, and began plunging his erection into my mouth with hard thrusts. At last he was using my mouth entirely for his own pleasure. Simone stopped caning me, and I felt her fingers pushing into my sex. I gasped and choked and snorted. I was so close.

I could feel the throbbing in Matt's shaft that I knew meant he was on the verge of releasing his sperm. I waited, trembling, and straining against my bonds, for the first jet of his delicious seed to splash against the back of my throat.

And then Simone's fingers, wet with my juice, slid up to my anus, and pushed inside, and flexed and twisted, and my pent-up orgasm flared inside me. As the waves of pleasure rolled over me I thrust my head forward, again and again, to take all of Matt's tender hardness into my mouth. The base of the shaft vibrated against my tongue, and my throat was suddenly flooded with his salty seed. My own orgasm was so overwhelming that his jets of sperm were met by my cries of joy. I couldn't swallow, and his cream spilled out of my lips around his shaft and dripped from my chin.

And that, dear diary, was what I learned this morning.

When I look back at my life with Eloise in the cottage, I realise what a childish brat I was. I've learned so much in the last few weeks: how to be obedient, how to behave properly, and above all how to have the most fun it's possible to have. It's so good to be grown-up. From now on I'll know how to have just as many spankings and orgasms as I want – and that means lots. I think Mummy would have been proud of me.

The only trouble is, I've started to think about having to leave here at the end of the summer. I think I've got over my infatuation with Matt now: I mean, I still like taking his penis in my mouth, and I still think he's gorgeous, but I'm sure that there are lots of other gorgeous men in the world who will let me lick their erections. I'll miss Simone though, with her lithe brown body and her mischievous grin and her cruel hands.

From the notebooks of Celia Bright

A slave becomes very sensitive to her master's moods. D is usually so controlled, so careful, so even-tempered. Even when I've been disobedient or careless, and he has to punish me more severely than he likes to for his own enjoyment, he remains calm and good-humoured.

Therefore I knew, when I detected a change in him, that I was not imaging it. I had noticed for several weeks that he seemed tired: he still liked to watch me display myself for him, and masturbate under his instruction, but he seldom took an active part himself. When he delegated to Thomas the task of keeping my buttocks marked with the whip, I became convinced that something was wrong.

With a self-regard that would have earned me a severe chastisement had D discovered it, I assumed that D was losing interest in me. I am thoroughly ashamed of my egotism. I thought that I must be failing him in some way: that I wasn't devoted enough to him, that I was losing my looks, that I was becoming dull.

Last night I could stand it no longer. During dinner, which was served even earlier than of recent times, it had obviously been an effort for him to maintain even a desultory conversation with me. I was wearing a new corset, in white, which was painfully tight, and I was sure I looked more than usually alluring; his only acknowledgement of my costume was a weary smile. By the time we retired to the study my heart was pattering in my breast and my eyes were prickling with tears. I had convinced myself that he was tired of me. Words cannot express the dread and misery that I felt. I thought – how stupidly wrong of me – that no pain could be worse.

'Kneel by the fire, Celia,' D said to me, as he lowered himself stiffly into his chair. 'Let me see you in the firelight.'

I knelt, turned slightly towards the glowing logs, on the rug, so that D was able to see my bottom. I waited, with my head lowered, for his instructions.

I waited until my forehead and the tips of my breasts were reddened and glowing in the firelight.

At length I dared to turn my head, and I looked over my shoulder. D wasn't even looking at me: he was staring into the dark corner of the room with his head resting on his hand and no expression on his face.

I threw myself at full length on the floor and kissed his feet. I begged him not to leave me or to set me free; I pleaded with him to punish me as severely as he could so that he could be in no doubt about my devotion to

225

him; I urged him to tell me in what ways I had displeased him. I doubt whether he understood more than one word in ten, as I was incoherent with emotion and weeping floods of tears.

By saying my name over and over, and stroking my hair, he managed to calm me. He guided me on to his lap: I think it occurred to me then that once he would have plucked me from the floor and lifted me in his arms as if I weighed no more than a child.

He told me I was perfect; that he wanted no other woman, slave or free; that I was the only light in the gathering darkness.

I didn't understand everything he said, but I could not doubt his sincerity. It is hard now for me to credit my own selfishness, but I was reassured and happy. When he admitted that he hadn't been attentive enough, I teased him, and agreed with him.

'It's my fault,' he said, stroking my breasts with fingers that seemed to me to be trembling with excitement. 'I've made you accustomed to service and discipline, and now I'm not using you or punishing you enough. I must do better.'

I could only agree. 'It's been ten days since you last used my anus, master,' I chided him. 'And even longer since you took me out with the pony cart. Thomas whips me every other day, but it isn't the same as being whipped by you.'

He seemed to be emerging from his black mood. He even laughed, briefly. 'I will make it up to you when I can, Celia,' he said. 'I am, indeed, very preoccupied at the moment. But that doesn't mean that I have any right to ignore your needs and desires in the meantime.'

I understood him to mean that for a temporary period he would have to continue to neglect me, and that he would therefore make arrangements for me to be used and punished in other ways. I knew better than to ask for information about what was to be done to me.

'It's been too long since we had a party,' he said. 'You need to be attended to urgently, Celia. I'll see who is free

226

to come here tonight. I should think that quite a few will rearrange their engagements once they know that you are available. Would you like me to do that?'

D proposed to give me to whichever of his friends were free to come and use me. I knew from experience that several of them were cruel and that I could be sure of an exhausting evening. The prospect made me shiver with desire.

'I want you,' I said, even though it is not a slave's place to express her own wishes. 'I'm happy to serve your friends, but will you be there, too, master?'

'I'll be there,' he said.

'Then I'll be content.'

An hour or so later the first guests began to arrive. I was waiting for them in the playroom. I was kneeling in the centre of the room. I was wearing nothing but my slave collar and a blindfold. Even the rings through my pierced nipples and labia had been removed.

I heard people enter the room; I heard murmured conversation, and footsteps. I gained the impression that as time went by there were more people present, and that they were gathering around me. Occasionally I would start as a hand touched me.

Everyone was talking in whispers so that I couldn't overhear their conversations. I was sure they were discussing me. I heard brief phrases: '. . . or whip her first . . .'; '. . . only her mouth and her arsehole . . .'; '. . . the leather one . . .'; '. . . the hood, now . . .'

Blinded by the velvet band across my eyes, I imagined them appraising me body as they planned how they intended to use me. I felt my breasts tingling with anticipation, and my labia parting and becoming moist.

Suddenly my arms were grasped and I was bent forwards. The blindfold was unwound from my head, but I was given no chance to look about me as a tightly fitting helmet was pushed on to my head. I did my best to keep still as the rubber garment was tugged into position and made secure.

It was a helmet I hadn't worn before. It covered my eyes and my ears, and was tied tightly at the back of my

227

head. My hair, gathered into a tail, escaped through a hole in the top. It obscured my vision more completely than the blindfold, and also prevented me from hearing. I formed the impression that the people around me were talking loudly now, but to me they sounded like a crowd murmuring in a distant room. The hands that had been holding me released me, and I resumed my kneeling position.

I heard a voice, perhaps a little louder than the others. It seemed to have a questioning tone, but I could detect no specific words. Then I became aware of someone close at my side. I felt a pressure on the helmet over my left ear.

Suddenly I could hear a voice as clearly as if my ears were uncovered. It was D's. 'Can you hear me now, slave?' he said.

I nodded. 'Yes, master,' I said.

'Very good,' D said. 'I have told my guests that you are theirs for the evening. They will do as they wish, for as long as they wish to. You must do your best to please them, and you will obey every instruction you are given, by me or by any of the others. Do you understand?'

'Yes, master,' I repeated. The pressure on the side of my head ceased, and I was once again deaf and blind.

I have no idea how many of them there were. Perhaps half a dozen. Enough, certainly, to ensure that there were only brief interludes when there wasn't an erection pushing between my lips or into my anus; enough to ensure that whenever I was being penetrated I was also being smacked.

But first of all I was whipped. I felt a leash being clipped to my collar, and I was led away on all fours. As I followed the tugging of the leash those walking behind me started to chastise my bottom. I have become familiar with the different types of searing and stinging caused by the application of different instruments, and I knew that the strokes landing on my left buttock were those of a cane, while those on my right were from a leather strap.

I was grateful for the helmet that encased my head. There were going to be no visual or auditory distractions: I would be able to experience nothing but the rigours of the punishments, the teasings and penetrations of the most sensitive parts of my body, and the taste of the sperm and the sex-juice that would be released on my face and in my mouth. I would know nothing of the people who were using me, but I would be continuously reminded that I was being used. As the first strokes burned unheralded lines of fire across my buttocks, I felt the knot of tension in my stomach untie itself, and I became calmer even as my sexual arousal increased. I hollowed my back and began to sway my hips from side to side, in order to present a more attractive target. D had instructed me to please his guests, and I was very, very content to do so.

I was brought to my feet. My wrists were tied together and pulled above my head. I felt pressure at the side of my head. 'Dance, slave,' a voice said in my ear.

I pranced, pirouetted and shimmied as the whipping of my bottom continued. There are a couple of D's friends whose chief delight is to watch me dance while I'm being whipped: when they come to D's parties they bring recorded music for me to perform to. Without music I had to create my own rhythms, and I found it very stimulating to base my dance moves on the irregular fall of the cane and strap on my buttocks. I hope I looked pretty as I danced. My bottom was ablaze, and as ever when I'm being punished on my bottom I began to feel a yearning need for something to fill my rectum.

The whipping stopped. I assumed that each guest had by now had at least one turn. I hadn't been given any more instructions, however, and I knew better than to do anything other than to continue to dance. I was, in any case, lost in reverie: my bottom and my loins were throbbing with heat and arousal, and the lips of my sex felt hot and heavy between my thighs. As I gyrated my hips and pressed together my legs I began to feel the first tremors of an orgasm.

I felt a hand on my shoulder, and then others grasping my breasts. 'Stop,' said a voice in my ear.

My legs were parted and my ankles were tied down. Fingers and thumbs closed around my nipples, and created a sweet tension in my breasts as they pulled me forwards. My breasts were stretched into cones of exquisite sensation as I bent forward as far as my bonds would allow. The fingers continued to squeeze my nipples as the whipping of my bottom resumed. This time only the strap was used, as first on my buttocks and then upwards between my parted thighs.

I don't know whether it was being enclosed in the helmet or the relief of knowing that D still wanted me, but for some reason I was in the mood to be severely punished. Sometimes it takes a while for me to accept and enjoy a whipping on my private parts: the pain is atrocious, of course, and until I become accustomed to it I sometimes feel as though my insides want to curl up. This time, however, I responded immediately, and I angled my bottom up to meet the strokes; the pressure on my nipples pulsed in time with the gasps and cries I uttered as the strap struck my open wetness.

The whipping was interrupted briefly while a gag was placed in my mouth; when it resumed the only expression I could give to the climax that was building inside me was a murmur of moaning and stifled gasps.

I didn't come, however, as the whipping stopped before I had quite reached the point. My nipples were released, and for a few moments I stood in my bonds, oblivious to everything about me as I tried to re-order my excited nerves and senses.

My wrists were untied, only to be secured again behind my back. They were pinioned at wrist and elbow to a fixed horizontal pole which pressed into my back so that my chest was pushed out. My ankles were freed and were immediately tied once more, so that my legs were kept apart. I got the impression that I was now attached to a framework or structure, although I couldn't be sure. Hands touched my breasts, my but-

230

tocks and my sex. I felt fingers at my lips, and when I opened my mouth the fingers pushed inside. They were wet and sticky and tasted strongly of sharp musk: I realised I had been given a taste of my own sex-juice, which I was producing so prolifically that I could feel it trickling down the insides of my thighs.

The hands at my breasts became more insistent: they squeezed and pulled the flesh. I felt the familiar ticklish roughness of cotton cord: someone was tying up my breasts, constricting them into balls of sensitivity. They began to throb with heat. I felt a wide strap being cinched around my waist, pulling me tightly against a beam that must have been a little lower than the one to which my arms were tied, and I sensed that I was being prepared for another chastisement.

Sometimes D likes to bind my breasts before he canes them, and I steeled myself for the expected streak of fire. Instead, I felt fingers holding the distended orb of my right breast – and then a single, sharp point of agonising intensity at the edge of my nipple.

As my senses righted themselves and I controlled my frantic gasps for breath I knew that I recognised the sensation – just as a second point of searing pain burrowed into the nerves of my other nipple.

D's guests were decorating my breasts with pins. D had done this to me twice before. On those occasions I had been cradled in his arms, and he had murmured reassuring nonsense to calm me as he heated the pointed ends of the pins in the flame of a gas burner, to disinfect them and make them more painful, and then pressed the points, one at a time, under the surface of the skin of my breasts. When D had put pins in my breasts he cuddled and comforted me; he used only a few pins, and he pressed them gently so that only the tips pierced my skin; and I cried out and sobbed and, in the end, had orgasms that racked my body. The pins had round glass heads of different colours, and looked attractive placed above and below the areolas of my breasts.

D's guests were less considerate of my comfort. Their aim was to decorate my breasts more thoroughly than

D ever had, and in the process to make me suffer for their enjoyment.

Unable to see or hear, I had no warning of where or when the next needle-sharp, burning point would touch and pierce me. Gagged, I did not even have the satisfaction of being able to release the shock of each new pain as a scream. Securely bound, I could not move, or react, or do anything to protect my outthrust, rounded breasts. I could do nothing but surrender my flesh and my shrieking nerves to their ordeal.

At first I clenched every muscle in my body each time my tender skin was pierced, so that I thought I might break the frame against which I was bound. Later, as I grew to anticipate the pain, I merely shuddered and groaned each time a new pin was pressed into the nubbly skin of my nipples. My tormentors must have interpreted my juddering moans as evidence of sexual arousal – and they were not mistaken. I was climbing towards an intense orgasm.

Through the jagged darts of pain and pleasure that were crossing between my breasts and my sex I was dimly aware that someone was standing behind me. I felt the material of a man's jacket press against the backs of my pinioned arms, and then the unmistakable touch of a penis – hot and hard – nudging between my buttocks. At last my arse was going to be fucked.

The bulb of the erection slid through the wetness at the entrance of my vagina, and despite the gag I released a loud whinny of sheer delight. The penis, which had seemed so hot a moment before, felt cool against the furnace heat of my sex.

No more pins were pressed into my breasts. As I fought to control the waves of pleasure that were coursing through my body I pictured my breasts, constricted into tight spheres, with the nipples surrounded by concentric circles of coloured pin-heads. Although it was only the epidermis that had been pierced I felt the throbbing deep within my swollen globes, and as pulses of energy as if I had a rigid conductor from my breasts to my sex.

232

I struggled in my bonds to push my bottom back to accept the probing hardness which was now thoroughly lubricated with my juice. The head was at my anus now, pressing against the ring of muscle.

Then my breasts were ablaze again, with sudden sharp stabs of pain. The cords around the orbs were loosened, and then the pins were being extracted, quickly and without finesse. I screamed through the gag, and my anus opened to receive the hard shaft. As my rectum was filled and stretched I came, releasing a long, drawn-out wail of ecstasy. My breasts flamed; the stiff penis thrust ever more deeply into me; I writhed and shuddered in the throes of a climax that seemed as if it would never end.

When the penis and the last of the pins had been pulled out of me, my breasts, vulva and anus were anointed with soothing lotion. I came again. I was untied, and allowed to sit on the floor. The gag was removed from my mouth. I felt the rim of a glass touch my lips, and I opened my mouth to receive a drink of water. I rested for a while, and no one touched me. The helmet was not removed from my head.

I felt a tug on the leash attached to my collar. I knelt, and then presented myself on all fours. I was led a few steps to a low couch, which I climbed on to. I presented myself again. Hands held my buttocks apart while my anus was whipped with a narrow strap; during the whipping an erect penis entered my mouth, and I licked it in time to the smacks of the strap until it spurted sperm into my throat. At that point the whipping stopped, and a lubricated phallus was pushed into my anus. Gentle fingers caressed my sex, and I came for the third time.

Each orgasm seemed easier than the last. It was as if my body was turning into a vessel of pure pleasure.

I was turned on to my back and my ankles and knees were secured so that my legs were held apart and folded back until they were almost touching my breasts. My wrists were tied at my sides. I sensed a mass looming over my head, and then my face was engulfed by the warm, sweet wetness of a woman's sex. I kissed and licked, while something was done around my clitoris to create an excruciating stinging. As the woman began to tremble with an orgasm, a vibrating phallus was pushed slowly into my vagina. I came, gasping into the woman's sex, and then, as the phallus was left inside me, I came again.

The phallus stopped vibrating but remained inside me. A harness was fitted around my waist and tightly between my legs to keep the phallus in place. My limbs were untied, and I was allowed a few moments' rest.

I lost count of how many times my mouth and anus were penetrated, and how many times I climbed up to and flew from the clifftop of orgasm. I was caned on my breasts while a man used my arsehole, and on my bottom while a woman used my mouth. The phallus in my vagina vibrated from time to time, in short bursts that kept me on the brink of arousal or for long periods during which I thrashed my limbs and cried out with series of climaxes.

At last I was too weak to obey commands, and D's guests took turns spanking my bottom. This, it turned out, was their farewell to me. Half asleep, I was only dimly aware of being picked up and carried into a darkened room. The helmet was removed. Someone kissed my eyelids and lips. I slept.

When I awoke I lay still for a while, piecing together my memories of the previous evening. I didn't want to lose a single recollection. The taste of sperm still filled my mouth; my breasts, buttocks, anus and sex felt sore, but not as much as I had expected.

I was in one of the guest suites. As I bathed I inspected my body: the pins had left hardly any traces around my nipples; my bottom was criss-crossed with welts and lines, but hardly any more so than after a standard punishment. I should have felt stiff, I thought, and weary. Instead I was rejuvenated. Naked, and glowing from the bath, I set off to find D.

He was in the study. The curtains were still drawn across the windows, and I didn't see him at first. Only his hand was visible, curled in the circle light cast by the lamp on the desk.

When my eyes had grown accustomed to the gloom I saw that he was wearing the suit he had had on the previous evening. He hadn't been to bed. He had, however, retrieved the morning post. Unopened envelopes were strewn across the desk. He had opened just one letter: he was holding it crumpled in his outstretched hand.

Refusing still to understand I saw that his shoulders were moving. Then I heard his sobbing; his long, hopeless cries of despair. At last I knew.

In the middle of August I found myself once again taking the slow, rickety train towards the cottage. The weather had broken at last, and the sky was filled with the grey, rolling clouds that had deposited overnight rain in such quantity that when I left the city the gutters were still streaming and gurgling.

Eloise had been reading more from Celia's notebooks, and wanted to experiment with being tied up while suspended from the ceiling. I liked the idea of experimenting with Eloise while she was tied up, and so I readily accepted her invitation to visit.

By the time I reached the front door of the cottage water had penetrated the soles of my summer shoes. As I waited for Eloise to open the door my desires had been whittled down to one: to remove my shoes and dry my feet. But Eloise didn't appear at the door, and I had no alternative but to venture once again on to the sodden lawn in order to circumnavigate the cottage and find a way in.

As I went round the north wing of the cottage I saw that lamps were alight in the dungeon outhouse. The door was ajar.

I heard voices from within as I approached. Eloise was not alone. I was surprised: in fact, to be honest, I was strangely affronted. The dungeon in the outhouse was supposed to be a secret, known only to me, Eloise and Anne. I placed my bags on the floor, took off my jacket and folded it over the bags, removed my shoes and damp socks, and made my way quietly towards the illuminated area from which the voices were emanating.

I saw Eloise first. She was standing in the wood-panelled space that I had anticipated would be the venue for our activities: the wooden partitions created a three-walled room which contained little furniture but which was well equipped with heavy metal rings and pulleys set into the two thick beams that ran across the ceiling. Loops of chain and rope hung like grim festoons. I was surprised to see that Eloise wasn't wearing one of her summer frocks. Instead she was dressed appropriately for the occasion in a corset of black leather, over which she had a loose voile blouse, and black stockings and shoes. She occupied the centre of the chamber, apparently troubled neither by her state of near-nudity nor by the ominous chains and hoists above her head.

I called out to her, and she turned. I smiled to see that she was holding the front of her blouse together: this did nothing much to conceal her breasts, and it revealed that she was perhaps not as self-confident as she was trying to appear.

I was able to see beyond her, and glimpsed a man sitting in a chair. I stopped in my tracks. It had never occurred to me that Eloise's other guest would be male.

My surprise must have shown in my face, because Eloise pouted and beckoned me towards her. She pulled me into a reassuring embrace and, while it was pleasant once again to inhale her perfume and to feel her stiff nipples pressing into my chest, I would have preferred to make a more dramatic entrance.

'Michael, this is Ben,' she said.

I exchanged a nod and a smile with Ben, who stood up to shake my hand. He was a tall, well-built chap with salt-and-pepper hair, a lined face and a keen gaze. I would say he was a well-preserved fifty-year-old. He was wearing a tweed suit that I would have found unbearably hot for the time of year.

'Ben owns land locally,' Eloise said, as if that was enough to explain his presence in the midst of Celia's secret collection of bondage equipment.

'Don't worry, Michael,' Eloise went on, as she could see that I was still having difficulty coming to terms with the situation. 'I still want to be tied up and hung from the ceiling. That's why we're in here. But I thought it would be fun to have two men at once. I can if I want to, you know.'

I agreed with the best grace I could muster. I didn't want to disappoint Eloise; I didn't want to have had a wasted journey; and, I suppose, I was reluctant to appear less ready and willing than the newcomer Ben.

'I've been showing Ben some pictures from Celia's notebooks,' Eloise said. She wiggled her bottom as she bent to pick up the pages lying beside Ben's chair. 'I think these two positions would do. You could suspend me like this to start with, so you can both smack my bottom and one of you can fuck me. Then, if you turn me over, I can have one of you at each end, and you can do what you like. I won't be able to stop you.'

I looked at the two pictures. One was a grainy photograph, and the other a reproduction of a drawing in the oriental style. Both positions would entail using a number of padded bars, each held up by at least two chains and, at least for the second position, the chains would have to be on pulleys so that the height of the bars could be adjusted. I would be required to co-operate closely with Ben in order to prepare the equipment.

I nodded sagely, as if I was an expert on mechanics, and gave Ben the slightest of smiles. 'Let's get on with it, then,' I said.

I must admit that Ben knew how to arrange chains and pulleys. When it became clear that he had the expertise and the physical strength to set up the equipment more quickly than I could, I left him to it and instead buckled heavy cuffs around Eloise's wrists and ankles. I used the strongest cuffs I could find in the cupboards because, in the first of Eloise's two chosen positions, all of her weight would be suspended from her four extremities. And although Eloise isn't heavy, it was important to ensure that she was as comfortable as possible in what was inevitably going to be an onerous position. The cuffs were wide bands of thick leather, each secured with two buckles and lined and edged with soft material.

As I fastened the cuffs around her limbs I tried to engage Eloise in conversation.

'Who is he?' I hissed up at her as I worked at her ankles.

'I told you,' she said, ruffling my hair. 'He comes from around here.'

'And does he come here often?' I asked through gritted teeth. Eloise was making no attempt to conceal her sex, and I could see that her labia were already moist and enlarged. I wondered how long Ben had been at the cottage before I arrived.

'Well, I have to keep myself amused while you're not here,' Eloise said teasingly. 'Ben's very strong. And he's not as strait-laced as he looks. Although he likes me to be laced up tightly.' She ran her hands up the front of the leather corset and cupped her breasts.

I bit the inside of her right thigh.

Ben was as efficient as he was taciturn. He had set up two separate arrangements of chains and bars, so that we would be able to transfer Eloise from the first to the second without any delay. Within a few minutes we had attached Eloise's cuffs to the first, simpler array of chains and had hoisted her into the air.

A single short chain of sturdy links hung from a pulley set near the ceiling. It ended in an iron ring to which other chains were clipped.

One of these was very short: to its lower end both of Eloise's wrist cuffs were secured, so that her wrists were held together and her arms were lifted straight above her head. A leather sleeve was wrapped around the chain just above the connection to her cuffs, so that she could grip the chain in her hands and thus take some of the weight that would otherwise be supported entirely by her wrists.

Two longer chains also hung from the single heavy chain. These were attached to the two ends of a spreader

238

bar, which was thus hanging horizontally just below and in front of Eloise's cuffed wrists. Eloise's ankle cuffs were clipped to the two ends of the bar.

Eloise was hanging by her wrists and ankles. Her arms were stretched straight upwards on either side of her head; her legs were held wide apart by the bar, so that I had an unobstructed view of her face and her breasts – and, for that matter, of her sex, gaping wide and clearly well lubricated, and of her anus. The muscles of her arms and thighs were taut. The part of her body nearest the floor was the curvaceous W of her bottom, which made a very tempting target.

Ben had had the same idea. As I stroked and slapped the rounded buttocks, and let my fingers probe upwards into Eloise's unprotected arsehole, Ben went to the side of the room and began to pull on the chain that ran to the pulley, so that Eloise was lifted higher.

'I'll hoist her for whipping,' he said. 'And lower her again for fucking.'

He was a man of few words, but I couldn't disagree with his plan. Despite the discomfort of her position, Eloise was bright-eyed with excitement. I knew the signs well by now: when she was aroused her pale blue eyes became brilliant, and her cheeks and breasts flushed pink. The viscous liquid trickling from her open vagina down to her anus only confirmed the diagnosis.

'This is so wicked,' she said happily as she was winched upwards. 'I hope you big, strong men are going to punish me.'

Eloise's hopes were not to be disappointed. Her bottom and sex, suspended at the level of my chest, presented a target that anyone would have found irresistible.

Ben returned, carrying two leather tawses. I took one: it wasn't one of the heaviest, but I knew it would sting. And Eloise would be getting two simultaneously.

'I'm left-handed,' Ben said. 'I'll stand to her left. You take the other side.'

Ben and I took our places on either side of Eloise's pendant hindquarters.

'I'll strike across the top of the area, like this,' Ben said. He swung his tawse, and it landed with a loud crack across the back of Eloise's left thigh. Its tails curved into the wet opening of her vulva. Eloise cried out, and discovered how little she could move in her bondage.

'You strike upwards, across the curve of her arse cheek,' Ben went on. 'After six, we'll change: you aim across the top, and I'll whip the arse cheek on this side. We'll give her thirty-six in total – at least to begin with.'

There was something disconcertingly mechanical about administering the punishment. I had to keep count of my strokes, for one thing, which meant I couldn't concentrate on watching Eloise's reactions. Ben worked like an automaton, with a stern expression fixed on his face.

Nonetheless, Eloise's buttocks and the backs of her thighs developed a pleasing ruddy glow and Eloise, at least, seemed to be enjoying the experience. She shook her head and uttered a little cry each time the two tawses landed on her flesh. Her vulva, tormented by the tails of one tawse and then the other, took on a darker shade of pink as it opened like the petals of a flower.

After we had administered the thirty-six strokes that Ben had decided would be appropriate, we stood back to contemplate the results of our labours. Eloise was breathing deeply, her breasts rising and falling, and as she rested her head against her arm her face had an expression of beatific contentment.

Then her eyes flew open and she said, 'What next?'

In answer Ben put his hands to his crotch, unfastened the front of his trousers, and extracted from within them an erection of a size that might, I confess, have been even more impressive than the best that I could achieve. I must confess also that punishing Eloise had not wrought its habitual effect on my own member, which was perkily interested rather than rampantly raring to go. I decided that the time was not propitious to engage in a cock-flashing contest, and my trousers remained buttoned up.

Eloise had turned her face away, pretending to be shocked by Ben's crude exhibitionism. However, she couldn't help glancing at the upright column of flesh rearing from the folds of tweed, and I'm sure I heard her moan with disappointment when, without a word, Ben turned and strode out of her sight.

He went only as far as the wall, however, where he pulled on the chain which lowered Eloise towards the floor. He stopped when he judged that her sex was at the same height as his erection, and when he returned to the centre of the room he didn't pause but walked up to Eloise and inserted his erection into her vagina. Eloise threw back her head and groaned as the thick cylinder of flesh slid deep inside her and her raw thighs and buttocks met rough tweed.

I may have been wrong, but I thought I detected a brief smile of satisfaction appear on Ben's lips. He put his hands between Eloise's legs and grasped her breasts, making her groan again. Then he pushed her away, until only the tip of his penis was touching her.

He pulled back his hands, and Eloise swung towards him again, impaling herself on his stiff prick. His hands shot out, squeezed her breasts, and pushed her away; she swung back, sliding on to his penis and pressing her backside against the scratchy material of his clothes. He entertained himself in this fashion for some minutes, swinging the helpless Eloise back and forth, off and on his erection. Eloise seemed to find it entertaining, too: she began to quiver in her bonds, and to make a keening noise which indicated to me that she was entering a pre-orgasmic state.

But Ben, it seemed, didn't want Eloise or himself to reach a climax yet. He stopped pushing Eloise away and, with his penis still inside her, he reached up to unfasten her right ankle from the bar. He looked over his shoulder at me. I shrugged, and ambled over to release the other ankle.

As the second arrangement of chains and bars was ready, we led Eloise towards it immediately and had her lie face-down on the floor. Once again it was Ben who operated the pulley which lowered the central hook from which the other chains depended.

Every part of Eloise's body seemed to be sensitised. Each time I touched her, to fasten her cuffs or simply because I was fascinated by her glowing skin, she shivered. Her limbs were limp, and the few words she spoke were slurred with desire. Her bottom was bright red from her punishment.

As before, her legs were held wide apart by a bar between her ankles. A wide sling of black leather supported her stomach. A second bar, very well padded, lay beneath her outstretched arms and her collarbone. Her wrists were attached to the ends of a third bar. All three bars, and the sling, were suspended on chains from the central hook. Each set of chains was adjustable, so that once we had hoisted Eloise off the ground we could arrange her as we saw fit.

The sling, hanging from the hook on only a short chain, did most of the job of supporting Eloise's body. By shortening the chains which held up the bar between her ankles Ben and I were able to unstraighten her legs, so that her knees were pointing towards the floor and her bottom was gently rounded. And by shortening the chains which supported the bar beneath her arms we lifted her head and shoulders a little. Her arms we left outstretched in front of her.

'Front or back?' Ben asked me.

I hadn't thought about it. And, now I had to make a choice, I found I didn't really mind. I looked at Eloise. Her rounded, roseate hindquarters were tempting; so, too, were her pendant breasts and her languidly smiling mouth. I gave her a questioning look, in case she had any preferences, but when she caught my eye she merely broadened her smile. She had been whipped and made aroused, she was comfortably helpless in her bonds, and now all she wanted was to feel two hard cocks inside her.

'Front,' I said, and went to look for a short, thin wooden rod: if Eloise was going to make me share her body with another man, then I would allow myself the pleasure of making her tits dance and smart while I came in her mouth.

Ben made final adjustments to Eloise's chains, ensuring that when I was standing between her outstretched arms I could easily move her mouth on to my erect penis, and shortening the chains on the ankle-bar so that Eloise's splayed knees were alongside her hips and her bottom was as open as possible.

I can't deny that it was interesting – in fact, let's face it, it was arousing – to watch Ben as he methodically prepared to bugger Eloise. Particularly as I had one hand in Eloise's dark hair as she licked the tip of my penis and the other, holding the thin rod, stroking and pinching and slapping her breasts.

Ben had a jar of ointment, and was applying handfuls of the cream to Eloise's sore buttocks. From time to time he also applied a hefty smack. I could see that he was concentrating more and more on smoothing the cream into the widely stretched furrow between her buttocks, and when he began pushing his hand forward insistently I knew that he was opening Eloise's anus with his fingers and pressing lubricant into her.

Eloise began to pant and moan. I pressed my hand down on her head, so that her mouth was filled with my erection and, having given both of her nipples a final, hard pinch, I started to swing the rod up against her hanging breasts.

Ben's erection, smooth and shiny within its prophylactic covering, looked enormous. Even my swollen penis was not enough to silence Eloise's groan when Ben introduced the tip of his member into the funnel of her arsehole and pressed forward.

Eloise bucked and writhed in her chains as Ben nudged his hardness into her. It was all I could do to keep her head fixed on my erection. Ben stopped pressing forward when, I judged, he was sure that his glans was firmly inside her.

He looked at me. His face was, I thought, still remarkably expressionless considering the sensations that he must have been experiencing. 'You come first,' he said. 'Then Eloise. Then me. OK?'

I shrugged. 'OK.'

He started to spank her bottom then, using both hands to apply loud, hearty smacks to one buttock and then the other. Eloise wriggled, but there was nothing she could do to move her sore bottom away from the regular slaps or to dislodge the staff of hard flesh that was holding open her anus.

I wasn't giving Eloise many opportunities to use her lips and tongue on my penis, but nonetheless the warm, wet interior of her mouth was having its effect, and I knew that I wouldn't be able to hold back my orgasm for much longer – particularly in view of what Ben was doing to Eloise just an arm's length in front of me. I continued to whip her breasts lightly for a while longer – Eloise finds mild discipline very stimulating, and I had some idea of the maelstrom of ecstatic sensations that must have been created throughout her body by the combined effect of what Ben and I were doing – until I could feel the seed throbbing and boiling in my balls.

I dropped the thin rod and with the palm of my hand caressed the pendant globes that I had been punishing. Eloise's body seemed charged with electricity: she trembled at every slightest touch. I could tell she was as ready as I was. Beads of perspiration ran from her shoulders and pooled in the small of her back.

I allowed Eloise to lift her head, so that only my glans was inside her mouth. Immediately she began to twirl her tongue around the sensitive bulb.

'Now,' I grunted to Ben.

He stopped smacking Eloise's bottom, and leant forward so as to push his erection further into her. I used both hands to squeeze Eloise's breasts. I felt my sperm come streaming through the centre of my penis, and I cried out as the first jet spurted into Eloise's mouth.

After the third pulse of come I opened my eyes again. Ben's groin was now almost touching Eloise's bottom. He had one hand resting on her coccyx, and the other was out of sight between his body and hers. He must have been touching her, however, because even as my orgasm in its final throes spat trickles of sperm into Eloise's throat, she began to pant and writhe and cry out.

I withdrew my member and Eloise, lost in a frenzy of sensations, began to toss her sperm-spattered head from side to side. Ben, moving with unaccustomed animation, thrust his hips back and forth with increasing speed as Eloise's cries became louder and less coherent.

Her orgasm seemed to go on for minutes, but at last her wails began to diminish and her head drooped. I heard a stifled exclamation from Ben, and saw that his face and body were still. His eyes were unfocused. Eloise uttered a shuddering gasp, and I knew that she could feel Ben's penis, lodged deep in her rectum, at last shooting forth its load of sperm. Her body trembled with an aftershock of orgasm. The chains holding her jangled.

'That was quite wonderful,' Eloise said, taking a breath between each word, as Ben lowered her to the floor and I began to unfasten her bonds.

I stroked her damp skin, and found myself wondering whether there was time to take the last train back to the city that evening. It wasn't that I didn't want to spend more time with Eloise: I simply knew that Ben wasn't likely to be much of a conversationalist. Dinner *à trois* would be an uncomfortable affair.

And I was impatient for Anne's return. I know the kinds of things that are taught in the Private House, and so I was sure that Anne would by now be trained to participate in and enjoy just the kind of entertainment that Ben, Eloise and I had engaged in. I imagined Anne in Eloise's place, her slim, lithe, golden body held open and supported by the bars. I felt her mouth engulfing my erection. And I saw not Ben but Eloise, or Stephanie, standing between her legs and pushing an oiled phallus between her well-whipped buttocks.

I couldn't wait for the summer to end.

Part Three

RETURNING

The Private House
31 August
My dear Michael

I know, I know, I should have written more frequently. I'm truly sorry, and I'm looking forward to seeing you again so you can punish me very thoroughly. I've been so very busy, you see: Jem depends on me more and more to oversee our activities abroad, and whenever I'm back here she likes to show me off to her visitors, and make me do disgraceful things. You know I can't resist being made to perform.

This will be my last report about Anne, of course, as she is due to be sent home soon. She has apparently proved to be a delightful student. I had a meeting with her Mentors today and I think they're both going to miss her. She has a remarkable ability to inspire affection in everyone who knows her.

After some initial reluctance, which was hardly surprising, Anne took to her training very well. She clearly has a natural aptitude for many of the skills and disciplines that she has learnt here, and she has absorbed completely the ethos of the Private House. In some areas she has been almost too enthusiastic.

I'm gleaning much of this information from the dossier that has been compiled on her while she's been here. It's interesting to compare her dossier with her mother's: she looks so much like a taller, younger version of Celia, but when you look at the accounts of their training here you find subtle differences. It makes one wonder how much of a person's personality is inherited from his or her parents, and in what proportions, and subject to what subsequent influences.

248

Well, Anne will leave in three days' time and you'll be able to see for yourself how well she has learnt her lessons here.

My last trip overseas was to the director of one of our Far Eastern partners. Jem says that he was very taken with me – my big tits getting me into trouble again! – and that she had some difficulty clinching the deal she wanted without having to promise that I would be part of the consideration. In the end she persuaded him to settle for a keepsake – which means that you've got another commission. Jem has offered him a painting of me: I'm to be naked, bound with ropes, in the eastern style, and apparently it must be clearly visible that my breasts are tightly cinched and well marked with a cane. I imagine you'll enjoy capturing that image on canvas.

Let me know when you can fit me in.

Always yours

Amanda.

From the notebooks of Celia Bright

I have pasted a copy of the letter on the opposite page.

There is no cure. There is no hope. D will have some months of normal life – they cannot predict how many months – and then the decline will be swift and irreversible.

I cannot bear it. And if the news fills me with such sickening, paralysing despair that I have no capacity for any other feeling, how much more must it overwhelm my master?

At first we could only hold each other and weep. Then, when we had no more tears left in us, I made D tell me everything. I refused to accept the diagnosis: I insisted that the doctors were wrong, that there must a remedy, that research could be undertaken. I denied the possibility that D could be taken from me, until he was roused to anger by my thoughtlessness, and for almost the first time he shouted at me until I was quiet.

I can't help being angry with him. He is going to leave me. He is going to leave me alone. I do not know how I will survive without him.

We wept again. Then D tried to reason with me. I had lived without him before, he reminded me. I had been successful in my career, and content. When I realised that we were discussing my future, that D was wasting minutes of his precious time in worrying about me, I burst into tears one more time.

I said that I would refuse to live without him. I would not outlive him by so much as a minute. He meant everything to me. He was my world. We must buy poison, I urged him. We would take it together. Neither of us need live without the other. We would cheat his illness.

D was amused at first at my hysteria, and then appalled when he realised that I meant what I said. He was tearful, and then angry with me again for wanting to go to the grave with him. His only consolation, he said, was the knowledge that I was alive and well: how did I dare to threaten to snatch away the one lamp that remained alight in his universe of darkness?

I fought back. To me he was the universe. Without him I could not exist. What right had he to condemn me to live on without him? It would be a living death. How could he want me to suffer?

And so we argued back and forth, and wept, and held each other, until at last we had no more words to say and no more tears to shed, and we were lying in each other's arms on the rug in front of the dying fire.

We were almost asleep. Instinctively my right hand went into his lap, where it found that his manhood was stiff and straight. Drowsily I unfastened his trousers and curled my fingers around the warm shaft: I find it comforting to hold him there. With his eyes still closed he began to kiss me, and I cradled his head against my chest so that he could nuzzle my breasts.

Soon I felt the familiar thrills of arousal, and I awoke enough to start undressing D. He had slipped one hand behind me and between my buttocks, so that he could caress my anus, but with the other he helped me to remove his clothes. We were soon naked, and still half dozing, and kissing and stroking each other as if we were new, young lovers.

We became more awake as we excited each other. I was shivering with the tremors that precede a climax, and I knew that D was also close to coming. I yearned to feel his member pushing into me and filling my rectum. I murmured, and began to turn over in order to adopt the position, but D was lying on me and kissing me urgently. The hot, hard tip of his erection was between my thighs, and then touching my sex, and I was suddenly lost in a swirl of sensations.

At the back of my mind I was sure that something was wrong, but the pulses of pleasure overwhelmed all my doubts and all my training. D was inside me, and moving his body against mine, and nothing else mattered. I was already starting to come: as the streaks of desire zigzagged through my body I felt my muscles contract around D's erection. I heard him cry out hoarsely, and he buried his face in my neck as he pumped his seed into me.

When we were both still, I understood what had happened. I extricated myself from our embrace and knelt beside him. His sperm trickled from my sex and down the insides of my thighs.

'Master,' I said, 'I'm so sorry. I've disobeyed you. Please punish me.'

D rolled on to his back and looked up at me. He had a sheepish smile on his face, and for the first time in weeks he seemed relaxed and cheerful. 'What on earth are you talking about?' he said.

I could hardly bring myself to admit my crime. 'Master,' I whispered, 'I wasn't paying attention. I was enjoying my own pleasure, and I should have been thinking only of yours.' I felt a tear roll down my cheek. I had disobeyed one of the fundamental rules, and he was clearly going to make me spell out my fault. 'I took you into my vagina, master. And I let you remain there, and come there. Look.' I hung my head, gestured helplessly with my hands at my wet thighs, and burst into a fit of sobbing.

I waited for D to pronounce his judgement. Perhaps I would merely be whipped particularly severely. Perhaps he would let some of his friends use my anus and my mouth, over and over until he was sure I would never again forget how to take him inside me. Perhaps he would introduce me to some cruel device that would keep my anus open for hours at a time.

Needless to say, there was an element of wishful thinking in my fearful imaginings.

But D merely reached up and stroked my face.

'We'll do it that way from now on,' he said. 'We'll make love in the traditional manner. And without any form of contraception. If we're lucky, I may be able to give you a reason to carry on without me.'

It took me a few moments to understand his meaning. When I did, I threw myself on him and covered his face with tears and kisses.

'I will conceive,' I promised him. 'I will conceive. But,' I added, after a while, 'you will still tie me up and punish me, won't you, master, before we make love?'

D laughed. 'Of course,' he said. 'I'll whip you and fuck you every day, while I have the strength left in me.'

The dew that sparkled on the lawn was the only hint of the changing season. The sun shone still with the warmth of summer, and the walls of the cottage shone brilliantly white as I strode towards the front door.

If there was a spring in my step it was because I could hardly conceal my excitement: Anne was due to arrive home, and I had risen at an unconscionable hour in order to be ready to greet her.

When Eloise answered my rap on the door my grin of surprise and delight was unfeigned. Eloise never looked less than pretty, but as the summer had progressed she had started to experiment with her clothes and her make-up, and to welcome Anne home she had put her newly discovered techniques to excellent use. Instead of one of the floral frocks that she used to wear, she had slithered into a skin-tight dress of jade-green silk. It had a high, oriental collar, long sleeves and a long skirt, but although Eloise was thus entirely covered the effect of the dress was to invite inspection of her body: the thin material clung to every curve. It was apparent that she was wearing nothing else: her nipples, excited by the touch of the silk, were as prominent and clearly delineated as if her breasts had been washed with a thin coat of green paint. The dark triangle of her pubes was visible, as was the gap between the tops of her thighs where I delight in inserting my hand.

Eloise had taken considerable care with her make-up, too. She used to favour a simple look which relied for its effect on the contrast between the dark curtain of her bobbed hair and the blue brilliance of her eyes. Today she had outlined her eyes in black, placed a touch of green and a touch of pink on her lids, shaped her cheekbones with highlights, and painted her lips a luscious dark purple. Her fingernails and toenails were painted to match. She looked quite extraordinarily striking.

I imagine I said something inane such as, 'Gosh. You look good enough to eat.'

Eloise merely smiled, stepped back, beckoned me over the threshold, and turned to lead me indoors.

I remained for a moment on the doorstep, too surprised to move. Eloise had revealed the truly daring aspect of her jade-green dress: it had no back. From her shoulders to her knees the dress was held tightly together by a series of ribbons. The green silk was held close together at her waist and towards her knees, emphasising the swell of her bottom. Each ribbon was tied in a bow, and each bow constituted an almost irresistible temptation to untie it.

'Come along, Michael,' Eloise said over her shoulder. 'Anne will be here soon.'

From the diary of Anne Bright
3 September
By the time I reached the cottage I was beginning to think that it hadn't been such a good idea to have myself parcelled up like a present.

The idea was that Eloise would take delivery of this huge parcel, and she'd have no idea what was in it, and

253

then when she opened it she'd find me inside, gift-wrapped for her. It seemed like a sweet thing to do for her, and everyone at the Private House thought so too.

But I was beginning to have my doubts. Not because I was tied up and squashed into a box: I've got quite used to that sort of thing, and the only inconvenience of it is that once I'm tied up and I know I'm quite helpless, I can't stop myself feeling very sexy and wanting to be spanked. And of course in my box there was no one to play with me.

No, the problem was that, as I felt the wheels of the courier's carriage trundling beneath me, taking me ever nearer to the cottage, I began to wonder what would happen if Eloise happened to be out. Or if she decided to leave the parcel unopened for some reason. Or if the parcel were to be delivered to the wrong address.

I was securely bound. The inside of the box was padded, and I was lying on my back on cushions on the bottom of the box. I've been allowed to keep my collar and my cuffs, and I wore them today to show them off to Eloise. My right wrist cuff was clipped to my right ankle cuff, and my left wrist cuff to my left ankle cuff. Then a chain round my knees had been attached to the front of my collar, so that my legs were drawn up to my chest. Otherwise I was completely naked. Hanging from my right ankle – this was my idea, too! – was a notice saying, 'A present for Eloise. Prepare for use by applying a sound spanking.'

I wasn't really worried, though, because I wasn't gagged. If I thought something was wrong I could always shout until someone rescued me. Actually, it was quite exciting to imagine being unwrapped by a complete stranger: what would he or she do to me?

My fantasies were interrupted when I felt the carriage stop. I heard the doors opening, and felt the box being tilted on to a barrow. The box was wheeled a short distance, and then I heard the courier knocking at a door.

'Delivery for you,' I heard him say. 'Just sign here, please. Shall I wheel it in for you?'

'Yes, please.' It was Eloise's voice. My heart leapt.

I heard the courier swear under his breath. He let the barrow tip forward with a jolt. I know now, of course, that his reaction was due to the sight of the back of Eloise's dress. Then he recovered, and I was wheeled into the cottage.

I suppose I should have expected Michael to be there. I didn't mind: after all my lessons I know I like men almost as much as women – as much, actually, when I'm in the mood for a man. And Michael is attractive, and all through the summer I remembered how agile and cunning his fingers can be!

I could hear Eloise and Michael discussing the parcel they had been presented with. They guessed that I could hear them, and they were pretending that they had no idea what could be inside such a large box. They prevaricated, and said they couldn't undo the knots, and talked about leaving it unwrapped until tomorrow 'because it might be for Anne, and she'll want to open it herself.'

I could tell from the tone of their voices that they were just trying to keep me in suspense. And it was working: as I lay on my back with my knees up and chained to my neck, anticipating the kisses and smacks I'd get, I could feel my sex juice beginning to seep from between my labia.

At last they began to untie the cords and tear off the outer wrapping. Once the box was unwrapped it was easy to see that the top would simply lift off. The sides of the box were designed to fall outwards once the top was removed, to reveal me lying naked and bound on the cushions.

It worked! Almost as soon as I was aware of daylight spilling into the box the sides fell away. 'Hello, Eloise,' I shouted. I was understandably excited to be home. 'Here's a present for you.'

I hardly recognised Eloise. Well, that's an exaggeration. I mean of course I recognised her, but she looked stunning and glamorous, and I told her so immediately.

255

Michael, of course, as usual managed to look both rumpled and sophisticated.

It was Michael who drew Eloise's attention to the note hanging from my foot, and to the fact that I was visibly aroused. They decided to spank me and make me come before they untied me – after all, as Michael said, it was impolite to refuse a gift. But Eloise did unwrap the chains from round my knees, because she could see that they were indenting my skin, and she knelt beside me and held my legs up while Michael used his belt on my bottom.

I don't know how many Michael gave me: more than the statutory eighteen, I think. But I didn't mind, because Eloise leant forward and started to kiss me, and soon I was enjoying both the smacking and the kissing too much to want either to stop. When Eloise started to rub my left nipple to the tempo of Michael's smacks, though, I found it all so lovely that I just let the orgasm come and take me. I opened my legs so that Michael could aim for my vulva if he wanted to, and when I stopped pulsating with pleasure Eloise was still kissing my lips and I realised I was crying.

It's terrific that women can love each other so easily. I hadn't realised how much I'd missed Eloise. I'm so glad to be back with her.

Delightful though it was to whip Anne's perfect buttocks and watch her melt into a gooey climax with Eloise, I was impatient to discover what she had learnt at the Private House. I have known several graduates of the disciplinarian regime there, and each has proved to be thoroughly trained in the arts of the pleasure-slave.

Therefore once Eloise had unfastened all the bits of Anne that had been clipped together, we cleared away the box and its wrapping and I had Anne show us some of the positions she had learnt.

As Anne demonstrated the litheness of her body, as well as its considerable beauty, by adopting a series of outrageously lewd postures, I began to wonder whether she had been the assiduous student that figured in Amanda's infrequent reports. Clearly Anne had learnt many submissive positions: her manner, however, seemed insufficiently subdued. I had expected to hear from her no more than 'Yes, sir', and otherwise to speak only when spoken to. I'm sure that such is the routine in the Private House. But Anne was chattering to Eloise, providing a commentary on each position and giggling when Eloise pointed out even lewder possibilities.

I interrupted Anne's display. 'Very good, Anne,' I said. 'What else did you learn while you were away? Were you taught about how to please a man?'

'Oh yes, sir,' the blonde minx replied, 'I'll say. And how to please a woman,' she added with a glance at Eloise.

'Well, let's have a practical demonstration,' I suggested. Watching her calisthenics had aroused my imagination, and both my carnal desire and my exasperation needed a release. 'Come and kneel in front of me.'

'Yes, sir,' she said eagerly. Hearing her say the words I had for so long looked forward to made me begin to feel content at last, although I would have been happier still were it not for the suspicion that the tone of Anne's voice conveyed the additional message: 'and about time too!'

At last I had the beautiful girl where I wanted her: kneeling in front of me, her grey eyes shining with anticipation as she unfastened my trousers.

Anne had been taught well at the Private House. Her fingers and lips touched lightly and delicately, and I found myself sighing with pleasure before she had even leant forward to take my straining erection into her mouth.

'Eloise,' I called out. I had to organise the proceedings before I became lost in the delights of Anne's mouth. 'Come here, my dear. Kneel alongside Anne, but facing the other way.'

As Eloise approached and, taking care of her flimsy dress, knelt gingerly next to Anne, I drew the belt from the loops of my trousers.

'I'll whip you while I'm using Anne's mouth,' I told Eloise as I untied the bows that held the ribbons across her bottom. 'And I'd like you to play with Anne's arsehole. At the Private House they usually teach students to enjoy that.'

Anne looked up at me. She widened her eyes and nodded, and then closed her eyes and smiled blissfully as Eloise's fingers found their target. Eloise lifted her bottom towards me, and I began to swing my belt in a series of slow smacks that were intended to bring a gradual glow to the pale buttocks presented before me.

As I lazily whipped Eloise, Anne started to use her lips and her tongue around the rim of my glans. I leant forward, urging her to take the whole bulb into her mouth, and so that I could more readily see Eloise's hand exploring Anne's arsehole.

I could feel the climax approaching. I was content.

From the diary of Anne Bright
3 September (continued)
The trouble with men is that they lack stamina. That's the conclusion I've reached.

I mean, it was lovely to have Michael's penis in my mouth – he really does taste quite yummy – especially with Eloise doing all those naughty things to my bottom. And I was very pleased when Michael had his orgasm: he had a really happy expression on his face, and I wanted to cuddle him. His sperm tastes nice, too.

But afterwards, although he was very strict about giving me instructions, and although he had me and Eloise performing some very specific acts for him, I could tell his heart wasn't really in it any more. Eloise and I were quite pleased, to be frank, when he finally went upstairs to have a lie down, and we could be alone together.

I think Eloise has learnt as much as I have! The things she's done while I've been away. Michael doesn't know the half of it, apparently. We had so much to tell each other. And, best of all, we couldn't keep our hands off each other's body. Eloise looks so sexy these days. I can't resist her.

So, all in all, we didn't get very far round the dungeon, which is what Eloise calls the outhouse where all of Mummy's equipment is set up. She was going to show me all the bits and pieces that she'd used during the summer, but we didn't get further than the first bed. The bed was the sort that has leather straps attached all round the edge, and there was some rope nearby, and a little cane, so we didn't need to wander any further. We just settled down to a long afternoon of tying each other up, and caning each other's bottom, and licking each other in all the rudest and most sensitive places, and gossiping.

It was the best homecoming imaginable.

Eloise has a really wicked imagination. I can tell we're going to have lots of fun. She made me come over and over again while she was caning my breasts. They're still sore now! I'll pay her back tomorrow.

I didn't see Michael again until we had dinner. By that time I was wearing a rubber outfit I'd found in the dungeon: it was black and very shiny, with cut-outs for my bottom and my poor tender breasts. Michael must have liked me in it, because I discovered that he had another erection. I got him to spank my bottom, and then I used my breasts and my mouth to make him come again. After that he seemed completely exhausted, the poor thing.

I wonder if I'll ever see him again?

Anyway, must stop writing now. It's late, and Eloise and I still have a lot of catching up to do. I can't wait for tomorrow!

Anne, I understand from talking with Eloise, left for college a couple of weeks after she returned to the cottage. She was alive with enthusiasm for continuing her education, Eloise said, although I think I detect there something of the rose-tinted view with which educators often view their charges. I suspect that Anne's desire to go to college had more earthy motives: her college would be an ocean within which she would find swimming schools of other students – young men and young women, in their sexual prime, with whom she would be able to practise her new-found skills. With the education she had received at the Private House added to her native beauty and charm, she would be a shark among minnows.

Eloise will remain at the cottage, although it seems that her sojourn there will not be the spinsterly exile she once imagined. She intends to hold parties. In the dungeon. Whenever possible they will be timed to coincide with Anne's visits, but knowing Eloise's newly discovered appetites I suspect that there will be frequent visitors at all times. Celia's master's collection will be put to good use, I'm sure.

I have returned to the city: back to the studio, back to Stephanie, back to preparing Amanda for her sitting. I lead an enviable life, I think.

And I don't know whether I'm wearing the rose-tinted spectacles again, but I reckon I can congratulate myself on playing some part in helping Anne and Eloise to find their true natures. Or is that just too fanciful?

NEW BOOKS

Coming up from Nexus, Sapphire and Black Lace

Grooming Lucy by Yvonne Marshall
September 2000   Price £5.99   ISBN 0 352 33529 7
Lucy's known about her husband's kinks for a few years, but now she wants to accommodate them herself. She knows it won't be easy – she has heard how extreme his tastes are – and she's asked some special friends to arrange a unique training course for her. But her husband's not the only man with extreme tastes, and some of his friends have their own ideas about how to train Lucy.

The Torture Chamber by Lisette Ashton
September 2000   Price £5.99   ISBN 0 352 33530 0
Catering for every perverse taste imaginable, The Torture Chamber is an SM club with a legendary reputation. Inside its exclusive walls, no fetish is too extreme, and the patrons know how to make the most of every situation. When Sue visits in disguise, she realises that she cannot visit again – the intensity of her reactions frightens her. But others at the club will stop at nothing to share in her special education.

Different Strokes by Sarah Veitch
September 2000   Price £5.99   ISBN 0 352 33531 9
These stories celebrate all aspects of the pains and pleasures of corporal punishment. Disobedient secretaries, recalcitrant slimmers, cheeky maids – dozens of young women, and a few young men too, whose behaviour can be improved only by the strict application of a hand, a slipper or a cane. A Nexus Classic.

Tight White Cotton by **Penny Birch**
October 2000   Price £5.99   ISBN 0 352 33537 8
Thirteen girls relate their experiences with the depraved spanking fanatic Percy Ottershaw, from his headmaster's daughter to Penny herself. From 1950 to 2000, his life has been dedicated to getting his girlfriends across his knee, pulling down their tight white cotton knickers and spanking their bare bottoms. Otherwise, he is polite, considerate, and always willing to indulge the girls' fantasies – from wetting their knickers in the street to being tarred and feathered.

Peeping at Pamela by **Yolanda Celbridge**
October 2000   Price £5.99   ISBN 0 352 33538 6
When four cheeky girls are recruited to live, rent-free, in a large house near Cambridge, it doesn't take them long to realise that their benefactor has more in mind than their welfare. Every room in the house is filled with hidden video cameras, which are all linked up to a number of voyeur websites. They also realise that their weekly stipend varies according to how much spanking they receive – which leads to increasingly exhibitionist behaviour. By the author of *The Discipline of Nurse Riding*.

Lingering Lessons by **Sarah Veitch**
October 2000   Price £5.99   ISBN 0 352 33539 4
When Leanne Dell inherits a former boarding school, now an advertising agency, part of the deal is that she has to share it with an unknown partner. Arriving at the grand house, she finds herself a voyeur to a scene of bizarre chastisement. Her co-partner, Adam Howard, is administering a sound spanking to his pretty young assistant. In the weeks that follow, Leanne learns some lessons of her own; that her handsome new partner in business is a devotee of corporal punishment, and that arousal and shame are two sides of the same coin.

Devils's Fire by Melissa MacNeal

September 2000   Price £5.99   ISBN 0 352 33527 0

Destitute but beautiful Mary visits handsome but lecherous mortician Hyde Fortune, in the hope he can help her out of her impoverished predicament. It isn't long before they're consummating their lust for each other and involving both Fortune's exotic housekeeper and his young assistant Sebastian. When Mary gets a live-in position at the local Abbey, she becomes an active participant in the curious erotic rites practiced by the not-so-very pious monks. This marvelously entertaining story is set in 19th-century America.

The Naked Flame by Crystalle Valentino

September 2000   Price £5.99   ISBN 0 352 33528 9

Venetia Halliday is a go-getting girl who is determined her trendy London restaurant is going to win the prestigious Blue Ribbon award. Her new chef is the cheeky, over-confident Mickey Quinn, who knows just what it takes to break down her cool exterior. He's hot, he's horny, and he's got his eyes on the prize – in her bed and her restaurant. Will Venetia pull herself together, or will her rough-trade lover ride roughshod over everything?

Crash Course by Juliet Hastings

September 2000   Price £5.99   ISBN 0 352 33018 X

Kate is a successful management consultant. When she's asked to run a training course at an exclusive hotel at short notice, she thinks the stress will be too much. But three of the participants are young, attractive, powerful men, and Kate cannot resist the temptation to get to know them sexually as well as professionally. Her problem is that one of the women on the course is feeling left out. Jealousy and passion simmer beneath the surface as Kate tries to get the best performance out of all her clients. A Black Lace special reprint.

Lured by Lust by **Tania Picarda**
October 2000   Price £5.99   ISBN 0 352 33533 5
Clara Fox works at an exclusive art gallery. One day she gets an
email from someone calling himself Mr X, and very soon she's
exploring the dark side of her sexuality with this enigmatic stranger.
The attraction of bondage, fetish clothes and SM is becoming
stronger with each communication, and Clara is encouraged to act
out adventurous sex games. But can she juggle her secret involvement
with Mr X along with her other, increasingly intense, relationships?

On the Edge by **Laura Hamilton**
October 2000   Price £5.99   ISBN 0 352 33534 3
Julie Gibson lands a job a a crime reporter for a newspaper. The
English seaside town to which she's been assigned has seen better
days, but she finds plenty of action hanging out with the macho cops
at the local police station. She starts dating a detective inspector, but
cannot resist the rough charms of biker Johnny Drew when she's
asked to investigate the murder of his friend. Trying to juggle hot sex
action with two very different but dominant men means things get
wild and dangerous.

NEXUS BACKLIST

All books are priced £5.99 unless another price is given. If a date is supplied, the book in question will not be available until that month in 2000.

CONTEMPORARY EROTICA

THE BLACK MASQUE	Lisette Ashton	
THE BLACK WIDOW	Lisette Ashton	
THE BOND	Lindsay Gordon	
BRAT	Penny Birch	
BROUGHT TO HEEL	Arabella Knight	July
DANCE OF SUBMISSION	Lisette Ashton	
DISCIPLES OF SHAME	Stephanie Calvin	
DISCIPLINE OF THE PRIVATE HOUSE	Esme Ombreux	
DISCIPLINED SKIN	Wendy Swanscombe	Nov
DISPLAYS OF EXPERIENCE	Lucy Golden	
AN EDUCATION IN THE PRIVATE HOUSE	Esme Ombreux	Aug
EMMA'S SECRET DOMINATION	Hilary James	
GISELLE	Jean Aveline	
GROOMING LUCY	Yvonne Marshall	Sept
HEART OF DESIRE	Maria del Rey	
HOUSE RULES	G.C. Scott	
IN FOR A PENNY	Penny Birch	
LESSONS OF OBEDIENCE	Lucy Golden	Dec
ONE WEEK IN THE PRIVATE HOUSE	Esme Ombreux	
THE ORDER	Nadine Somers	
THE PALACE OF EROS	Delver Maddingley	
PEEPING AT PAMELA	Yolanda Celbridge	Oct
PLAYTHING	Penny Birch	

ANCIENT & FANTASY SETTINGS

EDWARDIAN, VICTORIAN & OLDER EROTICA

SAMPLERS & COLLECTIONS

NEW EROTICA 3		
NEW EROTICA 5		Nov
A DOZEN STROKES	Various	

NEXUS CLASSICS
A new imprint dedicated to putting the finest works of erotic fiction back in print

AGONY AUNT	G. C. Scott	
THE HANDMAIDENS	Aran Ashe	
OBSESSION	Maria del Rey	
HIS MISTRESS'S VOICE	G.C. Scott	
CITADEL OF SERVITUDE	Aran Ashe	
BOUND TO SERVE	Amanda Ware	
SISTERHOOD OF THE INSTITUTE	Maria del Rey	
A MATTER OF POSSESSION	G.C. Scott	
THE PLEASURE PRINCIPLE	Maria del Rey	
CONDUCT UNBECOMING	Arabella Knight	
CANDY IN CAPTIVITY	Arabella Knight	
THE SLAVE OF LIDIR	Aran Ashe	
THE DUNGEONS OF LIDIR	Aran Ashe	
SERVING TIME	Sarah Veitch	July
THE TRAINING GROUNDS	Sarah Veitch	Aug
DIFFERENT STROKES	Sarah Veitch	Sept
LINGERING LESSONS	Sarah Veitch	Oct
EDEN UNVEILED	Maria del Rey	Nov
UNDERWORLD	Maria del Rey	Dec

Please send me the books I have ticked above.

Name ....

Address ....

....

....

.... Post code........................

Send to: **Cash Sales, Nexus Books, Thames Wharf Studios, Rainville Road, London W6 9HA**

US customers: for prices and details of how to order books for delivery by mail, call 1-800-805-1083.

Please enclose a cheque or postal order, made payable to **Nexus Books**, to the value of the books you have ordered plus postage and packing costs as follows:

UK and BFPO – £1.00 for the first book, 50p for the second book and 30p for each subsequent book to a maximum of £3.00;

Overseas (including Republic of Ireland) – £2.00 for the first book, £1.00 for the second book and 50p for each subsequent book.

We accept all major credit cards, including VISA, ACCESS/ MASTERCARD, AMEX, DINERS CLUB, SWITCH, SOLO, and DELTA. Please write your card number and expiry date here:

....

Please allow up to 28 days for delivery.

Signature ....